Give Me Chocolate

A Kelly Clark Mystery

Annie Hansen

HF
Publishing

Dedication

This book is dedicated to my husband, Brent Hansen, and to my parents, Tom & Gail McCarter.

Chapter 1

Late in the evening on a warm Tuesday night in early June, Nikki and I worked in the kitchen of her specialty dessert shop, Chocolate Love, as she finished up for the day. My sleeveless top and cotton shorts stuck to my body, and my long, brown, wavy hair hung limply down my back even though the air conditioning was on full blast. The heat in the kitchen was unbearable this late in the day, but it was better to be here in the company of my sister than up in my apartment.

Heat was nothing compared to the loneliness I faced up there. We sat at a small table in the old Victorian home Nikki's family converted into a chocolate shop years ago, off of the hustle and bustle of Third Street in Geneva, Illinois. Geneva was a beautiful, small town located about an hour west of Chicago nestled on the banks of the Fox River. Trees lined the streets, and large, bright pots filled with assorted flowers marked every corner.

The town was a high income community with a population of about nineteen thousand people. I was lucky to have the opportunity to live here. I didn't believe there was any real danger here, it wasn't a high crime city by any means, but after going through what I did three years ago, it was difficult to feel safe anywhere.

"You'll never know if you don't try it. Sometimes taking a risk can actually make your life better," my younger sister, Nikki, said, while signing a time card for one of her employees at Chocolate Love.

"Yes, but speed dating is not just about taking a risk, it's a guaranteed disaster. And as far as I'm concerned, this girl is off the market for good. I'm never dating again. Period," I said, pulling my hair into a ponytail. It was time for me to give up on trying to wear my hair down in some sort of style. The day was just too hot for a hairstyle. Besides, I wasn't really looking to impress anyone.

The store was deserted because the majority of her staff had already gone home. Nikki signed off on some final paperwork for the day, so she could prepare to head home as well.

Chocolate Love had been in Nikki's husband's family for two decades. When her father-in-law, Bob Connors Sr., was diagnosed with heart disease, he retired. He wanted to pass the store on to a family member and was thrilled when Nikki had enthusiastically stepped up.

"Okay, you're right, Kelly," Nikki laughed. "Forget I brought it up. Just thought it might be time for you to get back out there. You're wasting away up there writing that damn book while all the fun passes you by. You're only thirty-three. You act like you're sixty-five, in bed every night at nine o'clock and up at the crack of dawn. Where's the fun? That's all I'm saying. Where's the fun in your life right now?"

"First of all, I'm hardly wasting away thanks to your desserts. Second, the crack of dawn works for me because I like to start writing first thing in the morning. It's when I'm the most productive. I thought I was making progress, and you were happy for me."

"Of course, I'm happy for you. I just want to see you, you know, *better*." She paused to fiddle with the pen she held in her right hand. "You know. Like you were before."

I grimaced as her comment hit me like a truck. It was too painful to talk about what Nikki was referring to. It was hard enough holding my head up back in my hometown after what happened three years ago. Divorcing a man who attempted to murder his pregnant mistress left me with a huge stigma. And having the whole event splattered all over the national news only made things worse for me. Being the ex-wife of a convict was not exactly the role I dreamed of when I was a little kid.

Instinctively, I wanted to shut Nikki out, but I knew she was just trying to be a good sister and good friend to me. She was a good friend to me. My *best* friend. She took me in and gave me an apartment to live in rent free above Chocolate Love after I was left penniless.

Living here these past few months had been great for me. It was a familiar place that gave me a lot of comfort and joy on a daily basis. Nikki had done amazing things for the store in the last two years. She gave the entire building a new coat of light blue paint with red accents, remodeled one of the kitchens, and added more windows to the front of the store for customers to watch the preparation of the chocolates. Being here amidst all of this excitement and development continually lifted my spirits during a rough transitional stage of my life. Not to mention all the free desserts. Plus, I couldn't help but think, if this store could resurrect itself, why couldn't I?

"Please, Nikki, can we just let it go for now?" I felt defeated when Nikki talked about getting "better." What was that supposed to mean? I was never going to be the same person I was before.

"Yes, of course, we can."

She brushed her hands over and over her apron. To a normal person, it might look like she did it to rub off excess flour or sugar left over on her hands from baking in the kitchen. But to me, it was a head's up to what was next.

"What?"

"What do you mean?" Nikki asked innocently.

"You're doing the hand thing on your apron again."

Nikki was five-foot two-inches tall, but her firecracker personality made her appear larger than life. A dark, modern bob accentuated her eyes, which were the same color as the chocolate ganache she put on her fudge cupcakes.

"One last thing, and we'll drop it. Have you thought about going back to see Dr. Bruce?" she asked, referring to my psychiatrist.

I was trying my best to put my tragedy in the past. Rehashing it was not doing me any good. Why meet again and again with a shrink to repeat the same thing? I already knew I needed to put the past in the past and rebuild. Everyone just needed to shut up about it and let me do it my way.

"No. Not right now. I want to take a break and concentrate on my book. Writing is the only thing that makes me feel better."

Before I could say anything more, the back door opened and slammed shut.

"Here you are. Why haven't you answered my phone calls?" my older sister, Adelle, said. From her tone, it was obvious she wanted something. Which was nothing new. She always wanted something.

"I left my phone upstairs. We've been chatting."

"Is everything okay, Kelly?" she asked, pulling a chair out at the table to sit down next to me. Her form fitting yoga attire hugged her body and accentuated her large breasts. After popping out three children, she still had the body of a fit eighteen-year-old, even though she was a few years older than me.

"Everything is fine." As soon as I said it, I regretted it.

"Good. Mike and I want to know if you can baby-sit for us tomorrow night. We need a date night."

She sank lower in her chair and gave me her sad puppy look. Most of the time it was hard for me to say no to that face, but not now.

"I'm sorry, but I can't do it. You know how I feel about the weekday baby-sitting. I'm up so early in the morning to work."

"Oh, I know. I promise we won't be out late. We'll just grab a sandwich and talk for a bit. Please, Kelly? You know things have been tough for Mike and I lately." She pulled my hand into hers and pled with her eyes. They watered as though she was on the verge of tears. Her beautiful, long, blond hair fell forward, cascading around her shoulders. It wasn't what I wanted to do, but I chose to give in rather than deal with a nasty confrontation.

"Will you promise to be home by nine?" I could handle a couple of hours. It would be nice to hang out with her kids.

"Absolutely. Like I said, just a sandwich. I'll see you at six." She bounced out the door and left before I could even confirm six would work for me.

"That one is unbelievable," Nikki said.

"I know. It would be great to hang out with the kids though. And if she and Mike are having problems, they probably need to have some alone time." I justified her behavior like I always did. It was easier.

"Then hire a baby-sitter for God's sake. They can afford it. You don't work for them. And the only problem Mike and Adelle are having is how to count all that money of theirs."

"Nikki, don't start. Please."

Nikki sighed and turned her back on me. It felt like a slap, but I knew it was only so she could shut down the computer and continue to close up the shop.

"She takes advantage of you, Kelly. You don't see her asking me to baby-sit."

"You? She doesn't ask you to baby-sit because you hate kids," I said with a note of humor in my voice.

"I do not!" Nikki laughed.

Nikki got up to turn off the lights. She locked the back door and walked with me to the front of the store.

The store was set up so customers could walk in through the front door, view the chocolates being made through a glass enclosed work room to their left and then continue down the hallway into the store. Once inside the grand foyer, there was a winding staircase on the right, a bathroom straight ahead, and the actual store on the left.

In the foyer, Nikki made sure things were locked up properly for the night. A number of break-ins had been reported in the last month from her neighboring shop owners. Chocolate Love remained untouched, but I understood Nikki's concerns.

"I'll see you in the morning?" she asked.

"Sounds good. I'll be here. Good night." I climbed up the curving staircase to my apartment.

My apartment door was located at the top of the landing. When I moved in, Nikki added another bolt lock to my door, per my request. The house was always locked up at night when the store closed, but being doubly secured made the space more livable.

After making a turkey sandwich, I sat down in front of my computer to check email. I was happy with the pages I had written today for my new book, so I made no plans to revise tonight. Usually, my evenings were filled with reading over what was written during the day and making changes. Some nights I skipped it because I needed a night to re-charge. Tonight was one of those nights.

I noticed right away the majority of my mail was junk mail and advertisements. That was easy. Delete. Delete. Delete.

But my heart stopped when I scrolled down to the one email of substance. I could see there was an attached photo thumbnail. My gut urged me to delete the email immediately, but I couldn't stop myself and opened it.

"Oh my God."

A picture of a two-year-old toddler with rosy, red cheeks and blond, curly hair appeared on the screen. She wore a white bathing suit with red cherries on it. Shining, blue eyes gazed into the camera, and the smile on her face lit everything up around her. She held on tightly to someone who was out of the frame of the picture.

I just wanted to let you know Caroline turned two today. You are the reason this little angel is here. I can never thank you enough. We'll never forget you.

Love Always-
Mandy and Caroline

My first reaction to the email was to back away quickly from the computer screen. My sudden movement caused me to knock over the chair. I ran to the bathroom, barely making it inside before vomiting into the toilet.

* * * * *

After a terrible night's sleep, the alarm rang at 5:30 a.m. the next morning. For one brief moment, I allowed myself to think of Steve and where he would awaken this morning. Hopefully, he would wake there for at least another seven years, per the judge's sentence.

My mind wandered back to that horrible night.

9-1-1, what is your emergency?
My husband... I found... He's going to kill a woman.... Please, you have to stop him. She's pregnant.

"Not a good way to start the day," I said aloud to the room. The tee shirt I slept in was soaked with sweat. I'd become accustomed to that. My body always responded to my nightmares by producing mass quantities of stress sweat, as I liked to call it. Groaning, I pulled my shirt over my head and tossed it into the laundry basket at the foot of the bed. Another day of fighting off the ghosts.

I glanced down at my body now clothed only in my undergarments. The sight of my hipbone sticking out at a weird angle caught my attention. Nikki was right; the stress had taken off some pounds and not in an attractive way. A gaze into the mirror across from my bed revealed a too-thin, haggard looking woman with messed up hair, dead eyes, and swollen lips.

"Who is that?" I asked myself.

Maybe I wasn't doing as well as I thought. I wasn't restricting what I was eating; it was just that the fireball of anxiety in my stomach seemed to turn the calories I ate to ash. Today will be better. I vowed to eat more today and work less. Maybe even think less if that was possible. The only way I knew how to do that was to start my day off with a run. Not conducive to my weight gaining goals, but it just had to be done.

My feet stretched to touch the pink area rug strategically placed under my bed, so my toes wouldn't freeze during the winters. Shuffling slowly along, I dressed in running clothes, and wandered into the kitchen to pour a cup of coffee. As I headed out the door, I grabbed my iPod. Without my music, the run was miserable. My breathing was off and my stamina low. With my music, I was able to glide along and get my three miles in just under thirty minutes.

Walking down the staircase, all ready for my run, I noticed the lights in the kitchen on. The first shift probably came in very early today. Nikki made sure someone was in at 6:00 a.m. to start any of the baking that had to be done for the day. Usually it was her favorite and oldest employee, Fran, who came in early.

Fran had been with Chocolate Love since the store opened over twenty years ago. I knew my sister trusted her to be here before anyone else to start the big projects for the day.

"Fran?" I called.

I walked into the kitchen and called out her name again. It looked deserted. The schedules for the day were still up on the wall, and the tables as they were the night before. I didn't remember leaving any lights on last night.

Just in case Fran was in the basement, I left everything on. The back door was still locked, which wasn't unusual because Fran always locked herself back in until the other employees arrived. I knew she was always careful about working here alone in the morning.

Outside, the humidity washed over my body like a steam shower. Chicago in June was like running in a jungle. After powering up my iPod, I began my run down Third Street.

Third Street was considered the Historic District for Geneva. The red cobblestone streets were lined with all different kinds of quaint shops and up-scale restaurants. Some of the restaurants got deliveries at this hour, so a few trucks were parked up and down the street. Early morning commuters rushed south on Third Street, either on foot or on bike, to get to the train stop that took passengers east toward the city, or further out west.

Chocolate Love was in a great location being only a couple of blocks from the station. In the evenings when commuters came home, it got a lot of foot traffic.

After my three miles, I returned to the store. The back door was unlocked now, and I saw Fran and another early morning employee, Miguel, mixing cupcakes in the kitchen. One quick glance at the chopped carrots on the table told me their work would result in carrot cake cupcakes, my favorite.

"Hey, guys!" I chirped as I walked in.

"Good morning," Miguel said

Nikki's employees were used to me coming in, a hot, sweaty mess. I whipped through the kitchen as fast as possible so the room would not absorb any of my nasty smell. Once I got to the staircase leading up to my apartment, I chugged the water bottle I left there earlier on my way down.

"You were in early this morning, Fran," I yelled back toward the kitchen. "What?"

Fran poked her head out of the kitchen. Her salt and pepper gray bob swung back from her face. She had on her tortoiseshell glasses that she wore when working on a project involving small details, along with her usual apron.

"Look at you. You are a ball of sweat. Get up in the shower before you stink this place up," Fran said. "I don't know what you're talking about. I was here at my regular time, six o'clock." Fran stood just below five feet, a good six inches below me, but loved to boss everyone around. It was hard to be offended by it because she was so lovable.

If it wasn't Fran here this morning, then who was it?

Chapter 2

My mind raced with random thoughts in the shower. Did Steve come here to kill me?

I shook my head and laughed out loud. *Impossible.* I knew where he is. Maybe a call to my lawyer was a good idea to make sure he was where he was supposed to be, just to assure myself.

The ringing of my landline phone interrupted my worrisome thoughts. Wrapped in a towel, I hobbled into the living room to the small, white table near my desk. The clock on the table read 6:15. My feet were still dripping wet, causing water to pool on the hard wood floor.

"Hello?"

The line went dead.

Weird. I looked at the phone and then hung it back up. There was no way to know who it was because the vintage phone did not have caller ID.

This day was not starting out well. First, the lights on in the store, and now crank calls. Did I dare ask, what was next?

Behind me on my nightstand table in my bedroom, my cell phone rang.

"Darn it," I mumbled, turning and running back toward the bedroom.

The ringing stopped just as my hand grabbed hold of the phone. Who could be calling me this early?

My old editor, Maggie Murphy, used to call me first thing, but it was definitely not her. She quit the agency a year ago. Another editor took over when she left. She hadn't called me back in months, because I wouldn't write the kind of story her publishing company wanted.

"The public needs to hear Kelly Clark's side of the story. Are you going to let him do that to you and not speak your peace? You're a hero. All of the slighted women in the world will love you. Your book sales will explode."

She said it enthusiastically, but it sounded fake to me. My answer was no then, and it was still no. Hence, the cold shoulder.

No voicemail, but my phone read one missed call from Adelle. Odd. Why would Adelle call so early? My stomach sank, wondering what the trouble was. That had to be her on the landline as well. A double call could not be a good thing this early in the morning.

"Are you coming tonight?" My goddaughter, Cindy, squeaked into the phone on the other end of the line when I called back.

"Of course, I'll be there. Where else would I be? Did you just call me, Cindy?"

"Yes," she giggled.

Hearing Cindy's voice made me relax. She had a rough year at pre-school last year, but she was a tough cookie. She would be entering Kindergarten in the fall, and it was causing some stress in her life. She could be a little eccentric compared to the other kids with her glasses and her obsession for books. I just kept telling her it was good to be different, and yes, the glasses did indeed mean she could be a writer someday like Aunt Kelly.

"I have to go. Mommy is coming," Cindy whispered into the phone.

The phone abruptly hung up. The thought of Cindy figuring out my phone number and making the call to confirm tonight made me laugh. She was sweet, and I was grateful for her call. She brought me back to the present, so I could forget my past. Somehow, I had to leave the worries about Steve behind if my goal was to make a new life for myself.

I snuck a peek at the clock.

Nikki would be up at eight-thirty with coffee. It was a morning ritual for us. That gave me a couple of hours to get some work done before she popped in.

* * * * *

"Good morning!"

Nikki bounced through the door like the ball of energy she always was in the morning. She had on her signature black top and black pants with her pink Chocolate Love apron over it.

"Check this out! It's a flyer I found on the front door this morning. We are joining a yoga class!"

Nikki plopped down in a high back chair next to my desk and set down a cup of coffee and a muffin for me next to my computer. *Bless her heart.*

"Nightmares again last night?" she asked. Her eyes widened a bit when she sat across from me.

"Mmph," I mumbled softly. Taking a second to swallow the muffin, I tried again. "Why do you say that?"

"You've got some nasty dark circles under your eyes. I'm not trying to make you feel bad. You just look a little frazzled. I've got a new under-eye concealer you should try. It does wonders for me."

Instead of responding, I shoved the rest of my blueberry muffin in my mouth and chewed. I was serious about putting some weight back on. I didn't want to look at that crazy woman in the mirror every morning.

"Here have mine as well," Nikki said, pushing her plate closer to me. My smile caused crumbs to fall out of my mouth onto my black sweatpants. Oh well. Another stain on these old pants wouldn't hurt.

Saving my work for the morning, I grabbed the cup of coffee, inhaling the

13

strong scent. There was a cinnamon undertone this morning.

"There's something I need to tell you, Nikki."

"What's wrong? Yoga? You don't want to do yoga?" Nikki asked in a panic.

"No, it's not that. Yoga sounds good. I think it would be fun."

I sipped my coffee, considering my thoughts. It was easy to talk to Nikki. There were no walls between us. She was always there for me when I needed someone to dump my troubles on. And if there was anyone who would understand my worries, it was her.

Nikki's eyes locked with mine.

"Tell me," she said.

"I got another email from Mandy last night. It's like the one from last year."

"I knew it! I went to bed thinking about that last night because the little girl's birthday is coming up. Delete it." Nikki slapped her leg.

"No, I can't do that." My hands jumped to the keyboard in protection.

"Kelly, why not? It's torture."

Good question. Why not delete it? Mandy was a constant reminder of my past.

I shrugged my shoulders. "Maybe there's a small part of me that wants to hear from Mandy and see little Caroline every year. It makes me physically ill seeing her, but to see those shining eyes, that little, angelic nose and rosy lips, makes me feel something inside."

Pride, maybe? She wasn't mine, of course, but to some degree, I gave her life. Little Caroline was here on this earth because of what I did.

"I don't feel like she's doing it to torture me. Besides, it's nice to see the baby," I whispered, my throat constricting over the word baby.

* * * * *

"It appears as though you may need to start IVF in order to get pregnant. As your doctor, I would recommend it. You have to consider the costs though, Kelly. There is a chance this will not be covered by your insurance."

"Let's go for it, honey," Steve said, pulling my hands into his. His eyes were a mixture of hope, joy, and baby fever. "We both want a family." He leaned in to kiss me. "I love you," he whispered.

Nikki reached out and placed her hand over mine, pulling me back to the present. I noticed her eyes were slightly full of anxiety, echoing mine. As much as Nikki could serve up some tough love, she had a soft heart and knew when to back down.

"Can I see her?" Nikki asked quietly.

"Of course."

I turned and opened the email on the desk in front of me.

There was baby Caroline in all her glory, smiling back at us. It was much less painful today looking at the photo than it was yesterday. It may get easier every year, if Mandy chose to keep it up.

"Wow," Nikki said. She leaned in, her face close to the picture.

"Yeah, I know."

We both stared at the computer screen and allowed some time to pass. I heard the sound of cars motoring down Third Street, the bark from a neighbor's dog, and the door downstairs opening and closing as more and more employees came in for their shifts.

"Will you reply?" Nikki finally asked.

"I haven't thought of that yet. I didn't last year. It's kind of weird to be in communication with her, right?" I rubbed my temples lightly and took a deep breath.

Nikki's eyes glazed over as she leaned back in her chair.

"You know, I used to think so, Kelly. She seems genuinely grateful to you. Her tone is not antagonizing at all."

She hid her face in her coffee cup before continuing.

"I've spent a lot of time being mad at Mandy. But in a weird way, she did you a big favor by blowing it all up. Look at what a monster Steve is. You didn't know that until she came along. None of us did. What if *you* would have had a child with him? He could have made your life hell."

As usual, Nikki was right.

"Yeah, I know. Scary, huh? It's still hard to let him go sometimes. We had such a great relationship together, but he's not the Steve I loved." I lowered my eyes to my beloved sweat pants. Even these nasty old pants were a reminder. They were a gift from Steve when I got my first book deal. He had always been so supportive of my dream. He'd handed these to me and said, "Congratulations, babe. You'll be working from home a lot from here on out." Somehow, I had blocked that memory from my mind until just now. It made me want to burn them.

Nikki nodded her head.

"Maybe I *will* write her back." I sighed, running my fingers through my hair.

"Can't believe I'm saying this, but you should. She didn't know what she was doing. Steve lied to her, too."

Steve duped us all. Sometimes I forgot how this was still hard on Nikki. She was very close to Steve. She had introduced me to him through a friend of a friend at her old job, when she was in advertising sales. I knew she beat herself up about what happened more often than I. She shouldn't. There was no way of knowing how things would turn out.

"Okay, enough of Steve. I want to talk to you about what happened this morning. When I left for my run at about five-forty, the lights for the shop were on. Fran said she didn't get in until six. Did we leave lights on last night? I could have sworn we turned them all off."

"Hmmm, that's weird. What lights were on exactly?"

"The lights in the back kitchen. I thought someone was here early to prep for a catering gig, or something."

"No, there shouldn't have been." Nikki's brown eyes popped up to the ceiling.

"Fran will be in early tomorrow morning. Hmm, that is odd. No one was scheduled to be here this morning. Were the doors locked?"

"I know the back door was because I had to open it to get outside."

"What about the front door?"

"You know, I'm not sure. Never looked. I didn't think to go back and check after opening the back door. I just assumed it was Fran because she's usually the first one here, and she normally locks herself back in."

"Let me talk to the rest of my staff. I didn't notice anything missing this morning. The majority of the cash went home with me yesterday. The only thing left was my usual one hundred dollars in the drawer. Miguel opened the register this morning and didn't mention any cash missing." Her hands wiped at the non-existent sugar on her apron.

"Maybe I should look into that alarm system after all," Nikki said, more to herself than to me.

"With the other break-ins, weren't the stores visibly disturbed and money taken?"

"Some of them were. Some were not disturbed at all. Nothing looked out of place to you?"

"No. It looked exactly the way it always looks when Fran is in and about to start her day. The lights were on, but nothing was out yet. I assumed she was reading recipes somewhere, or bringing up supplies from the basement."

"Assuming both doors were locked, I'll just start by asking everyone who has a key if they came in." I could tell by the way she refused to look at me, Nikki was not telling me something.

"How many people have keys again?" I asked, trying to pull her eyes back to mine. That was the problem with those chocolate ganache eyes. You could never tell when they darkened with emotion.

"Six, no, wait, seven. Myself and Bob," she said, referring to her husband. "You, Adelle, Fran, and Miguel. Mom and Dad as my just in case."

"Can you believe in a moment of panic I thought it was Steve this morning? Like he escaped prison to kill me, or something. Isn't that crazy? We'll probably be notified if he breaks out of maximum security prison." I chuckled nervously and pulled my hair back into a ponytail on top of my head.

Instead of Nikki laughing with me, her hands continued up and down on her apron in an anxious gesture.

Chapter 3

Three hours later, I took my lunch break downstairs in Chocolate Love. Nikki and I had lunch together around noon most days. Then I took a short break to either take a quick nap or help her frost cupcakes. If the writing for my morning had gone well, I frosted cupcakes.

The physical activity of frosting somehow connected the synapses in my brain where all of my best plotting happened. If my ideas were beyond blocked, I would lie down for thirty minutes to try and reboot.

This afternoon, we worked in the kitchen at one of the stainless steel high top tables, piping cream cheese frosting onto carrot cake cupcakes. Chocolate Love had a very specific way of frosting their cupcakes. Nikki was adamant we do it precisely the way our mother taught us back when we used to bake in our parent's kitchen in Geneva. The frosting was swirled counter clockwise three times until it capped off in the center with our signature flick of the wrist.

After my third tray, I stood back to admire my work. Mom would be very proud.

"Voila!"

Nikki didn't react. She sat hunched over at her desk working on paperwork.

"It says here Francis Enterprises ordered five dozen carrot cake cupcakes for their launch party tonight. Why do I only see three dozen there?"

Nikki had been in a bad mood ever since our talk this morning, and it was wearing on me.

My eyes scanned the kitchen for more trays. It wasn't Nikki's style to take her frustration out on her employees, but for her own stress level, I hoped the cupcakes were here somewhere. Plus, it was in my best interest to keep frosting. The process was helping me work out the scene I planned to write this afternoon.

"Shoot. They're not here," Nikki said. "Fran will have to help me whip up two more batches. I hope we can get this done before she leaves."

"I'm going to head back upstairs and get back to work."

Nikki peeked out of the kitchen into the front of the store. At this time of the day, Fran was normally assisting customers at the front counter.

"I'm probably going to work with Fran on the cupcakes and then head straight to Francis Enterprises. You're still heading over to Adelle's tonight after work, right?" Nikki called over her shoulder.

"Yep."

"I'll stop upstairs and say hello sometime this afternoon. If I miss you, see you in the morning?"

"Sounds good," I replied, untying my pink apron and setting it on a countertop.

"And don't worry about this morning. We'll get to the bottom of this, Kelly. I still have to talk to Miguel. Also, Elizabeth covers morning slots from time to time if I'm busy. It was one of them for sure. I'll speak to everyone by the end of the day."

Nodding my head, I waved goodbye.

"Don't forget about yoga tomorrow," she said, smiling.

"Tomorrow? I didn't realize it was starting that soon."

That didn't leave me a lot of time to figure out a way to back out. I was pretty sure Nikki worked it that way on purpose.

"Six o'clock on Thursday evenings in Batavia. You're going to love it. Bye."

Batavia was the town directly south of Geneva. She didn't give me a lot of details, which led me to believe she was holding out on me. What was I about to walk into?

The rest of the afternoon I chugged away at the book. It was a good day for me. This was the third book in my series about a young woman, Mary, who solved mysteries in California. It was kind of a mature Nancy Drew meets modern day California girl. I was finding it a little strange to write about California now that I no longer lived there.

In the past, if a landmark was needed in a scene, I drove there to check out the details. Now everything was completely from memory. The Internet was helpful, but it was always better to use a location I'd recently traveled to. Maybe it was time to relocate my Nancy Drew to Illinois.

Before I knew it, it was five-thirty. Hunger pains wrestled around in my stomach. A quick peanut butter and jelly sandwich was the best I could do with the limited amount of time left.

I threw on a nice pair of khaki shorts, ran a quick brush through my hair and reapplied a little mascara and lip gloss, not wanting to disappoint Cindy. She put my grooming habits under a microscope when she saw me. She was always overly curious as to what I was wearing and how I'd done my make-up.

The plan was to bike to Adelle's house, which was only a couple of blocks from downtown. If she came home at the time she promised, it should still be light out, so biking home safely would not be an issue.

I cut through Chocolate Love to head out the backdoor to get to my bike. Nikki had an area for people to lock their bikes in between Chocolate Love and Crystal, an eclectic, high end jewelry store in the building next to us.

I was always pleasantly surprised at the number of customers Chocolate

Love had at this time of day. Third Street got a second burst of energy from the commuters coming home. A lot of families met mothers and fathers at the train. I assumed somehow the kids figured out a way to convince their parents for a Chocolate Love treat before dinner.

When Nikki took over Chocolate Love, she created an outdoor seating area, accommodating up to thirty people. The area included a large patio and white Adirondack chairs facing Third Street. It was a huge success. Customers loved to people watch and socialize.

Tonight was no exception. The majority of the seats were taken.

Just as I unlocked my bike, I noticed one of the seats was filled by someone I knew. Seeing him made me freeze on the spot.

Jack. It was Jack O'Malley. The last I heard, he had moved to Europe after he received his law degree. Why was he back in town?

There had always been a part of me that knew I would run into him again someday. His family still lived in the area. I was just not prepared for it to be so soon and here at Chocolate Love.

Jack and I were high school and college sweethearts. We met as freshman at Geneva High School during French class. A friendship developed, and by the time we were juniors, we were dating.

We did the long distance thing for a few years in college until I ended things. My reasoning had been we met each other too young and should date other people to make sure it was right. We never did get back together. One of us was always dating someone else or living in a different state. It never seemed to be the right time for us.

After a while, I had met Steve and life moved on. The rumor was Jack married, too.

I wondered why he would choose to sit himself in front of my sister's store. Surely, he knew the connection to Nikki. Everyone in town knew Nikki owned this store. For that matter, everyone in town probably knew I lived up above the shop.

This was certainly not the time to catch up. I wasn't ready.

It had been a little over ten years since we last saw each other in a Geneva grocery store. He had been quiet and reserved, like he had a wall up. I left the store thinking he probably didn't care to see me again.

He looked good now. Great, in fact. He was a big guy, standing almost six-foot five-inches tall, with muscular arms, a big chest, and long legs. I remembered he always had to bend down to kiss me. Physically, he had not changed much. If anything, he looked more solid, like he firmed up any baby fat he had left. Not that he had a ton.

His dark hair was cut short, and he was casually dressed in shorts and a tee-shirt. That strong jaw line I always loved was still there. His hair had grayed a bit on the sides, giving him a distinguished, confident look. I always felt charged by an electric current around him. We were friends for almost three years before we started dating. When the spark finally lit, it started a flame that had never completely gone out. At least, for me that was.

Shaking those thoughts out of my head, I realized I hadn't thought about a man that way for a very, very long time. It felt good. As bittersweet as it was, at least I wasn't thinking of Steve.

At that moment, Jack stood up to reach his arms out to a toddler running at him from the direction of the train. He bent down to pick up the little girl and threw her up to the sky. When he caught her, she allowed him to cradle her close to his chest. A series of giggles escaped her mouth as she snuggled into him. A woman, who I assumed must be her mother and his wife, followed close behind.

Turning around to make a swift exit, I crashed right into a woman who had pulled up to use the bike rack. As our bikes collided, we both screamed before crashing to the ground.

In an instant, we were bound together like a bike pretzel, our legs, arms, and wheels interlocking.

"I'm so sorry," I said.

"For the love of God, try to pay better attention. Can't you see I'm an old lady!" the woman raged.

"Sorry."

A bit thrown off by her hostility, I yearned to get away before Jack saw me, or worse yet, tried to help.

I quickly stood up to right our bikes. A Good Samaritan walked over to help the older woman to her feet.

"Are you okay?" The woman helping asked. She was looking right at me, but I was too flustered to respond.

A quick glance in Jack's direction confirmed my fear. He, the woman, and the child, were all staring over at us. He caught my look and handed the child over to the woman, as though he planned to help.

"I just want my damn chocolates," the old woman yelled and stomped off in the direction of Chocolate Love.

"Thank you," I said to the Good Samaritan, who snickered lightly to herself. As quickly as possible, I got on my bike and took a short cut behind Chocolate Love in order to avoid riding past Jack. Without looking back, my legs peddled as fast as they could in the direction of Adelle's house.

What a close call, that was.

Chapter 4

"Hello," I called out.

I let myself in Adelle's house through the front door. No matter how many times I visited, the awe of walking into the front entrance never went away. Adelle's husband, Mike Stefano, worked for his family's construction business. They had been very successful in Chicago for many generations.

Mike was the prime candidate to take over once his father retired. This five thousand square foot home they lived in was built as a model when the company decided to expand out into the western suburbs. Adelle and her husband took it over once a larger, grander home was built for clients to see.

The two story foyer glowed with natural light from the large window atop the gargantuan front double doors. Radiant beams of light shot out in all directions from the crystal chandelier hanging above the Brazilian, cherry floors. My mother's reaction the first time she saw that chandelier was priceless. "Jesus," was all she said. Now, every time I looked at it, Mom came to mind.

"Aunt Kelly!" a chorus of kids yelled out.

The shrieking came from the top of the winding staircase leading up to the second floor. All three kids were positioned there ready to come charging down. It reminded me of the old Brady Bunch episodes we used to watch as kids when all the kids would line up and march down in a single file. Frank, Cindy, and Craig raced down the stairs like a thundering herd of elephants.

"I'm first!" Cindy yelled.

"Look out," Frank screamed as he tried to push past Cindy.

Little Craig got lost in the shuffle. He toddled down the stairs still a little unsure of his steps. Halfway down, he stopped and began to cry because he must have realized he had no chance of keeping up with his older siblings. Frank reached me first and threw his arms around me at the waist. Cindy was close behind. She grasped her arms up, asking to be picked up. To my left, I heard the double doors to Mike's office slam shut.

"Don't mind him," Adelle said. She floated down the stairs and scooped up Craig. She was dressed in an elegant wrap dress with her hair falling around her shoulders in waves. It almost looked like she was wearing extensions, but I knew her better than that.

"He's on a business call. He's been crabby today."

Craig's fussing calmed when Adelle dropped him in my arms. I reached down and scooped up Cindy with my other arm. Even though my back felt like it was going to break, it was worth it just to see the huge smiles on their faces.

"They are fed and bathed. You know the routine. They should all be in bed by seven-thirty because we have a big day tomorrow. We're going to the zoo for a play date. Frank can stay up till eight to watch his Batman show on TV, if that's all right with you."

"Can we play book store?" Cindy whispered in my ear.

"Yes, we can," I said. I widened my eyes to convey my excitement for her suggestion. My reaction made her laugh.

Cindy was wearing the nightgown I snagged for her from Chocolate Love. It had the logo on the front, a big cup of hot chocolate next to a cupcake with the saying "Give in to the Craving."

Adelle turned and made her way into the kitchen. We passed through the large sunken family room, which was my favorite. The other rooms in the house were too fancy to hang out in for my taste. How she managed to keep things intact with three kids running around, I had no idea.

In my opinion, this room was comfortable and classic at the same time. It had an extra large plasma TV and an over-stuffed suede sectional couch where I'd been known to doze off from time to time. This room also had a space behind the couch with a small desk and computer set up. It was where the kids did their homework or played on the computer. Mike and Adelle both had their own private offices elsewhere in the house.

The walls of this room were loaded with family pictures from all of their travels: the family at Disney World, Disneyland, Atlantis in the Bahamas, Cancun, and their trip to San Francisco. They made sure to take a big family vacation at least two times a year.

"Where are you going tonight?" I asked Adelle. The kids were still hanging on me like little monkeys. Craig put his face directly in front of mine, so it blocked my view of Adelle.

"We're going to catch dinner at Wildwood in town," she said, referring to one of my favorite restaurants right in the heart of downtown Geneva.

"Do you want us to bring you something back?"

My mind raced to their signature chicken dish I ate the last time I was there. My mouth watered thinking of it, marinated in garlic and herbs, roasted to perfection.

Steve and I went there a few years ago when we were visiting my sisters. The night had seemed so perfect at the time. Now I couldn't help but wonder if he had been cheating on me then while I sat there oblivious at Wildwood. Had it already started by that point?

"Kelly?" Adelle's voice interrupted my thoughts.

"What?"

"What were you just thinking of?" she laughed.

22

"Nothing."

"You had that look you get on your face when you plot your stories," she said, coming closer to me and scooping up Craig. As soon as he was in her arms, he started to wiggle out.

"Give Auntie Kelly some space, Craig. You can smother her later."

"It's okay," I said, stretching out my arms to welcome him back onto my lap.

The sound of Mike's shoes clicking on the floor told us he had finished up in his office.

"You're right. Thinking of my story," I said quickly.

"Sweetie, are you ready?" Mike asked. He was dressed in a sport coat and dress pants. His wavy, black hair was combed to perfection. Just seeing his attire made me worry. It didn't appear like these two were going out for a quick sandwich.

"You're just heading out for a sandwich, right?" I asked in a wary voice. Things had been going so well with the book. I knew it would be horrible to lose momentum at this point in the game. I needed to stick to my early morning work schedule.

"Right. We might grab a quick drink with a client afterwards," Mike said, leaning down to kiss me hello on the cheek. "We won't be late."

Adelle stood up and moved closer to Mike to pick something off of his sport coat.

"You look great, babe," she said. These two were ridiculously attractive when they stood next to each other. They had it all: beauty, success, money, great kids. I was happy for Adelle, but I had to work like crazy not to be jealous of her.

"All right then, we're off," Adelle said. She bent down to kiss the kids one by one. Mike was already out the door.

"And remember, you're always welcome to use the computer in the family room if you want to work."

I blew the comment off and didn't show any reaction to it. If Adelle had paid any attention to my work, she would know the evening was a horrible time for me to write. Instead, I said, "Have a good time."

Cindy started to pull at my hand to lead me down to the basement.

"It's all set up, Auntie Kelly. Are you ready?"

I smiled at Cindy and allowed her to pull me into her fantasy land.

In order to get all the kids involved, Cindy and I had to be flexible with our roles. Craig wanted to play the customer who messed up the entire store and left crumbs everywhere, in other words, himself. Frank participated as long as we allowed his G.I. Joe characters to work at the book store.

Being with the kids was refreshing, exhilarating, and exhausting all at the same time. I was blown away by their imaginations. It took me back to when Adelle, Nikki, and I were kids. Even then, I remembered how much fun it was to play together because of how different we all were. It was healthy for me as a writer to go back to that time and remember the process of allowing your imagination to take over. These three did it so effortlessly.

By the time I got all three kids in bed, I was exhausted. How did Adelle do this every day and still look the way she did? I always thought she secretly had help, maybe a live-in nanny that hid in the closet whenever someone came over. But I'd never found any evidence of it.

At last, I had a moment to myself and surrendered to the couch. I turned on the television more for the noise in the quiet house, than to watch something.

If my mind wasn't so sleepy, this would have been a great time to browse through Mike and Adelle's extensive library, a chance I didn't get very often. Although they weren't big readers, they *were* collectors. A huge array of classics, and not so classics, that would warm the heart of any avid reader. A lot of it was first edition: Tolstoy, Fitzgerald, Bronte, Irving, Stevenson, and so much more.

Unfortunately, reality television was about all my mind could handle right now.

At nine, I turned off the television and checked my email. Upon opening my account, a familiar email address popped up.

> *"Hi Kelly, I'm coming to Chicago on Sunday night. I need to see you. It's important." –Gina*

Gina Phillips was a so-called friend who leaked pictures of Steve and me to the press after the arrest. That year had been a record high for men killing spouses or lovers in the United States. Because my story had such a strange twist, a few networks wanted it to be the front runner.

A number of broadcasters had called me directly, begging for an interview. Many wanted to focus on a positive outcome rather than dwell on all the sadness. My story would show the world "What happens when abused wives struck back." When they couldn't reach me, they had found Gina.

Gina had been more than happy to give them everything they were asking. The media couldn't get enough of us at our wedding, honeymoon, and life in California. They painted me as the wholesome Midwest girl who got caught up in a firestorm of scandal.

Gina even shared with the press our story of infertility and our desperation for a child. It made Steve look even worse, because he attempted to kill his unborn child with Mandy, while trying to have a child with me.

I couldn't show my face in public for a long time. The press hounded me for months. The only thing that helped was the passing of time. Eventually, the media moved on to their next victim.

After that incident, I closed the door on Gina's friendship and never looked back. I couldn't forget how she betrayed me in order to get her own fifteen seconds of fame.

In the last two days, a Pandora's Box from my past opened. First the email from Mandy, Jack at Chocolate Love, and now this email from Gina. Why was all this happening now?

I deleted Gina's email, logged out of my email account, and stretched out on the couch with the intention of taking a quick nap. It was closing in on nine forty-five, and like usual, Adelle was late.

Lying my head down on Adelle's plush couch, I considered turning on the television, again. I felt my eyelids getting heavy over my eyes. My last thought before drifting off to sleep was about my book. I couldn't wait to wake up early tomorrow morning to write. It was my only peace. My only way of escaping the hell that was my life.

Chapter 5

"Kelly?" a familiar voice inquired on the other end of the line.

"Jack? Is that you?" A blush in my cheeks spread like wild-fire across my face as it kicked in what was happening. It was Jack, and he was calling me.

"It's me," he confirmed. His voice was soft and familiar. "Will you join me for dinner tonight?"

"Dinner?" What about the other woman he was with the other day? Wasn't he married? What about the little girl? "But, what about?"

"There's no one else, Kelly. There has never been anyone else."

His voice didn't sound right. It changed from the deep soothing tone of Jack's voice, to the rushed energetic tone of Steve.

"I'll pick you up tonight," he said, his voice clearly the voice of Steve now. "Be ready at seven. And don't forget to pick up a half a pound of turkey, sliced very thin, and a half a pound of Monterey cheese. The kids like it for their lunch."

* * * * *

What? Firmly awake now, I jumped up to a seated position and found my body once again drenched in sweat. Morning sunlight filled the family room, alerting me I was still at Adelle's.

It took a second to register Adelle in the kitchen on the phone. She was twirling her hair with her finger and sitting at the island.

"Can you pick that up on the way home tonight? We have turkey for today, but we'll definitely be out of it by tomorrow," she said. I assumed she was speaking to Mike. If he had already left for work, it was probably past eight in the morning.

"She's still asleep," Adelle said into the phone. "No, I'll tell her we were home by ten. She doesn't need to know it was after twelve. You know how she gets."

"Auntie Kelly, we're waiting for you," Cindy said from the kitchen. Craig was next to her clutching his beloved blanket. They were both dressed and ready for the day.

I could hear the cartoons that played in the kitchen. They probably had been sitting in there waiting for me to wake-up.

"Hey guys," I said, managing to mask my anger with a smile. It wasn't their fault their parents liked to take advantage of me.

"Good morning," Adelle said. She was dressed in a casual sundress, her hair done up in a trendy braid. I must have really been out cold in order to sleep through the entire family getting ready for the day.

"We're off to a play date this morning. We'll have to leave in about fifteen minutes. You're welcome to stay as long as you want."

"Adelle, you were supposed to be home at nine last night."

"We weren't home much later than that," she said, sitting down next to me on the couch. "You were asleep, so we figured we would let you rest. You must have needed the sleep if you slept in this late." She reached out and ran her hand up and down my arm.

"Adelle, I needed to write this morning."

It was frustrating to have an argument with her because she didn't understand my needs as a writer. Besides that, she lied her way out of it every time. I couldn't catch her at it, either. She wasn't one of those people who got tangled up in their own lie. She expertly weaved her way out of it without a drop of sweat.

"Honey, look, let's not make this a big thing. You were tired, you needed the extra sleep, the kids had a great time, and it's not much later than the time you normally start work. Please don't get yourself all worked up. If you want to, we can just throw your bike in the trunk. We'll drop you off at home on the way to our play date. You'll be writing by eight-thirty." She smiled and started to rub my arm again.

"Adelle, you don't get it, do you?" I growled. Adelle looked startled by my reaction.

"Kelly, maybe we can talk later," Adelle said, motioning to the kids. I got what she was implying, and she was right. It wasn't appropriate to have this discussion in front of them.

"Let's go in the kitchen and have a cup of coffee."

"We need to get to our play date."

"You can be a few minutes late." I stood and walked into the kitchen without turning to see if she would follow me. My slept in clothing clung to me in an awkward way, but I ignored it. I was too upset to deal with it.

Her large eat-in kitchen had black, granite countertops and white cabinets with an island in the center of the kitchen. The room was bright and inviting, lit primarily by the natural light from the skylights and bay window where the kitchen table was set up. I moved over to the cabinet next to the sink where she had her coffee cups and took one down for myself. After pouring myself a cup, I turned to find her seated at the island. Blowing matted hair out of my face, I took a quick sip of coffee.

"Where's Frank?" I wanted to make sure her oldest wasn't around the corner about to listen in to our conversation, as he tended to do.

"He's upstairs in his room."

"Want a cup of coffee?"

"No. Kelly? What is wrong with you? You're never this crabby."

Normally when I was in a situation like this with Adelle, I was always the first to fold. I hated the confrontation, the arguing, the frustration of trying to talk to someone who was so head-strong and so determined to be right, they would lie their way to victory. However, I was learning something about myself. If I always took that position, if I always tried to be the bigger person, I would become a very, very resentful person. This was exactly what was happening to me. It was time to stick up for myself.

"Adelle, don't turn this on me. I heard you on the phone with Mike. You came home after twelve last night and were going to tell me you were home at ten."

Adelle didn't even hesitate. "Why is this such a big deal? You always make a mountain out of a molehill."

Before she began to speak again, I cut her off.

"This is a big deal, Adelle. You don't get it. This book needs to be written because I have to support myself. I don't have a "Mike" to provide me with all of this," I said, waving my hands in the air, referring to our surroundings. "The best time for me to write is in the morning. You don't seem to understand that. You don't seem to *want* to. It's just push-over Kelly. Do you have any idea what I've gone through? Do you even care?"

"Kelly, I'm sorry," she said, surprising me. "You're absolutely right. I was inconsiderate last night."

She shocked me into silence. My anger melted away quicker than expected, like warm butter on a crescent roll. Adelle admitting she was wrong? It was what I had hoped for, but not what I was prepared for.

"Mike and I have been going through a tough time. We just needed a night out last night. We ended up seeing one of his clients at the restaurant and stayed to have a drink with him. We completely lost track of time. They finalized a deal last night, so we couldn't leave when we planned to. Mike's business is doing fine, but in this economy, he needs every order he can get."

"Are you guys going to be okay?" My irritation was gone now that she had brought up her and Mike again. My thoughts turned to the kids. Mike and Adelle had to be okay. Those kids needed them to be.

"We'll be fine. It's just that Mike has been working so much to keep his company going. It's put a lot of stress on both of us." Her hand reached up to play with her large diamond earring.

It wasn't like Adelle to allow anyone to see her sweat, especially me. She whined and exaggerated to get you to do things for her, but this time felt different. She didn't let anyone see behind the perfect curtain. She always asked me to baby-sit so she and Mike could have alone time, but she had never used the stress of his business as a reason. It was a little off-setting to me.

"I didn't realize you guys were under so much stress. You never talk about your finances. Forget about last night. It's not a big deal." My hand reached out to grab hers.

"We'll be fine, Kelly. Like I said, we just needed a night out. We really appreciate you staying over last night. The kids adore you. Let me take you home. You have to get home to work. I feel terrible about your morning deadline."

Just like that, she was back to perky Adelle.

"Well, it's not a real deadline. It's just my time to work," I said, feeling foolish now.

"Right, well, either way, it's important to you. Let me get the kids," Adelle said, jumping up from the chair.

I sat at the island for a minute going over our conversation in my mind. Only after she left the room did it sink in that Adelle never addressed the real problem. She gave me a little nugget of information about her life, just the tiniest hint they may be struggling financially, and then glazed over what happened last night. We didn't talk about me. We never talked about me. And we certainly didn't talk about the fact that she lied last night and took advantage of me.

It was time to get out of this house and back to my apartment. I was tired of feeling like I was being worked over. I needed to commit to some stronger walls around my fortress. Heaven knew it was time.

Chapter 6

By the time we got to Chocolate Love, it was close to nine in the morning. It took longer for us to get the kids out of the house than planned.

"Thanks for the ride, Adelle." Grabbing my bike from the back of the SUV, I waved goodbye to the kids.

Instead of stopping to see Nikki in the shop, I went straight upstairs to take a shower. What a night!.

While my hair conditioner set, I leaned my forehead against the cool tile of the shower wall. Letting the hot water beat away the balls of stress in my upper back, I tried my best to relax.

Sometimes I couldn't help but think it would be healthier for me to move away from Adelle. Of course, moving away from her meant moving away from her kids and Nikki, which was something I didn't want to do. It was impossible right now anyway.

Steve's voice in my head stiffened the muscles in my body, ruining any progress I'd made to relax.

> *"We may have to start taking on some debt to continue with these treatments, Kelly. It will be worth it in the end. We'll have a family."*

Rinsing the conditioner from my hair, I stepped out of the shower onto my pink, fluffy bath mat. While wrapping a large towel around me, I heard someone knock on the apartment door. It had to be Nikki. She probably heard me come in, or heard the shower on.

"I was hoping you would come up," I said, pulling the door open. Surprisingly, it wasn't Nikki, but Fran in front of me. She held a large cup of coffee and a shopping bag.

"Look who finally decided to come home." A smirk spread across Fran's face, her dark eyebrows moving up and down in suggestion. "Good morning, Kelly," she said, smiling up at me. Standing in my large door frame, I was reminded of how petite Fran was. What exactly she was suggesting, I wasn't sure.

"Thanks for the coffee. I stayed at Adelle's last night to baby-sit the kids," I said to discourage anymore suggestive eyebrows.

"Oh," she said, not bothering to hide the disappointment. Her eyes reached past me to see into the apartment. Although Fran and I had spent a lot of time together downstairs, she had never been up to my place. I stepped to the side and waved my arm to beckon her in.

"Please, come on in."

Fran was a refreshing distraction from all of my frustration from last night. Plus, anytime Fran walked into a room, she brought a ray of sunshine along with her. I respected and cherished the time when we were together. I needed her sunshine this morning.

"Let me just go run and throw on some clothes," I said, making my way back to my bedroom. Located right off of my living room, I didn't have far to go. The door sat slightly ajar, so we could talk while I dressed in cut-off sweatpants and a Chocolate Love tee-shirt. Combing my hands quickly through my hair, I stole a quick glance in the mirror. Shrugging, I gave up on my hair. Fran was not going to care.

"I don't have any coffee to offer you this morning, Fran," I called out to her.

"No coffee for me. Just bringing yours up because Nikki asked me to. She felt bad she had to miss your regular coffee time because of a meeting with a potential new client. I came up at eight-thirty, but there was no answer. You didn't head out for your run either this morning. I was worried you might be sick, or something. When you came in a couple of minutes ago, I heard the shower on, so here I am."

"That's very thoughtful of you." Stepping out of my room, I took my cup of coffee from Fran.

"I was supposed to be here at eight-thirty, but things changed."

"Changed, huh?" Fran commented, while bending down to look at one of my framed photos on my side table.

"Yes."

Fran's comment made me wonder how she felt about Adelle. Nikki was not one to gossip. She might talk to me about Adelle, but she never said anything negative about her to anyone else, especially an employee.

"You were here early this morning again?"

Fran motioned her finger at the picture. My nod affirmed her unspoken request to pick it up. It was the one of me accepting an award at a Mystery Writers of America conference a few years ago.

"Yes," she said. "You look beautiful in this photo, Kelly."

"Thanks. It was taken after my first book was published."

"You look so happy." Her eyes crinkled, and a huge smile shined brightly on her face.

"I was."

"How is your new book coming along?"

"Ugh."

"That good, huh?" she laughed. "Don't worry, it will be great." She set the photo back on the table and turned to look squarely at me. "It's a real shame

31

what happened to you."

Her comment caught me off guard. Fran and I had never really spoken about my past.

"It's only going to make you a better writer now that you've gone through something so difficult. You have a gift, Kelly. If you stop now, he will have taken that, too."

"Thanks, Fran. I won't," I mumbled. My mind grasped for something to change the subject. Luckily, Fran picked up on my body language and did it herself.

"Hey, before I forget, Nikki wanted me to give you something." She moved back to the chair where she placed her shopping bag.

"What is it?" Curious now, I took a step closer to peer inside.

"Just a little something for tonight."

She ran her fingers through her hair and sat down. She was going to wait to watch me open it.

"There should be a little card in there," she said, pointing her finger at the bag. I had a feeling Fran acted as more than just the delivery person in this transaction.

I fished inside to find a little, square envelope. Whatever was in there looked to be hot pink and black. What is Nikki up to?

The card read:

Dear Kelly,

I have to be in a meeting all day. Here's a little something for you to wear to our first yoga class tonight. Don't worry, mine will not be the same color. Hehe. Pick you up at five-thirty. Class starts at six!

Love,
Nikki

At first glance, it appeared as though the bag held two separate items. One was a hot pink, fitted yoga top and the other, a pair of black yoga pants. I gave them a little stretch to see if they would show me any mercy. Because the bag still had some weight to it, I reached in again and pulled out a small tube of make-up.

"It's a new highlighter for under-eye darkness. I'm the one that turned Nikki onto this stuff. It works wonders."

"Oh," I said.

"Don't worry, honey, you look fabulous. Everyone could use a little help though, right? You should see my eyes before I apply that stuff. These early morning shifts wreak havoc on my dark circles," Fran laughed. "Not that I would ever change my hours. I love the early morning."

"Fran, what was Nikki up to?" I asked.

"She just wanted to do something nice for you. I'll tell her you love it.

Well, gotta go! Business calls!"

"Thanks, Fran."

Fran turned to go. Just as she was about to shut the door, she re-opened it and stuck her head back in.

"You're going to look great in that outfit. Good luck!" With that, she closed the door.

I had a bad feeling about this. Good luck?

* * * * *

The day trudged along. I felt well rested but still off from having spent the night at Adelle's. I just couldn't seem to get in the zone. Trying to keep my promise to myself, I made sure to eat three meals and break for snacks.

By the end of the day, I only had two new pages written. When I re-read them, the words didn't flow the way they should. Also, the main character's voice didn't work the way it did before in blending with the story. The character now sounded bitter and crass when I didn't intend her to be.

At five, I decided to delete my work and called the day a wash. Thanks, Adelle.

I spent the next thirty minutes dressing and primping for class. Fran was right about the under eye highlighter. My eyes looked less "night of the living dead" and more "old" me, as Nikki would say, when I examined them in my bathroom mirror. Since I had such luck with the under eye make-up, I decided to go ahead and apply blush, a little eyeliner, mascara, and lip-gloss.

Just as I was contemplating washing it all off, there was a knock at my door.

"Man, am I glad to see you," I said, letting Nikki in. She had on a matching outfit to mine except her top was a teal blue.

"You look fantastic," she said. Her short hair was pulled back by a bobby pin.

She turned me around and smacked my rear. "Look at that butt. And your eyes. You look so different today. You really look hot, Kelly."

"Do you think so?" I asked, trying to look back at my butt unsuccessfully.

Instead of continuing to strain my neck, I walked over to the full length mirror that rested against one of the living room walls. I couldn't help but notice the lack of curves where they once were, but somehow I did look better than yesterday.

"Where did they go?" I sighed, waving my hands up in the direction of my breasts. The weight loss had not been kind to them.

"They'll come back. Don't think about that. Day by day."

"I know. Thanks again for the outfit."

"No problem. You're getting there, sis. Okay, let's go."

Nikki seemed distracted and in a rush.

"Don't you want to come in for a minute? How was your day? Did you get a new client?"

"Sure did. We can talk about it in the car," she said, turning to head out the door. "I hear this class fills up quick. We want to get a good spot. I am so excited!"

I hurried to grab my keys and locked up. Nikki was already half-way down the stairs.

"Wait, we never talked about yoga mats. Do we need to bring our own?"

"I already picked up two for us today. They're in the car," she called up the stairs.

On the car ride over to Batavia, we discussed my adventures from the night before: my near run-in with Jack, the email from Gina, and my unexpected sleepover at Adelle's. Nikki was shocked and upset at the appropriate times during my stories, but still appeared distracted by something.

I was worried about both of my sisters, especially after the comment Adelle made about financial stress. My book better sell fast. I wanted to start paying Nikki some rent for the apartment and be able to support myself again.

We arrived at Shannon Hall, an old Catholic church in Batavia, with fifteen minutes to spare. The Batavia Park District took over Shannon Hall when the church's congregation decided to build a new church. Now the park district used it to host banquets, ceremonies, and classes.

Nikki was out of the car and rushing to the door before I could even undo my seatbelt.

As soon as I was out of the car, I hustled my way across the parking lot to catch up with her. She was holding the door for me and waving her hand in an impatient movement.

"Hurry up. I want to get close to the front."

The space was one large room with the instructor set up to teach on what used to be the altar. The setting sun shined through the stained glass windows at this hour of the day, shooting colorful beams of light all over the room. It was breathtaking. It must have been hard to leave this building behind when the congregation moved on to greener pastures.

The class participants were setting up their mats on the carpeted area that once held the pews.

"Over here. Please sign in first, and then choose a place for your mat," the instructor called out from atop the altar.

My heart stopped when I recognized her to be the woman Jack greeted yesterday in front of Chocolate Love. Her beautiful, chestnut hair was pulled back into a ponytail tonight, making her features all the more striking. Her eyes, a brilliant shade of green, stirred something in me.

"Come on," Nikki said, pulling me to the sign-up sheet. I froze in place, causing me to block the rest of the people entering the hall.

"Kelly, is that you?" the instructor asked, as I approached the altar. Her athletic, cat-like form jumped down from the altar and gracefully moved toward me. This can't be her. Her entire appearance had been transformed. She was a compact, lean and mean, fighting machine. Not the overweight adolescent that used to sit next to me when I went to Jack's home for dinner.

"Mari?" The confirmation in her green eyes told me my assumption was correct. This was indeed Mari, Jack's younger sister.

"Kelly!" she exclaimed, moving fast and catching me in a surprisingly strong hug. It wasn't the body I remembered hugging, but it was the same intensity I once knew very well. Mari was always very expressive with her emotions. If she liked you, you knew it. If she didn't like you, that was also made very clear.

When I broke up with Jack years ago, we had stayed in touch for a short time afterward. She was a teen when I was with Jack and having a hard time battling through life with an extra fifty pounds. I had always done my best to help her with her self-esteem and find a way to ignore all of the teasing and bullying she received when in school. We eventually grew apart, but she had often been in my thoughts throughout the years.

"Look at you!" I clasped her shoulders with my two hands. She wore a tight pair of light gray yoga pants and a pink sports bra that showed off her six pack of a stomach.

"You're a knock out! You look amazing," I told her.

"Thank you." Her radiant smile made it apparent she enjoyed the compliment. After a couple of seconds in her presence, it was clear her self-esteem was at a whole new level now.

"I finally got sick of being the fat kid and took some action by getting in shape. Then I topped it off by marrying a Marine!" she laughed. "We train for triathlons together now."

"And you teach yoga, I see. How long have you been doing this?"

The class filled while we spoke. Nikki was no longer at my side. Taking a quick peek in the crowd, I finally spotted her setting up out mats near the front. When I saw who she set our mats next to, my voice came to an abrupt halt.

Another set of green eyes stared back at me.

Chapter 7

Seeing Jack's confident smile made the room come alive as my senses revved up. My vision was clearer, and my nose picked up a few more scents in the room. Even the dust motes dancing in the sunshine became alive and vibrant. It was like the animal in me awakened.

Jack lifted his left arm up in a way of a greeting. He looked handsome in a white tee-shirt and a pair of old, blue sweatpants. The muscles in his chest pulled the tee-shirt tight in all the right places.

I didn't remember him being so muscular. He had bulked up a lot since college. Another equally muscular man was standing next to him, observing me. Jack looked at him and nodded in some kind of confirmation.

Nikki beamed back at me. So, that was what this was all about. She knew Jack would be here.

"I just moved back to the area," Mari said. "Our mother is not well. My husband, Dan, and I, as well as our little girl, moved back here a couple of months ago to help take care of her. It got to be too much for us to handle on our own, so Jack relocated here to help out. That's my husband standing next to Jack."

I lifted my hand up in response to Jack's greeting and gave him an awkward smile. He looked much more enthusiastic to see me than he had in the past. Of course, it was now ten years since we had last seen each other. Maybe he had gotten over any weirdness left over from our break-up.

"Go say hi to Jack," Mari said. "He would love to talk to you. I have to sign in the rest of the class. Can't believe how popular it has become. Maybe because it's a good mix of men and women. Looks like a great place to meet people."

She walked away from me. I was starting to believe Nikki and Mari planned this whole thing.

After I signed my name, phone number, and e-mail, as well as Nikki's, I passed it to the person behind me.

I gathered my courage and made my way toward Jack. Why did it feel so awkward to see him? Didn't he know what happened to me? It wasn't really a question of did he know; more like how much did he know?

Could he still be angry at me for ending our relationship? Impossible. So many years had passed. It was ridiculous to even think he would have any feelings left for me at all. There had probably been many women in his life since we ended things. All I had to do was look at him to know that. Jack was a catch.

Hoping not to be caught, I snuck a quick glance at his ring finger on his left hand. Empty.

"Hi, Jack." My voice came out much softer than intended, almost a whisper. He surprised me by reaching out to give me one of his signature bear hugs. This close to him, I was able to confirm Jack had packed some serious muscle on his frame. He smelled just like the Jack I remembered, a mix of soap and sandalwood.

"Hi, Kelly. It's great to see you. You look great. This is Dan, Mari's husband." He moved over to give me room to reach over and shake Dan's hand. Dan greeted me warmly, but certainly took a moment to examine me. I could only imagine what stories he had heard from Jack. Hopefully, they were positive.

I stepped back onto my mat placed almost on top of his by Nikki. I shot her a quick glare before turning back to talk to Jack.

"Sorry. Let me just move this over a bit," I said, using my feet to try and push my mat off of his.

"Here let me help you." He bent down, as did I, to help maneuver it.

"Is this okay?" he asked, looking up at me at the same time I raised my head. Our faces were only inches apart. From this close I could see the few laugh lines he had developed around his eyes since we were last together. Jack with a few wrinkles. Mesmerizing. I wanted to reach out and run my fingers across his face.

"Kelly?" he asked when I did not answer.

Breaking from my trance, I stood up and did my best to pull myself together. He stood as well and placed his hands on his hips watching me closely. What just happened there?

"I'm sorry to hear about your mom. Mari told me she's not feeling well." Thank goodness Mari had given me that little piece of information. There was something for me to talk about. Otherwise, I worried I would just be smiling up at him like an idiot.

"Yeah, her heart's not great. She never took the best care of herself after Dad died. Now it's catching up with her."

I remembered Jack's mother, Peggy, was a widow at a very young age. I had never gotten the chance to meet his father. By the time we had started dating, he was long gone. It didn't surprise me that both of her children moved back to the area to take care of her in her time of need. She was a sweet lady.

"I'm very sorry to hear about your divorce. I'm glad you made it through all that okay." Although he did not come right out and say it, I knew what "all that" was referring to.

From the look on his face, Jack seemed to realize he had said something wrong and tried to back pedal. "We don't have to talk about that now. Or, ever, if you don't want to."

"It's okay," I said, taking the rubber band on my wrist and pulling my hair back into a ponytail. The task allowed me time to gather my thoughts and pull myself together. Jack held eye contact with me while I played with my hair. Suddenly, his eyes wandered down to his mat, which he moved a bit with his foot. Before they broke focus with mine though, I saw something in them. For the first time, I thought he was nervous as well.

"It was a disaster," I said, laughing an awkward giggle. "I'm just trying to move on with my life."

Jack smiled at me and nodded his head.

"What about you? What have you been up to?" I was dying to know his story. Seeing that he was not wearing a ring made me think the rumors about Jack were not true.

"I just accepted a job transfer to Chicago with my law firm. Mom is sick so, well, here I am," he said, opening his hands.

Even his hands looked like they had put on muscle. I stared at them for a minute, thinking back to the way they used to curve around mine when we held hands. I wondered would his hands feel the same to me now. Would his touch on my body be as familiar and comforting as it once was? Would it all be the same? Or even better? My mind raced back to the reflection I saw in the mirror today in my yoga attire. Could he even love me the same when he figured out how much of me Steve took with him?

I fought the temptation to ask him about the rumor that he was married. If he wasn't offering up the information, it didn't feel right to ask.

"Everyone, it's time to start. Please take a seat on your mat," Mari's voice called out.

"Enjoy the class," he said and winked at me.

The gesture made my heart flutter.

He didn't seem to be harboring any kind of ill-will toward me. I was always self-conscious of that. Maybe we could put all that in the past and be friends again.

I spent a few awkward seconds dancing around on the mat, trying to best sit myself down. My only hope was that my body didn't make any awkward noises. I gave Nikki one last glare. I wanted to kill her for so blatantly setting this up. Was I ready for this? My mind told me no, but my body felt differently based on its reaction.

It was great talking to Jack again. But did it have to be in a spandex outfit, twisting my body into a pretzel for the first time after all of these years? Couldn't there have been a little bit of a warm-up?

"Let's take a few deep breaths and raise our hands above our heads. Yoga will teach us to be aware of our breath, align our spine, and most importantly, strengthen our core muscles. Now bring your arms back down to your lap and take in three big breaths," Mari said.

The room filled with the sound of waterfalls and monks chanting. Mari's music gave another element to the class. It made the church hall even more stunning and peaceful at the same time.

"Let's lay back on our mats. Raise your arms above your head, close your eyes, and stretch your feet out in front of you. Lay as flat as you can. Make sure the small of your back is touching the mat. Go ahead and stretch," Mari said, elongating the word, stretch.

Jack and I lay next to each other on our mats. We were so close to each other it gave me the sense of feeling like we were in bed next to each other. I wanted to open my eyes and take a peek at him. The smell of him next to me was an intoxicating aroma. And it made me think back to our first date.

"I don't think I'm ever going to forget the way you smell tonight," Jack said before taking my hand and helping me into the car. We were both dressed up for our first date—a movie followed by dinner at Luigi's Pizza. At the end of the night, in his mother's Ford Explorer, he leaned in to kiss me for the first time. He took his time, reaching first to cup my face in his hands. With surprising finesse, his thumb slowly caressed my cheek while simultaneously pulling me in for...

Suddenly I felt Nikki nudge my side. My head jerked over to her. She motioned with her pointer finger for me to get up. The rest of the class was now in a seated formation with their arms above their heads. Quickly, I sat up and tried to copy what the rest of the class was doing. Beside me, Jack chuckled lightly.

"You okay?" he leaned in and whispered.

Had I fallen asleep? I was so relaxed and tired from being at Adelle's the night before, it was entirely possible.

"Yeah," I said, turning and meeting his gaze. His brow was lined in anticipation of my answer. He remained close to me, looking as though he wanted to say something more.

"Say it."

"What?" I whispered.

Jack shook his head and smiled down into his pose with the same sweet smile I remembered from so long ago.

"Nothing," he whispered back.

What was he going to say?

Through the rest of the class, I tried to remain as focused as possible. Jack's close presence was impossible to ignore. His body easily bent itself to the game of yoga like a pro. I had to refrain from blatantly staring at the way he was able to perform each pose with ease. Perhaps Nikki was right about me needing more time with the male gender. I practically had to keep myself from panting being this close to Jack. It was ridiculous.

The class ended after an excruciating forty-five minutes. Yoga was much harder than I thought it would be and was made more difficult by trying to remain cool. Mari spoke once more before closing the class.

"That was a great first class, everyone. I ask that you please spend a few minutes listening to a friend of mine speak about a local 5K charity race she is heading up in two weeks. Sharon Winters has raised over three hundred thousand dollars over the last year for cardiovascular programs here in the United States. Please welcome her and feel free to take a sign-up sheet on your way out. Thank you."

Sharon was an attractive blond, with hair cut in the adorable pixie style I saw a lot of Hollywood actresses wearing lately. She carried herself with confidence as she walked up to the altar and stood next to Mari. She must have been taking the class, because she was wearing a yoga outfit and had a slight shimmer of sweat over her body.

She spoke for a few minutes about the threat of cardiovascular disease in the United States and how the money she raised in the 5K would go to our local hospital. It was clear she was very passionate about the cause, so I tried my hardest to give her my utmost attention.

But I was distracted by thoughts of Jack. Should I ask him out for coffee? That might be a bit much. My old-fashioned tendencies felt the man should ask the woman. In this case though, it was not a date. It would be two friends getting reacquainted.

Before long, her talk ended, and we all rolled up our mats to leave.

I looked over to Nikki for a sign as to what to do. By the way her eyebrows bounced up and down, it was obvious she wanted me to move in for the kill.

"I'll see you later," he said, touching my arm. "I want to go ask Sharon some questions about the race."

"Sounds good," I said, feeling like I just got punched in the face.

"Let's go," Nikki said, pulling me in the direction of the door. "If he's not going to ask you out, we gotta leave him wanting more."

I turned to see Jack pointing at the sheet with the race information on it. Sharon's blond head bobbed up and down in confirmation. They laughed together about something on the piece of paper. A strange emotion ran through me. Jealousy?

Sharon and Jack seemed to be hitting it off. She reached her hand up and tucked her hair back behind her ear in a flirtatious manner. Her eyes jumped up and caught me staring at her. I quickly averted my eyes and left the building.

Chapter 8

"What *was* that?" I asked Nikki through gritted teeth once we were back in her car. The car felt like we had stepped into a furnace. She punched buttons on the dashboard to make sure the air conditioning was on full blast.

"That was step one of my master plan," Nikki said, beaming back at me.

"Nikki, don't pull that kind of stuff on me," I said, reaching over and punching her in the arm.

"Ouch. Come on, you're not seriously mad at me, are you? You liked seeing Jack. It's all over your face. Look at you, you're still blushing, Kelly."

I made a quick scan of the parking lot to make sure Jack wasn't anywhere near the car, and could possibly see us argue. He had to still be inside.

"Let's put the windows down until the air is cool," Nikki said.

"Not a chance. I don't want anyone to hear us."

At this point, I was annoyed with her, and now Jack, seeing he still had not exited Shannon Hall yet. That meant he was probably talking to Sharon what's-her-face.

"Mari was in the shop last week. She told me about the yoga class and about Jack being back in town. I swear to you, I was not going to go to the class. But then there was that flyer in the door. It felt like we were destined to go. And you were having such a bad week. My hope was that if Jack was there, he might cheer you up.

"Listen, I'm sorry, Kelly. I won't do anything like that again. I just want you to be happy. I thought seeing Jack would make you happy."

Now I felt bad for coming down on her.

"I am happy, Nikki. In my own way, I am happy." I threw my hands up in the air in frustration.

"I know. It's just me wanting to make things right."

"Why? Because you still think you made things wrong? That's just silly. You did not set me up with Steve. I met Steve at an event you happened to invite me to. Stop. Please. You are absolved of all blame you mistakenly think you should have." I made the sign of the cross over her forehead and laughed.

"Okay, okay. I'll stop," Nikki said, pulling me in for a quick hug over the steering wheel. A glance over her shoulder allowed me full view of the door to Shannon Hall. It began to open and a large muscular leg stuck out.

"Now take me home, Nikki."

Nikki pulled back and looked in the direction of the door.

"He's coming out, isn't he?"

Sure enough Jack's large figure stepped out of the door. He shielded his eyes with a hand and scanned the parking lot.

"Are you sure you don't want to give him one more chance to ask you out?"

"No. Let's go."

My finger pointed to the gear shift to make her move faster.

"But it wasn't completely horrible, right?"

Sighing, I thought of Jack's smell and his body next to mine on the mats.

"It wasn't completely horrible." I felt a nice rosy blush fill my cheeks.

* * * * *

The next morning, my alarm woke me at five-thirty. After a pleasant night's sleep, I was ready to run. Yesterday, the entire day felt off because I had not run first thing. That couldn't happen again today.

Last night after yoga, instead of turning on the television, I had spent a good two hours plotting my story. Seeing Jack had revved up some new ideas about romance for my character. In my mystery series, Mary did not have a serious boyfriend or even a love interest. It felt like the right time for her to have some fun. Plus, adding some zing into her life might draw a bigger reading base.

I poured myself a cup of coffee and waited for my brain to turn on. At my kitchen table, I doodled on paper while sipping my coffee. The caffeine kicked in almost instantly this morning, taking my good mood to the next level.

Spending time with Jack and Mari yesterday had been *refreshing*. When we started dating, I had been sixteen. Life had been full of possibilities. Nothing out of reach. A part of me still believed in fairytales at that point.

It felt that same way again this morning after so many years of hopelessness. And I liked the feeling.

My doodles formed what I imagined my character's kitchen to look like. It resembled the one I was in right now. A small, round, wooden table took up the majority of the space in the center of the room. The compact refrigerator, stove, and dishwasher huddled together on one side of the room, like soldiers ready for battle. The counter space was very limited, as well as the cabinet space. It was a kitchen for a single woman.

A noise from downstairs in the shop caught my attention. Sounded like someone was in the kitchen. It was one of those early mornings again for Nikki's staff. Last night, she admitted that neither Elizabeth nor Miguel were in early on Wednesday morning. Not able to pinpoint who left the lights on, it had stressed her out all day. I knew Nikki was worried about my safety.

I stood up from the table and went to my bedroom to put on running gear. According to the forecast last night, it was supposed to be very muggy first thing this morning. It wasn't in my comfort zone to bare my stomach, but on a day like today, it was tempting to run in just my shorts and sports bra.

I dressed quickly and made my way downstairs.

The kitchen appeared deserted, though the overhead lights were on and humming away. A batch of muffins sat out on the counter, filling the air with the rich aroma of dark chocolate. Someone was definitely here. Just as I reached the door, I tripped over something soft lying on the floor behind one of the tables. My entire body fell face first over what felt like a large sack of flour, causing my head to smack the tile floor. It was only when I tried to push myself up I realized the bag of flour had arms and legs attached to it.

Quickly, the buzzing overhead intensified. It sounded like I had kicked apart a bee's nest, causing them to swarm around my head. The room darkened and my peripheral vision became fuzzy and faded away. My mouth gathered an unnatural amount of saliva like I was about to vomit.

And just as suddenly the buzzing stopped, and the only thing left was the sound of my breathing, heavy and labored. Collapsing on the floor, I was aware of the cool sensation of the tile on my cheek. The shock of the cold floor distracted me momentarily from what was now right in front of me. When my eyes finally registered the image, I knew what I was seeing was Fran's pale face.

Even as consciousness slipped away from me, I willed her to open her eyes. Please Fran, be all right. Talk to me.

* * * * *

"Ma'am? Please try to wake up. We need you to wake up," I heard someone say.

"Her name is Kelly," a familiar voice said.

Opening my eyes, I could see I was still on the kitchen floor of Chocolate Love. Two EMTs hovered above me; one of them rubbed my arm. Why were these people all staring at me with such strange expressions?

"Kelly, my name is Mark. I'm an EMT. We're here to help you. Are you in any pain?" A young man stared at me with a look of worry on his face.

My eyes shifted over to his partner, who was considerably older.

"My head hurts," I squeaked out.

"You have a small bump on the right side of your head. Do you think you may have been hit, or could it have just been from falling and hitting your head on the floor?" Mark asked.

Do I think I've been hit? Why would I have been hit?

Suddenly, it was as if someone queued the theme song from the old *Twilight Zone* television show. My head turned swiftly in the direction where I last saw Fran. She was gone.

"Where's Fran?" I asked, trying to sit up. "Where did she go? She needs help. Where did you take her?"

"Kelly, please stay still. We want to make sure you don't have a concussion. You're going to bring on a very bad headache if you move too quickly," Mark said. His partner stood up and waved someone else over. When he stood, I was able to see the person who gave my name. He was initially blocked from my view, but now I saw Miguel. While he stared at me with red rimmed eyes, he chewed frantically at his fingernails. Why was he so upset?

A man in a suit stepped into the small circle of people around me and patted Miguel on the shoulder, as though dismissing him. He leaned in and said something so quietly I couldn't hear him. Miguel nodded and looked at me before stepping out of the way, allowing the man to kneel in front of me.

Before he could say anything, a commotion by the back door pulled my attention from the man.

"Where is she?" I heard Nikki's frantic voice call out. "Where's my sister?"

I tried once again to sit up, this time to see Nikki. The EMTs gently pushed me back down to the floor. Nikki's face appeared behind the man in the suit. She looked as though she had been crying.

"Is she dead?" I didn't really know who I was asking. It didn't matter who answered me. Someone, please just tell me.

"Oh, Kelly," Nikki said, trying to push her way past the small crowd to get to me. I watched as the older EMT placed a hand on her arm and said, "Give her a second." Nikki shot him a dirty look and pushed his hand away to get to me.

The fact that no one answered my questions about Fran said a lot.

Chapter 9

Two hours later, Nikki and I were in the Emergency Room at Delnor Hospital in Geneva. After what seemed like an eternity, an ambulance had transported me here to be evaluated. If it had been up to me, I would have declined because of my intense dislike for hospitals. However, the EMTs felt it best to get properly checked for a concussion.

Shortly thereafter I had been sent for tests. The CAT scan had determined I did indeed have a minor concussion.

Nikki and I relaxed in my room waiting for the doctor to come back with my discharge papers. He felt it would be okay for me to be released, as long as someone stayed with me tonight to check on my status every couple of hours. The plan was to stay with Nikki and Bob for the evening.

Nikki's husband, Bob, was out in search of some coffee for us. Knowing him, he would do whatever it took to hunt down the best coffee he could find rather than bring back nasty hospital coffee. I would not be surprised if he returned with Dunkin Donuts coffee, our favorite.

"The detective is supposed to meet us here. He has some questions for us," Nikki said. She had been a basket-case for the last hour after hearing Fran had not made it.

I had learned after much prodding Fran was still alive at the shop when the EMTs arrived, but died in the ambulance en route to the hospital.

Fran's family was already here in the hospital. She had one daughter and a sister that both lived in Chicago.

"I think I'm still in shock," I said. My body was lying down on one of the hospital beds, but my brain felt like it was floating in another universe.

It was still a mystery to me exactly how I fell. Every time I thought of the sensation of falling onto Fran's soft body, my stomach got nauseous. Did she see me? Did she feel me with her? It seemed so cruel and wrong that someone so vibrant like Fran would spend her last moments alone on a cold floor. My only hope was that my presence for that short time gave her some kind of comfort. Not that I was any help to her.

Nikki told me Miguel had already found her and was outside waiting for the ambulance to arrive when I tripped over her. They probably pulled up right at the moment I fell on top of her because the EMTs thought I was only out for a few seconds.

I was going to miss Fran. I really liked her. A tear ran down my cheek before I could stop it.

"Don't do it, Kel-ly," I heard Nikki's comatose voice say next to me when she looked my way. Her voice broke and she crumbled into a sob.

I reached my arm out to motion her over to the bed. She came over, and we hugged. It was a moment where we allowed the grief to take over.

It was hard to see Nikki like this. She buried her head in my chest and mumbled things I couldn't understand. It sounded something like "It's all my fault."

"Excuse me." A man's voice broke into our private moment. He stepped into the room. When he saw the state we were in, he put his finger up in the air, signaling he would be back. He was the same man in the suit I remembered seeing at Chocolate Love.

Instead of speaking with me at the shop, he had told me he would meet me at the hospital to discuss what happened, so I could get the medical treatment I needed.

Hearing the man's voice, I felt Nikki stiffen in my arms. She pulled away from me and sat up on the bed. Her short hair stuck up in all directions, and whatever was left of her make-up was now smeared all over her face. Nikki stood up to pour me some water and get us tissues.

"Let's try and pull ourselves together so we can talk to him. We have to figure out what happened to Fran. We can't just let her die like this," she said, wiping at her eyes.

"You don't think someone...." She handed me a glass of water, and my mind went blank. It was too difficult to say what was in my head right now.

Nikki wouldn't meet my eyes. Instead, she stepped over to the little mirror by the side of my bed and wiped off make-up from her face.

"Can I speak to you ladies for a moment?" The male voice called from the doorway.

I put my head back on the pillow and tried to find a comfortable spot. There was still a lot of pain, but we had to talk to him, especially if Nikki suspected some kind of foul play.

I took a deep breath in to prepare myself. Since my ordeal three years ago, anytime a member of law enforcement came near me, it made me cringe. It was like reliving the whole event all over again.

"Yes," Nikki said, stepping away from the mirror. "Please come in."

As he stepped into the room, what can only be described as a ruckus broke out in the hallway.

"Ma'am, you'll have to wait a minute. There are a lot of people in there right now."

"I *am* her sister," a voice said with a heavy emphasis on the word sister. There was a small shuffling of shoes on the tile floor before Adelle came into the room. A small smile registered on my face at the image of Adelle wrestling the nurse to get in. The nurse didn't stand a chance.

The nurse popped her head in. She didn't look like she had just lost a wrestling match. The shoe shuffling was probably just the sound of her coming from behind the counter to try and stop my sister.

"Kelly, Nikki, what happened?" Adelle shrieked. The situation certainly called for emotion, but this small room and my headache begged for a little less hysteria.

Adelle's presence made Nikki tear up again. Adelle quickly pulled Nikki into an embrace. I noticed Nikki stiffen a little while accepting the comforting gesture Adelle offered.

"My name is Detective Meyers. I'm with the Geneva Police Department," the man said in a way of greeting Adelle. "Did I hear you are Kelly's sister?"

"Kelly and Nikki are both my sisters," Adelle said back to him, still holding onto Nikki.

"I would like to talk to them briefly about what happened this morning. Do you think you can wait for a few minutes in the hallway?"

Unlike the brash detectives I was used to watching on television, Detective Meyers was very polite and calm.

"Absolutely not," Adelle said, ruining the Zen like atmosphere he brought to the room. "My sisters have been through a traumatic experience. I need to be here with them."

Detective Meyers opened his mouth to speak, clearly determined to change Adelle's mind. Rather than make him do all the work, I spoke up.

"Adelle, can you give us a minute? Bob is somewhere in the hospital searching for coffee for us. Can you see if you can find him? I don't think he knows which room I'm in."

Nikki slowly pulled away from Adelle and wiped the tears from her face. Adelle looked to Nikki for direction. Nikki nodded her head.

"Okay," Adelle said, pulling away and taking Nikki's hand in hers. "I'll be back."

She squeezed Nikki's hand before heading out the door. I saw her and the nurse exchange a look before her exit. They looked like two wild beasts bearing their teeth at each other to see who held the alpha position.

"I'm very sorry for your loss. Let's talk about Fran," the detective said. His tone was courteous and regretful. He motioned for Nikki to take a seat in the one chair in the room. Instead she sat on the bed and nodded to the chair in offer for him to take it instead. He sat down and pulled out a notepad from his inside suit pocket.

Detective Meyers ran his right hand through his thick head of light brown hair while reviewing his notes. I imagined he was deciding what he would ask us and what he would tell us.

"Kelly, you found Fran very early this morning. Is that correct?" He clicked his pen open.

"I was heading out for my morning run when I tripped over Fran lying near the back door." Nikki released a stifled cough next to me.

"At what time?"

Before I could answer, Nikki cut in. "Was Fran murdered?"

I sucked in a breath of air, shocked by the bluntness of Nikki's question.

"Tell me why you would think that," Detective Meyers said without missing a beat. The courteous mask he wore stayed completely intact.

"Because of the break-ins over the past couple of months. The other morning, Kelly noticed the lights were on before any of my staff was there. I am getting an alarm system installed on Monday..." Nikki's voice trailed off for a minute. "Fran came in early today to bake for an event we are sponsoring. I didn't..."

Nikki was not really making a lot of sense. Her thoughts seemed to be very scattered.

"We aren't pursuing this as a murder investigation right now," the detective said. "The doctors tell us there are no signs of trauma to her body. It appears she died from a heart attack." He sat in silence and watched us as we took in the information.

"Then, why are you here?" Nikki asked.

"I'm aware of the break-ins. We have been following them closely. I already spoke to your husband, Bob. He said you told him there was no sign of a break-in and nothing was missing from the store this morning. Is that correct?"

This guy was slick. He spoken to Nikki's husband already. He should have told us this from the beginning. No wonder it was taking Bob so long to get back here with the coffee.

"It was like that with some of the other break-ins in the neighboring stores. The shop owners I talked to have told me nothing was taken from their stories either," Nikki said defiantly.

"Without sign of a break-in or trauma, we have to close this case and rule Fran's death due to natural causes." His tone was still courteous, but had a finality to it.

"Fran was very healthy," she said, shaking her head no. "It doesn't make any sense."

"Let's just run through this one more time. Kelly, what time did you find Fran?"

I thought back, trying to remember the early morning. It felt like it all happened days ago.

"My alarm went off at five-thirty. I made a cup of coffee and then went downstairs. It was probably about ten to six?" I remembered doodling at the kitchen table, not in a huge rush.

"Tell me exactly what you saw. Anything you can remember."

I thought back, remembering. "When I came down, the lights were on and there was a fresh batch of chocolate muffins on the table. I didn't see anyone in the kitchen. Well, except Fran, when I tripped."

"Was that normal for her to be there so early?" he asked Nikki.

"Yes, she usually takes the earliest shift. Today she was in early to bake muffins for a meeting at the Geneva Lutheran Church. She had to be in by five to start the process. I was worried about her being alone, so Miguel was supposed to join her. He said he wasn't in until quarter to six because one of his kids got sick. He called Fran to explain. Miguel said she told him to stay home and take care of his daughter. He went in anyway once things were under control at home. He called Fran on the way to let her know to expect him. When he arrived, he saw Fran on the ground and called 9-1-1. He tried to resuscitate her when he saw she was not breathing. He said he considered going up to get Kelly's help, but didn't know if she was gone already for her run and didn't want to waste precious time if she was. After a few minutes, he ran out to go flag down the ambulance." Nikki's voice was heavy with sadness.

Listening to Nikki retell what Miguel told her explained a lot. I had no idea he tried to save Fran. My mind flashed back to the way his face looked in the kitchen behind the EMTs. No wonder he looked so anxious.

"Is Miguel a good employee?" Detective Meyers asked Nikki.

"Absolutely. The best."

Miguel was about thirty-five years old and supported two young children. He and his wife relocated here from the Dominican Republic five years ago to find a better life. He'd always been reliable and trustworthy.

"And the door was not locked when he arrived, correct?" he asked, making it clear he had already spoken to Miguel.

"No. Fran told him she would leave it open for him. When he called, he was only a few minutes away from the store. She was expecting him."

"No sign of a break-in. Nothing taken from the store." Detective Meyers closed his notepad.

The implication silenced us momentarily.

"How would we go about getting an autopsy? Who do we need permission from?" Nikki finally asked.

Chapter 10

U pon my hospital release, Nikki, Bob, and I headed to their home. They lived in a four square home within walking distance from Chocolate Love. It was considerably smaller than Adelle's, but my preference was to hang out here. I found it much more comfortable and inviting.

Built in the 1920s, it still had all of its original crown molding and stained glass windows. Like a mini version of Chocolate Love.

An elegant, wooden staircase was the main showcase in the front room of the four square. To the left was a cozy living room with a small fire place. The living room led into a dining room that served as the main eating area since the kitchen was too small to serve in. Though most of the time we ate at the small island in the kitchen.

The kitchen was Bob's territory. He was a fantastic cook, specializing in Mexican and Italian dishes. He always said things like "Nikki makes the desserts. I make the meals." He promised us a comfort meal tonight to help try to take our mind off Fran's death and other things.

On the drive home from the hospital, it began to pour. This made the temperature drop considerably. The bolts of lightning and the claps of thunder made it feel like the sky was screaming out in pain, the loss of Fran too much to bear.

Nikki and I dropped our shoes in the mud room and walked over to the living room. She plopped down on the couch, exhausted.

After we had spoken to Detective Meyers, we had been able to hunt down Fran's daughter, Amy, in the hospital to try and convince her to ask for an autopsy. Detective Meyers had said that by law, without suspicious circumstances, he would not be able to order an autopsy. However, the family could be consulted and request an autopsy if a reason was produced for it to be considered a suspicious death.

Amy had shocked us when she told us the family had a history of heart disease. According to her, Fran was on blood thinners and cholesterol medication. Nikki had no idea. She let things be after that so as not to upset Amy or Fran's sister, Jules, who was also at the hospital.

I was currently still in my running clothes from this morning. It would've been nice to go home and change, but I couldn't bear to go into the shop.

I plopped down on the couch next to Nikki and grabbed her hand in mine.
"Hot chocolate will be out in five minutes," Bob yelled from the kitchen.

That sounded good right now. The temperature outside was still in the eighties, even with the rainstorm, but the combination of the air conditioning and our chilly mood made it feel like a fall day. I pulled a blanket from the back of the couch and wrapped it around Nikki.

"If you want to go put some sweatpants on, you can go dig in my closet," she said. As usual, we were right in sync with one another.

"I will in a minute."

"I should have had an alarm system installed sooner," she said in the same creepy zombie voice she displayed at the hospital.

"Nikki, you heard what the doctors and Amy said. This was not about the break-ins. She died of a heart attack. It is *not* your fault."

"Yeah," Nikki said in a non-committal way.

Bob walked into the room with a tray and three mugs. A small bowl filled with marshmallows sat on the tray. Just as he was about to set it down on the coffee table, a huge bolt of lightning ripped through the sky followed by a loud clap of thunder, and the lights went out in the house. I stood up to help Bob set the tray down.

"Great," Bob said. "Just what we needed. I'm going to find some candles."

Although it was nearly 11:00 a.m., the room was dark and gloomy.

"It looks like the rest of the block is out as well. The lightning must have hit something," I said, peering out the front window.

Bob returned a couple of minutes later with a bunch of candles in his arms. He set them up on the coffee table and throughout the room. The soft candlelight brought a comforting presence to the room.

Fran, are you here? I pondered silently to myself.

"What will Chocolate be without Fran?" Nikki asked. "She loved working there. She always talked about the day she quit teaching to do something she really liked. The day after she quit her teaching job, she applied to Chocolate Love and has been there ever since. Twenty years," Nikki said in disbelief.

"She was awesome," Bob said. "When we first re-opened after the remodel and things were tight at the store, she approached me a couple of times to tell me to hold off on her paycheck, so we could keep the store open. I never had to do that, thank God, but there were times I thought about taking her up on her offer. We had some tough times trying to get things profitable again after the remodel expenses."

Nikki groaned next to me. In an effort to comfort her, Bob moved closer to put his arm around her. We were all on the couch squished together like sardines.

"I had no idea she was on medication. Why didn't she tell me? Those early morning hours must have been stressful for her," Nikki said.

"That's what she wanted. Trust me, as a morning person myself, those were the best hours in the day for her to work." At that moment, the lights flickered back on.

"Yeah," Nikki said, slipping back into her zombie voice.

We spent the next couple of hours like this, sharing stories about Fran and her commitment to Chocolate Love. Bob and Nikki decided to keep the store closed for the rest of the day and the following day to give everyone time to grieve. We bounced around a couple of ideas on how to best honor Fran, possibly by doing a free cupcake or chocolate tasting day.

Surprisingly, we did not hear from Adelle. As nutty as it was for her to appear like she did at the hospital, it was nice to see she cared. As the day went on, I became annoyed that she didn't call or stop by Nikki's house. She knew we were coming back here. Nikki was going to need a lot of emotional support the next few days as she fought her way through the grief.

Eventually, I made my way upstairs and pulled on a pair of Nikki's sweatpants and a clean tee-shirt. Because Nikki was considerably shorter than me, the pants didn't quite make it past my shins. A pair of long socks from her sock drawer made up for the difference.

Dressed now, I headed back downstairs to help out. All three of us made calls to other employees and Fran's friends to inform them of what had happened. At the hospital, Amy had given us a list of people she wanted us to contact. The calls were clearly emotionally draining for Nikki. She spent time on each call, answering questions about what happened. It would have been nice if Adelle was here to help out.

By three o'clock, I needed a break.

Bob was in the kitchen feverishly grating cheese for dinner, and Nikki was sitting at the island speaking to Fran's daughter, Amy, about the funeral arrangements.

"Oh, my God, it's just so hard," Nikki said, after she hung up. She finally caved and put her head down on the counter.

"We'll get through it. Please, take a break and go lay down," I urged.

"I think I have to," Nikki said, standing up and leaving the room.

We listened as Nikki's feet slowly made their way up the stairs and then stopped above us in the master bedroom. Bob and I stared at each other for a minute, both of our faces a combination of worry and fatigue.

"She'll be okay," he said simply and with determination.

Bob was kind enough to grab my cell phone and my purse from my apartment early that morning. Nikki had asked him to get my purse in case they needed my insurance information at the hospital. I walked into the front room and dug in my purse for my cell phone.

"Can you come over to Nikki's house? She can use your support," I texted Adelle.

I waited a couple of minutes for her response. When she didn't respond, I shot out another text.

"Adelle, where are you?"

I sat on the bench in the front room to wait for a reply. Finally, I gave up and slid the cell phone into the pocket of my sweatpants. She would get back to me as soon as she could. Or maybe she would just come on over. Maybe.

A few hours later, dinner was ready, but Nikki was not. We checked on her three times and found her dead asleep each time. I even had a nap myself during the time she slept. We finally chose to leave her be and ate dinner without her. She looked so peaceful; it felt criminal to wake her.

After dinner was cleaned up, I called the rest of the people on her list. We planned on posting the funeral details on Chocolate Love's website, as well as in the local newspaper. That way anyone in the community who knew Fran, which was a great number of people, would be able to attend. Since we didn't have the details yet from Amy as to what the date would be, I told most people to check in on the website over the next day or so.

By seven o'clock, all the calls had been made, and the kitchen was spotless. Bob and I watched TV while we waited for Nikki to come down.

My head throbbing, I knew I should go to bed, but I wanted to stay awake until Nikki came down. Hopefully, that would be soon. Just as my mind started to zone out, the front doorbell rang. Adelle. It was about time. Where the hell had she been all day?

Bob stood up to answer the door.

"I'll get it," I said.

Because the front door was all glass, the visitor could be identified before actually opening it. My heart stopped when I saw who it was.

Seeing her made me emotional all over again. Her presence confirmed the very thing I tried to avoid all day. The reality that something very, very bad happened.

"Hi, Mom," I said, opening the door.

Chapter 11

The next morning, Saturday, felt like a fresh start. Bob, Mom, and I were all up bright and early, huddled near the coffee maker in the kitchen, waiting for Nikki to come down. It was a treat with Mom here, but it was impossible to forget the real reason for her visit. The grief over Fran's death remained heavy in my heart.

"I'm headed over to the store first thing to check in," Bob said. He already had his empty coffee cup in hand.

"Why don't I go with you?" Mom asked. Her hair was cut shorter than usual and was streaked with gray. Mom didn't stand as straight as she used to. Overall though, I thought she looked great. Miami had been good for my parents. They had left at just the right time in their life. They still had energy to enjoy the beach, yet they had saved enough money from their careers to be able to enjoy their life in retirement.

I thought it was healthy for them to be away from their adult children. God knew our drama would suck the life out of them being here.

"Okay, sure," Bob said.

"I'll stay here and wait for Nikki," I said.

"Your father wanted to be here, Kelly. We just didn't have anyone to watch Mickey and Rooney on such short notice," Mom said, referring to their two dogs.

"Of course. We understand, Mom," I replied.

"It was important to me to get here quick. We panicked and decided it was best for Dad to stay there rather than scramble and try to find a kennel. Adelle was very upset when she called to tell us what happened," she said. "When do you think we'll get to see Adelle?"

Your guess is as good as mine, I thought.

At least Adelle had called her. In the madness of yesterday's events, Nikki and I had not thought to call our parents. Having Mom here would be a big help to Nikki and a source of comfort for us all.

"Should we call Adelle this morning?" Mom turned her dark brown eyes in my direction to observe me.

"Why don't you call her this morning?" I didn't bother addressing the fact that Adelle had been M.I.A. over the last twenty-four hours.

Mom had never fully accepted, or possibly refused to see, the selfish side of Adelle. She was forever making excuses for Adelle and her behavior. She had done it all of our lives.

"When did you talk to her last?" she asked.

"We saw her at the hospital yesterday and haven't heard from her since," I said.

"Did you try calling her?"

"I called *and* sent a couple of texts," I said, refusing to get irritated by my mother's tone. It was always a losing battle with Mom to try and explain Adelle's actions to her.

"It was very nice of her to go to the hospital," she said defensively.

"Who came to the hospital?" Nikki asked from the doorway. She stepped into the kitchen freshly showered and dressed. She had not styled her hair or put on make-up yet, but she looked a million times better than yesterday.

Nikki made her way over to the cabinet where she stored her coffee mugs and reached in for one before she kissed Bob good morning.

"Hey," Bob said, as he nuzzled her cheek. "You look much better today."

"I *feel* better. Who were you guys talking about?"

Mom made eye contact with me as though waiting for me to speak.

"Adelle," I said.

"Oh," she said nonchalantly. Even though she was the youngest, I'd always thought Nikki was the first one in the family to figure out not to rely on Adelle. It hit me then that she wasn't counting on her being here today.

"I have an idea to bounce off of you," Nikki said.

Bob poured her the first cup of coffee and handed it to her. He motioned for Mom's cup next and made eye contact with me for a second, raising one eyebrow. I handed him my cup in acceptance.

"We should keep Chocolate closed today and tomorrow," Nikki said. "If the funeral isn't held on Monday, how about a free cupcake day in honor of Fran? We could make mini-versions of the red-velvet one that was her favorite."

Yesterday, Nikki was practically comatose over the death of Fran. Today she was ready to whip up a zillion cupcakes. Her change in energy was a good thing, but it seemed like she was moving too quickly through the stages of grief.

"That's a wonderful idea, honey," my mom said. "That way the whole town of Geneva can honor Fran. We could even try to think of a name for the cupcake. Something like Forever Fran or Red Velvet Fran.

Mom seemed relieved to see Nikki had turned a corner. When Nikki had finally woken up last night, Mom was next to her on the bed, waiting to talk. She had burst into a crying session for over an hour. Maybe there was something to be said for getting all that emotion out of her.

"I just want Fran to be remembered. She made such a difference in the store. Someone's commitment for twenty years should be recognized," Nikki said.

"I'll call my dad right now," said Bob. "He and my mom called last night wanting to help out in some way. They would be thrilled to participate in Fran Fest. They loved her so much when she worked for them."

"Fran Fest!" Nikki said excitedly. "That's perfect, Bob!"

"Why don't I call Amy and see what progress she has made with the funeral?" I asked. "Then we could figure out what day would be the best to have Fran Fest? Would it be better to just bring the cupcakes to the wake or the funeral?"

"No. We can contribute cupcakes for the funeral, but we need something in the store that the general public can participate in. Not everyone will be able to go to the wake or funeral. Most people in town know Fran from the store. I want her to have a special day at Chocolate," Nikki said.

"I like it," I said. "That sounds good."

"And no hard feelings, Kelly, but I want to be the one to call Amy," Nikki said.

"Of course, not a problem. I'm here to help you."

It felt good to do something productive. The bump on my head was still there, but the painkillers had silenced any discomfort it gave me. I excused myself to head upstairs and pop a couple more pills before a quick shower and a dig through Nikki's closet for something decent to wear.

Her clothes would do for now, but it was time for me to go home and get some of my own stuff.

Once dressed, I headed back downstairs. I found Nikki and Bob in the kitchen working over a notepad. It appeared to be a rough schedule of the day. Her hair was styled and her make-up impeccable. I must have missed seeing Mom upstairs because she wasn't down here.

"Here's the plan," Nikki said. "I just spoke to Amy. The wake will be on Monday and the funeral on Tuesday. We'll close the store today and tomorrow, but open on Monday and Tuesday with limited hours. We need to re-open, or we will not do well this month. Fran would not want that."

"I agree," I said.

"Fran Fest will be Wednesday," Nikki said. "I have to run the numbers to see what we could do without going in the red, but I was thinking something like three hundred cupcakes. I'll spend this morning talking to the staff about it. Also, Bob's parents have volunteered to prep cupcakes Tuesday evening and work the event the next day."

"I'm in. The book is officially on hold for the next couple of days."

"No, Kelly," Nikki said. "I won't let you stop writing. You need to keep working on it."

As usual, she was right. If I lost momentum now, I would only struggle with the book. Things fell apart very quickly when I didn't write every day.

"How about this? I promise to work a little bit every day. It won't be at a grueling pace, but I won't shut down completely."

"The book is your number one priority," Nikki said firmly. "You join us when you can, however, you know Fran wanted that book done ASAP. She was your number one fan."

"You're right." I thought back to the conversation we had a few days earlier in my apartment when she brought my coffee up.

"You have a gift, Kelly. If you stop now, he will have taken that, too," Fran said.

"So you and Bob will head over to Chocolate. I am going to stay here to make calls and organize. We're just waiting to see if Mom wants to go with you. Sound good?"

"Sounds like a plan."

Nikki got up and walked over to the sink to wash out her mug. Bob looked at me like he was going to say something. Instead, he walked over to the sink to wash his mug out.

"One more thing," Nikki said. Her back was still turned to me.

"What?"

"You should stay here until the alarm system is installed, so you may want to grab some essentials," she said.

"But Nikki, you know there wasn't a break-in," I said.

Bob set his cup down and started to walk out of the room. He stopped to pat his hand on my shoulder as he brushed past me, but did not make eye contact.

When Nikki turned around to look at me, all the momentum she had pulled from within herself to keep it together since last night appeared to crumble before my eyes. She had that same look in the hospital: a combination of fear and acknowledgement that life could be unpredictable and cruel. And there was nothing to be done about it.

"Please," she said slowly. "For me."

"Of course, I'll stay," I said and pulled her into a hug. My tiny little sister allowed me to embrace her in my arms.

I shuttered slightly and wondered, what was she afraid of?

Chapter 12

After collecting my things from my apartment, I spent the day at Nikki's working with her on details for the next few days and pretending to write. We finally had all the details for the wake, funeral, and Fran Fest laid out. Every single staff member insisted on volunteering their time rather than being paid for Fran Fest. It was an incredible gesture considering how tight times were for most families and how bad paychecks were needed.

Nikki had already begun talking about how to bump up Christmas bonuses for everyone at Chocolate Love for the year as a thank you for their commitment and loyalty.

At eight o'clock that evening, Mom, Nikki, and I sat around the dining room table in Nikki's home with the spreadsheets for the baking process for Fran Fest. Bob was upstairs in the master bedroom on his laptop, putting together a eulogy he was co-writing with Nikki. She had asked Amy if it would be okay to stand up and say a couple of words on Fran's behalf. Bob's father, who was Fran's boss for many years, would also be speaking.

When the front door bell rang, we all looked up expectantly at each other, as if the other person should know who it was.

We heard Bob's feet coming down the stairs, so none of us stood up to get the door.

"I forgot to tell you, Nikki," Bob yelled. "Adelle called to say she was stopping by."

I snuck a peek at Mom and saw her eyes light up. I knew she had made two calls to Adelle during the day. I had heard her leave messages, asking Adelle to call her as soon as possible. As far as I could tell, her calls had not been returned.

Nikki's dark brown eyes met mine and then quickly went down to her sheets on the table.

"Hi, Mom!" Adelle said, floating into the room to sweep our mom into a hug. She was a lot taller than Mom and had to bend over to pull her into her chest.

"I'm so glad you're here, Adelle," Mom said, hanging on tight. She'd already changed into her pajamas and robe. When she reached up to hug Adelle, the sleeves of her robe slipped down and exposed the liver spots on her arms.

"Got your calls. I'm sorry it took me so long to get here. We had such a hectic day with soccer games and ballet. I got here as soon as I could," Adelle said.

Adelle let go of Mom and pulled out a chair next to her. We were quiet for a minute, carefully taking each other in. No one seemed to want to bring up the white elephant in the room-the fact that Adelle had been absent for a very crucial thirty-six hours.

Soccer games and ballet practice? Seriously? I didn't have kids, but I found it hard to believe there wasn't someone else to take her kids to their events so Adelle could sit with her sister. Or, maybe the kids could have skipped this one session?

Besides that, Mom was in town. Adelle being unavailable during this time was very strange.

"What's going on? What are you three working on?" Adelle asked, as she looked down at the sheets we had laid out in front of us.

"What's going on?" I asked her. "Adelle, where have you been? Nikki needed you. Why haven't you been answering our calls?"

"Kelly," my mom said in an authoritative voice, "that's enough. I'm sure Adelle was busy. She's here now. That's the important thing."

Nikki had been sitting quietly with her eyes down at the table. This wasn't like her. If anyone could stand up for herself, it was Nikki. She looked beaten down.

"Kelly," Adelle said in an exasperated voice, "I just told you, I've been super busy. You don't understand what it's like to have three kids. They don't understand what a crisis is. Life just goes on for them. I needed to keep things as normal as possible at home."

"Then how about a phone call? Or is your phone disconnected? How about telling Nikki you will be there for her as soon as you can. *Something*. Do you have any idea what the last thirty-six hours have been like for her?"

"First of all, I was there as soon as I heard the news. I dropped the kids on Mike and ran over to the hospital as soon as I found out. You guys acted like you didn't even want to see me, so I gave you space. What else could I have done? What do you *want* from me, Kelly?" Adelle reached out her arms like she was being nailed on a cross.

"How about some help with the calls, the food, and consoling Nikki. She just lost one of her best employees." Years of resentment poured out of me. I knew it was happening; I just couldn't stop.

"Try showing some compassion, Adelle. Some little act to show her you care. That you care about someone else besides yourself!"

"Kelly," Nikki's voice broke my rant. I stopped, my mouth left open, and met her eyes across the table. Her voice was weak and defeated. "It's okay," she said.

I closed my mouth and waited for her to speak again.

"Why don't you take a break and go to bed. You've been at this all day. Go to bed early, so you can get a lot of work done tomorrow," Nikki said. She was in her pajamas already and her make-up had been removed. Without the coverage, her cheek bones stuck out in harsh angles, and the circles under her eyes made her look sickly. Her normally flawless hair stuck out in different directions.

My perfect Nikki was crumbling right in front of my eyes. And it was killing me. All this time she had been so strong for me. The calm in my storm. Now, I was supposed to be the calm in her storm, and instead I had conjured up tornadoes with my screaming and yelling.

No one said anything as I collected my notes I wrote for Fran Fest. Some time to myself would be good for me. And probably best for everyone. I was exhausted and wanted to just crawl into bed.

"How about some chamomile tea?" Bob asked, breaking the silence. "Would anyone like some?"

"Yes," all four of us said in unison.

"I will bring yours up to you," he said to me.

As I started to make my way upstairs, I heard Adelle ask, "Is she okay?"

I ignored her comment as I headed up to the guest room. Nikki was right to make me take a break from that scene. I was half tempted to put on my running shoes and head out for a jog.

Missing my run today was getting to me. My normally mild temperament was a bit frayed already. Adding Adelle into the equation had turned me into a raging lunatic. After mulling it over for a moment, my exhaustion trumped the thought of a run. Instead, I decided to wash up and change into my pajamas. I grabbed the toiletries from my bag and nearly ran into Bob in the hallway.

"Whoa!" he said, as he tried to hold onto the mug he carried.

We both watched as a small drop landed on the khaki, Berber carpet beneath our feet. We waited silently for a second to see what type of damage I had done. Fortunately, the drop of tea landed on a darker section of the carpet and blended right in.

"We'll just pretend that didn't happen. Nikki will never know," Bob said, smiling. "Here, let me set this down for you in your room."

Instead of continuing onto the bathroom, I followed him into the guest room. The room was painted a soft pink, and the only furniture in the room was the small twin bed, a nightstand, and a white, antique armoire. I always hoped it would become a little girl's room when Nikki and Bob were ready to have kids.

"Bob, is Nikki alright?"

"Well." He pushed his round glasses further up his nose. As he bent over to place my mug down on the nightstand, his face must have gotten close to the cup because his glasses had a slight fog to them.

"Honestly, I don't know, Kelly. She's holding out on me."

"What do you mean?"

"I know when my girl's upset and when she's in control. I just can't tell this time. She's been so quiet."

"I shouldn't have gotten upset with Adelle," I said softly. Voices traveled in this small house, and I didn't want anyone to hear me.

"Ah, don't worry about it," he said. "You know, Kelly, you're the one she wants. She gave up on Adelle a long time ago. Don't let her absence this time bother you."

"I know." I sat down on the twin bed and pulled my feet up underneath me. "Normally, I wouldn't. I'm just over-tired."

For a second, Bob looked like he was contemplating sitting next to me on the bed. It was really the only place to sit down in the room.

He chose instead to lean against the armoire and fold his arms into each other. Bob was conscientious of people's personal space, so I guessed he was worried sitting next to me on the small twin bed would be too close.

"I tell you, Adelle is a hard one to figure out," he said.

"What do you mean?"

"Don't get me wrong, I love Adelle." He paused for a moment.

"Have Mike or Adelle ever asked you for anything, Kelly?" He squinted his eyes together.

Gee, have Mike or Adelle ever asked me for anything? Was he kidding? They ask for things all the time.

"Sure. They're always asking me to baby-sit, watch their house when they're gone, help them with taking the kids to soccer and ballet, help pack up for their summer house, and the list goes on." I paused to look at Bob. Something in his expression had changed.

This was clearly not what he was looking for.

"Wait, what do you mean? Asked what of me exactly?"

"That's all I meant," he said quickly.

"Bob." I tilted my head to the side.

"All I'm saying is they ask a lot. Not so much of us anymore. Since you moved back into town, they focus in on getting help from you. They're takers, not givers. I love them. They are our family. We've just learned to not expect much help from them. This tragedy has proven it."

These were pretty harsh words coming from Bob. He wasn't one to speak negatively of other people, so when he did, he had good reason to do so.

"I have to go check on the ladies downstairs. Get a good night's sleep, Kelly. I'll see you in the morning."

"Goodnight."

Bob's comments swirled around in my brain like cream mixing with a cup of black coffee. What did he really mean by his questions about Adelle and Mike? I set the bathroom items on the bed and reached over to grab the tea.

When I realized how hot it was, I placed it back down on the night stand and grabbed my laptop.

Having it with me gave me the ability to get work done while here. My email inbox showed new messages, the first one from Jack's sister, Mari. She had my address from the sign-up sheet at the yoga class. That class seemed like a million years ago.

The email was a general message written to the entire class to thank them for signing up. It also gave information on what we would learn in the next class. A website address linking to the 5K charity race was also listed.

I was a little disappointed the note from Mari wasn't a little more personal. It was nice to run into her and Jack. Just thinking about it brought a few butterflies to life in my stomach. It felt good to think about something else besides Fran's death.

The other two emails were junk mail from some of my favorite clothing stores. I deleted those, and swore never to give my email information out again. The last one was another email from Gina. Ugh.

Hi Kelly,

Did you get my message? I sent you an email a couple of days ago to let you know I was coming to town. There's something you need to know. It needs to be ASAP. Tuesday or Wednesday of this week at the latest.

Love, Gina

I closed my laptop down after reading her email. Who the hell did she think she was putting all of this pressure on me to see her? There was nothing she could possibly know that would be important to me. She knew nothing about my life now.

The image of Gina, long, straight, brown hair, slim figure, and average height, popped into my head. I saw the small, black star she had tattooed behind her right ear. The thought of that star made me shiver. It used to make her unique. Now it just made her all the more creepy.

Chapter 13

That night, I dreamt of standing at the foot of the stairs leading up to the front door of Chocolate Love. The store looked inviting as always, but there was something keeping me from walking up the stairs. An undefined hesitation had settled in my gut and kept me rooted there.

While trying to figure the source of my worry, I glanced around at my surroundings. It was a beautiful fall day. Leaves of all different colors blew across the stairs and front sidewalk. I looked down at my feet and noticed one of the leaves stuck to the laces of my running shoe. I had not realized I had been on a run, but sure enough, my arms glistened with sweat.

Third Street was picking up just as it always did after my run. A bus full of commuters zoomed by on the street. A gentleman passed by on his bicycle, and a woman pushed a running stroller on the sidewalk behind me.

My guess was that it was close to six-thirty. I couldn't remember waking or turning off an alarm, so I had no idea how long I had been out on a run. Based on the way the sky blended pink and gray, my guess was it was still pretty early.

When I looked back up at the door, it was wide open. The sensation of someone standing directly behind me caused me to turn, but when I did, no one was there. Fully spooked now, I wanted to get inside and back up to my apartment.

I made my way up the stairs, listening to the soft creak of the wood beneath my feet. When I reached the top, I noticed something heavy resting in my right hand that wasn't there a moment ago. My hand reflexively opened, and a metal object fell to the ground.

I bent down to the porch and saw a small silver key. It looked like my key to Chocolate Love. Normally, I kept it tied to the shoelace of my left shoe during my run.

A glance down confirmed the key was still tied to my left shoe. This wasn't my key then. So, whose key was it, and where did it come from? The overwhelming urge to get back up to my apartment rushed through me again.

I slipped the key in the pocket of my running shorts and grabbed the handle of the screen door. The main door was already open, so I walked through the doorway and entered into the small front entrance hallway.

The second door that led into the foyer was already open. These doors were never open this early in the morning. Nikki would never do that.

I glanced at the large grandfather clock Nikki kept in the corner at the base of the stairs leading up to my apartment. It appeared to be shaking slightly. Frightened, I stepped backward and tripped over the Oriental rug Nikki kept in the foyer.

The clock stopped shaking all of a sudden, and the bells signaled five o'clock. Five? *Impossible.* I had already been out for my run. Everything was wrong. The time, the key, the clock. I couldn't understand what was happening?

Just as the fifth bell struck, a haunting voice called out to me from the top of the staircase.

"Kel-ly...."

As frightened as I was now, I was drawn to the voice upstairs like a moth to a flame. My instincts told me to run out the front door as fast as I could, but I couldn't stop myself from finding out more about the voice at the top of the stairs.

"Kel-lyyyy," the voice called again. The tempo of the voice hypnotized me.

Instead of fear, curiosity took control of me and kept me in place, my eyes transfixed to the top of the stairs. There was no more hesitation. No more fear. It had left me now. I knew that voice.

Taking a step toward the stairs, my hand grabbed the rail and held on. Was I supposed to go up? Was she calling me upstairs? Or would she come down to meet me? Unable to wait, I took the steps two at a time.

"Kel-ly," the voice said again. It felt like a warning to stop, so I did. Had I angered her? I wanted to go to her, but I was unsure of what she wanted.

"I'm here," I called.

Her high-heeled shoe, glittering with sparkly sequins, was the first thing I saw. When she stepped forward, her ankle was revealed before her dress swooped down over it. Her skin was an unnatural white tone that matched the color of the dress. The beautiful ball gown barely made it down the hallway, hitting the spokes of the staircase on one side and the wall.

My eyes glanced up to the top of the dress cut in a sweetheart neckline. Her bosom was small but exquisite in the fit of the dress, showing the tiniest bit of cleavage. A single pearl hung from a silver chain around her neck and fell just above the dip of the front of the dress. Her face was covered by a veil, but I already knew who it was.

"Will you help me?" she asked, her voice full of excitement. In her hands she held a small bouquet of white flowers. "He's waiting for me!"

I rushed up the stairs to meet her, no longer afraid.

"May I?"

"Of course," she said, as though she was waiting for me to ask.

My hands reached for her veil and lifted it over her face. Before me stood a young Fran on her wedding day. Her face looked exactly the same as when I knew her except for a few wrinkles absent.

She smiled and flashed the same perfect teeth, a bit whiter than I remembered. Her hair was pulled back into some type of chignon at the base of her neck.

"How do I look?" Her smile was a bit shaky and her eyes glowed bright.

"You're beautiful."

"Is it time?" she asked.

I didn't know what to say. Fear was back and taking control of my emotions again. It was Fran's smile that did it to me. She didn't look like herself. She was never this anxious or nervous. I was starting to get the overwhelming sensation again that everything was wrong. And that I had no way of controlling it.

"Is he waiting for me? He's still waiting for me, right?" Her voice was even more anxious now.

Fran grabbed my hand, and her fingers felt icy cold.

"Can you check to see if he's still there?" The way she asked the question told me she didn't want him there at this point. Things were changing quickly.

"Please, walk halfway down the stairs and peek into the kitchen to make sure he is gone." Her hand squeezed mine a little tighter, making me all the more uncomfortable.

"No, I don't want to," I said. "I'm scared."

"Please, Kelly," she begged. Her cheeks filled with a blush, a clear contrast to the rest of her skin that gave off a soft white glow.

She released my hand and tipped her chin up. With some hesitation, I turned and made my way down the stairs.

A look back at Fran revealed she was still at the top of the stairs, but she was no longer the young bride. She had become an older version of herself. The one I knew from Chocolate Love.

Halfway down the stairs, I bent my knees to peek into the kitchen. From this angle, I could only see a portion of the kitchen. Sure enough, I saw legs that looked like they belonged to a man.

I stood up slowly and turned around to look at Fran. There was someone there in a wedding dress, but it was no longer Fran.

It was the woman that broke up my marriage.

Mandy.

And the front of her dress looked like there was a big balloon stuck under it where her flat stomach should have been.

"Is he there?" she asked.

I glanced away from her quickly and stood for a moment on the stairs, trying to figure out what to do. I needed to get the hell out of here. I should have listened to my instincts to begin with. My body started to tremble, and my hands covered my mouth to keep from screaming.

I forced myself to squat further down and look back into the kitchen. The further I tilted my head, the more of him was revealed. First his torso, then his large chest covered in the pumpkin colored sweater I bought him for our first Christmas together. His hands rested on his hips in an impatient stance. I knew it too well.

My eyes traveled further up his body, to his large muscular neck that bulged with veins when he was angry, as he appeared to be now. Finally, my eyes moved up to his familiar face fixed in a determined and aggressive stare directly on me.

Steve.

Here at Chocolate Love.

I stood up abruptly and ran back up the stairs. I needed to get as far away from Steve as I could.

Mandy was there now at the top of the stairs holding baby Caroline, who was swaddled in a blanket.

"Is he coming?" she asked, clearly terrified.

"Go!" I screamed.

Footsteps slammed on the floor behind me as Steve ran from the kitchen into the foyer. It wouldn't take him long to get up the stairs.

"Go into the apartment and lock the door!" I screamed again.

"No! I'll never make it," she screamed back. Her voice was a mix of fear and determination.

"Please, take her! He's coming!"

To my horror, Mandy tossed the baby to me. Caroline came at me like a football thrown too high for me to catch. I jumped up to reach her but lost my balance, falling backwards down the stairs.

The bundle passed over my head, and I reached my hands outward to make one last effort before I felt the sensation of falling. A deep sadness poured over me. All I could think of was if Steve would catch the baby. Would he even try?

As I fell, my eyes jumped back to Mandy. She was crying and screaming at the same time. Her face began to change into another familiar one. Before I could make out who it was, things began to go dark. My last thought was of complete despair, knowing the baby would not live through the fall.

"Kelly!" Steve screamed behind me. "Kelly, wake up!"

I woke suddenly, drenched in sweat, my heart racing a million miles an hour. My first feeling was relief to be out of the nightmare, but then desperation overwhelmed me again. I couldn't save Caroline.

Clutching at my sweat drenched shirt, I worked to control my breathing. My mind raced to the negotiating tactics it always did when I woke from one of my crazy nightmares. Put me back. Give me another chance. I made these pleas and demands silently in my head to whoever controlled the nightmares. Was it God? But how could it be? How could He put me through this hell every night? Why? Hadn't I been through enough?

Finally, it kicked in, as it always did, that there was no going back. I would have to accept the outcome of my horrid nightmare. Whoever was the master of my mind during these dream times had pulled the curtain shut tonight.

While consciousness pumped through me, making me come alive back in the real world, something came into focus. The outline of a female form sat on the edge of my bed. I was not alone in this room.

Chapter 14

I bolted up in bed and pressed myself back against the headboard, trying to get as far away from the woman as possible.

"Stay away from me," I said, pulling the sheet up to cover my body.

As my eyes adjusted to the dark, the figure turned ninety degrees to face me. I could no longer see the profile of her face. She reached her arm out toward me.

"No!" I screamed. My eyes closed, terrified to feel her touch.

"Kelly," Nikki said in a soothing voice. "It's just me."

My eyes popped open. The hand I thought was reaching out to grab me passed by my face and reached over to the nightstand to turn on the small Tiffany lamp next to the bed. The room filled with the soft glow of the multi-colored lampshade.

Unable to speak, I stared at her instead.

"You were talking in your sleep. Are you okay? Were you having another nightmare?" She moved closer to me on the bed.

Nikki's eyes, her face, her voice. I knew it all so well. This was real. She was *real*. Not the night terror that gripped me so fiercely a few moments ago.

Every inch of her face and every emotion that played out on it was familiar to me. And the look on her face right now was one of concern. If I felt stronger, I would tell her I was okay.

"Come here," she said, embracing me. "It was just a dream."

I crumbled in her arms and broke into tears.

Nikki and I shared a room growing up. Back then when I had nightmares, she would crawl in my bed and tell me the monsters were not real and that we would have pancakes in the morning.

The next day, I had always woken up to pancakes. Years later I found out Nikki made sure to tell my parents what had happened. My parents never knew how to stop the night terrors, but they had known how to comfort me afterwards.

My dad had always asked the same thing, "How goes it, Missy?" He sat with me at the table, stealing glances at my face. As an adult, he told me this was the one thing about me that was the most difficult thing to handle as my father. Apparently, I was a very easy kid to raise, but my parents had felt completely helpless about the nightmares.

The night terrors had died down a lot as I grew to be an adult. But sometimes, during a stressful time, the monsters came back. When I became a writer, my mom said, "Maybe creative people need those terrors to help spark their special talents?"

Whatever these were, they had been a dark presence in my life for a long time. No one understood the intensity of these nightmares. They were impossible to explain because I couldn't bring someone to the scene and expose them fully to the emotions experienced during the dream. If anyone were to understand though, Nikki had the best ability to.

"Tell me what it was about," Nikki asked, as she stroked the back of my head.

"I don't want to talk about it," I said. My breathing was still coming out in jagged gasps.

"We don't have to."

"He's not…" What? What did I want to ask? He was not here? He was not coming back to get me? He wasn't angry with me anymore? Nikki couldn't possibly confirm any of these things.

"He's not getting out for seven more years," she said, as she pulled me closer.

It wasn't enough, but it was all we had right now.

After a few minutes passed, I pulled away from Nikki and sat up.

"What time is it?"

"It's a little after five," she said.

"Is anyone else up?"

"No, just us. Do you want to get up and go for a run? It might make you feel better."

I wanted to, but I still felt groggy. My body was half asleep even though my mind was fully active. I needed the physical activity to align them.

"Can we have some coffee first?"

"Of course. I'll go down and fire up the coffee machine while you get dressed." She was already dressed in her workout clothes.

Twenty minutes later, we were out in front of Nikki's house. It was a little bit cooler than normal. The drop in temperature would make for a pleasant run. Since it was a bit earlier than I normally went out, it was a little darker than I was used to.

We started out on a slow jog. Nikki took the lead as far as what direction we headed.

She ran from time to time with me, but was not a devoted runner. Both Nikki and Adelle belonged to a local health club associated with Geneva's hospital, Delnor. They swam together in the indoor heated lap pool. Swimming allowed a much needed bond for Nikki and Adelle to develop. It was a bond that kept the peace.

"I've been thinking about something," Nikki said. By this point we had run for about a quarter of a mile in the direction of Chocolate Love.

"Do you remember the woman who spoke at our yoga class, Sharon Winters?"

I was surprised to hear Nikki mention Sharon. I thought Fran Fest would be the first thing we would discuss.

"I remember her," I said.

Bringing up the yoga class made my thoughts go to Jack. Despite all that had happened in the last couple of days, he was still on my mind. I couldn't get those few moments we shared out of my head. His smile and the way he looked at me had stayed with me. I felt a little bit ridiculous, holding onto something so slight. All he gave me were a few moments of interest and that delicious smile of his. Afterwards, he made it clear he wanted to go talk to Sharon.

"Ouch," Nikki said, pushing her hand into her right side.

"Feeling all right?"

"Yeah. It's just a cramp. I need to work through it."

We ran for a couple of minutes in silence while she breathed in through her nose and out through her mouth.

"Better?"

"Yeah," she said. "I was thinking. Do you remember the race Sharon talked about? It's for some kind of heart charity."

"Yes."

"Do you want to run in it with me? We could do it together to honor Fran's memory. We're doing Fran Fest, but it will be over in a couple of days. This could be something we could do on top of that."

Nikki had her stride now; she looked much more comfortable.

"Sure! I'm in."

We ran for a moment in silence.

"I don't remember any details about it though. When is it? How far is it?" I asked.

"I wasn't paying close attention either. We could email Mari though, and see if she could send us some information. Actually, did you get the email from her last night about the class?"

"Yes. Now that I think about it, there was a link to the charity race in the email."

"I didn't have a chance to read through the whole thing. I skimmed it over before I went to bed. We can check it out when we get home," she said.

We approached Chocolate Love on our right. The store looked different this morning. I wondered if we'd ever be able to see it the way we once did. Hopefully, Nikki could continue to thrive and keep it going as the fun, family place it was.

There was a small banner already up over the front door. Without a word, we both stopped in front of the shop.

The banner read:

In loving memory of Fran Harper, we will host Fran Fest on Wednesday, June 16th, from 10:00a.m.-3:00p.m. Free cupcakes and coffee. We miss you, Fran.

The Staff of Chocolate Love

"Bob and his father worked on this yesterday," Nikki said. Her voice was much calmer than I thought it would be. I, on the other hand, had to fight back tears.

Nodding my head, it was best for me not to speak at this point.

Nikki walked around to the side of the building where the bike rack was.

"Where are you going?"

"I just want to see something."

It was about quarter to six now. It hit me then that this trip was anything but spontaneous. I followed Nikki around to the side of the building. She stopped and looked over at the jewelry store next to Chocolate Love. She glanced back and forth between the two buildings.

"What are you looking for?" I asked.

"Where's that dog?"

"What dog?"

"You know, the dog we hear barking. They are new to the neighborhood, whoever his owner is, since I don't know him. How come we don't hear him now?"

I stood very still and listened. She was right. There was no dog barking.

"Why isn't he barking at us now?"

"That's a good question. I don't know."

Nikki turned on her heel and headed toward the back of the building.

"Now where are you going, Nikki?"

She made a complete circle around the building, looking in every window she could reach. I followed and watched silently as her head whipped back and forth taking in details she did not share with me. We ended up back at the front door.

"See, no dog."

"Where are you going with this?"

"I don't know yet. Want to head back?" she asked.

I nodded my head in agreement, and she took off down Third Street to head back toward her house. Watching her go, my mind began to race.

Why was the dog so important? What kind of lead was Nikki following?

Chapter 15

The rest of Sunday was a whirlwind of activity.

In the afternoon, I snuck back to the peace and quiet of my apartment for a couple of hours to write on my desktop. The days off had not been kind to my writing mojo, and every word was a struggle.

Also, not living in the location where the book was set was posing more of a problem. It was probably time to relocate my character to Geneva. It was a quaint town with a lot of different usable settings. It would be just a matter of figuring out what would happen in her life to make her choose this area.

In my series, Mary owned her own antique store. While researching items for her customers, she would find something odd or strange about the item and then the story began.

I wrote from noon until four before calling it a day. It took me a good hour to get going, but once I was in the zone, things got cooking. It was so nice to be back in my little work cocoon. Throughout that time, I heard Nikki, Bob, and her staff moving around downstairs, prepping for the upcoming week.

Before heading back downstairs, I cleaned and tidied up my apartment. This was supposed to be my last night at Nikki and Bob's house. By tomorrow morning, the alarm system would be installed, so I could go back to my apartment without Nikki getting anxious. The store was scheduled to re-open tomorrow with shortened hours.

I closed up my apartment and headed downstairs to find Nikki and Bob. In the little hallway leading to the stairs, a chill ran up my spine. This was how my nightmares came back to me. The more time that passed, the more I lost the details, and my fear would fade. But once in a while, something would trigger a memory: a color, a scent, or in this case, a location.

I stood in the very spot where the bride-young Fran, old Fran, Mandy, and the mystery woman, had stood in my dream. My right hand grabbed onto the banister to prevent myself from falling down the stairs.

I closed my eyes to try and remember the rest of the dream about Fran. The clock. I remembered that. My eyes popped open.

Sneaking a peek at the clock at the bottom of the stairs, I noticed it read four-twenty. That clock would never look the same to me. I made my way down the stairs and stood in front of it. Standing about seven feet tall, my recollection of the clock was that it was an heirloom from Bob's family. Too bad. I wanted to ask Nikki to get rid of it, but I was sure it had a lot of sentimental value. From here on out, I had a feeling it would always remind me of my nightmare about Fran.

The sound of the front door opening grabbed my attention. No one was supposed to be coming in that way today if the store was closed. I stepped further into the foyer, prepared to tell whoever it was we were not open.

"Hell-ooo!" I heard Adelle's voice ring out.

Adelle and Mom came in carrying shopping bags. By the amount they held in their arms, it looked like they had bought out an entire store.

"Was that door open?" I asked.

"No, I have a key," Adelle said nonchalantly.

"Hi, honey," Mom said. "What's wrong? You look frazzled."

Because my mom was used to my nightmares, I could go into detail about the clock but chose not to. It was fine to sound like a raving lunatic in front of Mom. Adelle, on the other hand, had no patience for it. Whenever I tried to talk to Adelle about the nightmares growing up, she would brush it off and say something along the lines of "Did you eat chocolate before bed again?"

"I'm just burnt out from writing."

"How did it go? Did you get a lot done?" she asked.

"I did," I said.

Mom always read my work before I sent it off to my editor. She was my first reader on all of my books and gave the best advice. I didn't feel like talking about my work though, so I changed the subject.

"What is all that stuff?" I asked, pointing to the bags. Adelle and I hadn't addressed the harsh words spoken between us last night yet, which still made me feel horrible. I deliberately avoided doing that, hoping to show her I could move on.

"Nikki asked me to pick up some stencils for her," Adelle said.

"That was four hours ago," Nikki said, walking in from the kitchen. "Where have you been?"

"We got a little side-tracked at Geneva Commons," Adelle said, referring to one of our local outdoor shopping malls. "We both needed something to wear to the funeral," Adelle said defensively.

Judging from the amount of bags she was holding, she had bought enough to attend twenty funerals. So much for my worries about Adelle and Mike's financial crunch.

"I'm just dropping Mom off and heading home. I have to pick up the kids from the neighbor's and won't have enough room in the car with all these bags. Can I just leave them here and pick them up later?"

Adelle had stolen Mom away for four precious hours when she could have been helping Nikki get ready for Fran Fest. Mom held one small bag. Obviously, she wasn't the one shopping for herself. She was probably dragged around by Adelle like a personal assistant.

"What did you buy, Mom?" I asked.

"Just a little pair of earrings to go with the black suit I brought. It's a few years old, but it will be just fine. Because of the earrings that is," she threw in.

"What's the plan now?" I asked.

"Did you forget we are supposed to swim?" Nikki asked Adelle. As much as these two butted heads, they continued to swim every Sunday and Tuesday night at Delnor. It was a commitment they had kept for many years, even after Adelle had all of her kids.

"Shoot!" Adelle said. "Yes, I did."

I didn't want either of them to miss out on their time together since the exercise break always did a world of good for their sanity and their relationship.

"Mom, why don't you and I pick up the kids so they can go to Delnor?" I suggested, craving time with the kids. It would be a much welcome break.

"Are we still having dinner with Mom back at Nikki's house?" Adelle asked. "Mike could pick up the kids and head over to Nikki's. Wait, I forgot, Mike is meeting at a potential build sight tonight."

Bob walked into the room with a marker in his hand. I guessed he and Nikki were working on signs for Fran Fest. They probably had to start them without the stencils.

"Nikki, why don't you and Adelle go for your swim? Mom and Kelly can pick up Adelle's kids, and I'll head back home to make dinner. My parents will be joining us, too," Bob said.

"Okay, babe, thanks," she said, leaning in to give him a quick kiss.

"You'll feel so much better," he said, holding her close to him. I watched their interaction, thinking how nice it would be to have a partnership like these two did. It always seemed so effortless and genuine.

The evening turned out to be rather pleasant with all of us at the house together. It almost felt like a holiday if it weren't for the impending wake and funeral.

"Where are you, Kelly?" Nikki leaned in and asked at one point. I had been zoning out, deep in thought. She dropped some salad on my plate and passed the bowl onto her father-in-law, who was seated on the other side of me.

"I'm just thinking about Fran and her family. Sitting here with our family is making me think of hers. They're probably sitting down to dinner somewhere without her tonight," I said.

Nikki nodded her head. "I know. I was thinking the same thing. Excuse me," she said, getting up from the table abruptly. I knew immediately based on her reaction that I shouldn't have said that. Why pour more salt into the wound? From here on out, I needed to be more careful around Nikki.

* * * * *

Monday and Tuesday flew by at a hectic pace. There were many moments of sadness, but Fran's daughter, Amy, and her sister, Jules, had done an excellent job honoring her with a photo board filled with memories of Fran's life. Fran's husband had passed about ten years ago, but from all the pictures, you could tell their years together were happy and full. Nikki's staff had prepared a huge display of cupcakes in the shape of Fran's face. They used a digital picture of Fran and then meticulously worked from a graph of the image to break down the picture into some kind of map to build her face.

At the reception after the funeral, I couldn't help but cringe when people took cupcakes, as they were intended to do. It was like Fran's existence was disappearing as her face got gobbled up by family and friends. Knowing Fran, she probably would have had a good laugh at that though, so I tried my best to let go and watch people enjoy the treats.

"These turned out so good," Nikki commented, taking a bite of a cupcake. A bit of the cream cheese frosting stuck to the tip of her nose. I reached up with a napkin and wiped it off quickly.

"The secret to Red Velvet Frans, as they will forever be called, is the frosting. Fran always added more cream cheese than what was traditionally called for in a red velvet cupcake," Nikki said, smiling. Her mouth had turned an unnatural red color from the food coloring in the cake. I laughed and looked around the room.

Jack didn't attend the services. There was a part of me that secretly hoped he would be there. However, the attendance was overwhelming. I had no idea Fran had so many friends and family members. The general vibe was that this was more of a celebration of Fran's life, which is what her family wanted. The cupcake display helped to add to that mood. Nikki seemed to be in better spirits by the reception, which in turn helped me to relax.

Back at the apartment on Tuesday night, I rejoiced to be back in my own bed. With the new alarm system installed, I felt safe and secure. The events of the last few days had exhausted me too much to even think about break-ins.

On Wednesday morning, I woke up at four-thirty to do my run. That left me with an hour to write before heading down into the kitchen to help Nikki put the finishing touches on Fran Fest. The kitchen was already abuzz with worker bees at six-thirty. The first person I ran into was Nikki's father-in-law, Bob Sr.

"Kelly, good morning! Thanks for coming in so early. Ready for work?" he asked, stepping aside and allowing me to enter the kitchen. I walked into the rich cocoa smell of red velvet cupcake.

"You bet. Where should I start?"

"Well, looks like I'm the official coffee guy," he said, smiling down at me. He was a good fifty pounds lighter from when he ran the store due to a strict diet post his heart attack. Although his body had physically changed, his energetic smile was still exactly the same. Working in the store today looked like it was agreeing with him. "You should start with a nice cup of coffee. We made some for everyone coming in early. It's hazelnut, Fran's favorite. We'll start the big brew before we open. I'd love for you to test out the sample and see if it's strong enough."

I had already drank two cups of coffee this morning but didn't have the heart to tell him no. Besides, I could always use another cup of coffee, especially hazelnut. I wandered over to the coffee station and took a taste, giving Bob Sr. the thumbs up sign.

"Follow me. Are you okay with frosting duty for the Red Velvet Frans? Nikki tells me you're the best froster we've got."

"I am," I said proudly.

"Are you making sure you get paid for your frosting time?" he joked.

"Nikki helps me out, so it's only right I give her frosting time."

"Yeah, I heard. You guys stick together. You're really lucky. My Bobby is blessed to have married into a family like yours," he said, patting my shoulder quick.

An awkward moment passed when we could talk more about why I needed Nikki's help. Instead, Bob Sr. gracefully moved the topic onto other more pressing matters, like how I needed to frost three hundred cupcakes in the next couple of hours.

By twelve o'clock, the cupcakes started to run low. I couldn't believe how fast the cupcakes were flying off the shelves on a weekday. Didn't people have to work? Apparently, all you had to do was tempt people with a free cupcake, and they dropped everything to stop by.

Nikki didn't look frazzled at all by the fact that we were getting low. Apparently, she had anticipated it and had two hundred more waiting in the back fridge. We got to work on frosting those.

About twenty minutes into our second frosting binge, Nikki abruptly stopped and looked at her watch.

"You know what?" she said. "Why don't you take a break from frosting and go help out at the counter? We've got a mob out there."

I gave her a look like "Are you crazy?" We still had over one hundred to frost.

She leaned back in her chair to look at something in the front room. I turned to see what caught her attention. A swarm of people crowded their way to the counter. My guess was she was worried about the amount of people waiting for assistance.

"What about the rest of the cupcakes?" I asked, pointing dramatically at the large number of cupcakes we had yet to finish. My back was aching from bending over at the waist to frost, and my signature pink apron was covered in cream cheese frosting.

"We'll just hold off on the last one hundred to see if we really need them."

"Um, I think we're going to need them," I said with some sarcasm, shooting my thumb over my shoulder to the mania going on in the front room. At the rate these Red Velvet Frans were moving, there was no way we would have enough without frosting the remaining cupcakes.

"Okay, I'll go help. You're right. We're swamped," I said.

Setting my frosting bag down on the table, I pulled off my cream cheese icing drenched apron and put on a fresh one to be more presentable for the customers.

As soon as I walked into the front room, I knew immediately why Nikki wanted me there. Jack wasn't visible to me from the kitchen because the frame of the door blocked my view of him.

"Hi, Kelly," he said when my eyes met his. The blue polo shirt he had on made his bright green eyes stand out, and his mouth turned up into a killer smile. "We were hoping to see you here."

Chapter 16

I picked my jaw up from the floor and tried to reattach it to my face before speaking.

"Hi," I replied. A shiver of anticipation ran through my body. I had been hoping to see Jack again soon since the yoga class, but had not anticipated him coming to Fran Fest.

The customers in front of Jack got their cupcakes and moved to the side, giving him the opportunity to step up to the counter. He held the right arm of an older woman, who was hunched over a cane she held in her left hand. I tried to disguise my look of shock upon realizing this was Jack's mother, Peggy. She had aged so much in the last ten years it was hard to recognize her.

"I know. I'm old as hell," she said. Her lips turned up into a smirk on the right side. It looked as though the left side was unable to join in the smile, as if she had suffered a stroke recently. I moved around the counter, so I could be closer to them.

"No, you look great. I was just surprised to see you here. It's been a long time. Thank you for coming."

"Don't get old, Kelly. It's hell." She pulled her arm away from Jack and let go of the handle of the cane. She raised both of her arms, signaling me to come in for a hug.

"It's good to see you, sweetie," she said. My body fit into her snug embrace. This close to her, it was clear she had shrunk down significantly from how I remembered her. Our embrace felt completely different because of the change, but she still smelt exactly as I remembered. It was a mix of something sweet like chocolate chip cookies and baby powder.

"Great to see you, too," I said, letting go of her. Her embrace was strong, but it felt like it took a lot of effort on her part. I didn't want to strain her.

"I'm so sorry about Fran, Kelly." Her hand reached up to touch my face and lingered on the side of my cheek for a moment.

"Thank you." When she touched me, our eyes met, and for that moment in time, she was the nurturing, strong woman who was like a second mother to me back when I dated her son.

She reached back for her cane with her left hand. Jack was two steps

78

ahead of her, and placed the cane in her hand before she had to strain for it.

"We're so glad you're having this Fran Fest," he said. "We weren't able to make it to the services. Mom has been coming to Chocolate Love for years. She just loved Fran."

Jack appeared openly nervous today-different than he was the other night at yoga.

"Thanks. This was all Nikki's idea. We were all very fond of Fran, but Nikki was especially close to her. We wanted to do something special for her."

Jack and Peggy were now at the front of the line, and Claire, one of the employees, handed them two Red Velvet Frans. At that moment, two more employees came up to the counter from the back room. I was sure Nikki sent them in as more reinforcements.

"Thank you," Jack said to Claire.

He moved off to the side, still holding his mom's arm with one hand and two cupcakes with the other. They both looked like they wanted to stay and chat a little longer, but didn't know where to stand.

"Would you like to sit out on the patio?" I offered.

"We just checked for chairs on the way in. They're packed. We might have to take our cupcakes to go," Jack said. He had to maneuver his body closer to mine in order to allow a woman to pass by. I took in a whiff of Jack's smell, the same combo of baby powder and chocolate chip cookies today. He must have spent some time in his mother's house before coming here.

When he moved close to me, the buttons of his shirt shifted slightly, exposing his collar bones and the very top of his chest. His normally light Irish skin had darkened with a nice tan. It made me remember how much he loved going down to Lake Michigan in the summers when we dated to play volleyball on the beach. Hoping to not get caught staring, I diverted my eyes quickly.

Steady, Kelly.

"Would you like to come into the kitchen? We have a small table and chairs we keep around for our employees to eat lunch." A big part of me wanted to get them away from the crowd to a more intimate setting. I was enjoying being with both of them.

"Really?" Peggy asked. Her eyes widened. "I've always wanted to see the back of this place. This old house is so mysterious and quaint. I heard you live upstairs, right?"

"Mom," Jack said in some kind of a warning.

"What? I'm just asking if she lives here. Not asking to go see it," she said innocently.

"Kelly doesn't want us knowing all her business," he laughed. "Let's just take her up on her offer for the kitchen tour for now."

"Okay," Peggy laughed.

"We would love to see the kitchen," he said.

I directed them behind the counter, stopping in the doorway to the kitchen to allow them to go first. When Peggy passed me, she shot me a wink. Jack followed shortly after her and mouthed the word sorry to me.

It made me giggle.

"Don't worry about it." I casually put my hand on his arm. The feel of his muscular arm under my hand sent a zing through my body. It felt good to touch him. My hand lingered longer than what was probably appropriate. Finally, my brain sent a signal to my hand to cool it, and I pulled away.

"Wow, this is gorgeous. Very professional. It's not the way I imagined it," Peggy said.

"What are you saying, you old bat? You're surprised we don't have a junky kitchen?" Nikki asked.

My mind began to race, trying to think of a way to soften Nikki's words. When I saw the smile on Nikki's lips, I wondered if the stress of the last couple of days had turned Nikki a little crazy.

"Nikki!" Peggy said. "There's my girl. Where were you last night? We missed you."

Peggy and Nikki had met when I was dating Jack, but as far as I knew, they had not stayed in touch. Their familiarity confused me.

"And who are you calling old bat? I still kick your butt in the pool and don't you forget it!" Peggy said with a laugh.

"I swim with Peggy at Delnor," Nikki said to me. She walked close to Peggy and took her arm from Jack to lead her over to the table where she could sit and eat her cupcake. Peggy jumped at the opportunity to drop Jack's arm and be led by Nikki. It was obvious these two were comfortable with each other.

Nikki met my eyes for a second.

"I didn't go last night because we had Fran's funeral yesterday. We were all exhausted. I just wanted to stay home with my family," Nikki said.

"Of course. You must have been beat," Peggy said. She sat down at the table and dug into her cupcake. "Could you show me where the bathroom is?" she asked Nikki after a couple of bites.

"I'll take you, Mom," Jack said.

"No, that's okay Jack. I want to ask Nikki about something about the store anyway." Nikki was at her side in a flash, and they headed out of the room.

"You should see her in the water," Jack said, pulling a chair out for me to sit down at the table. He took another one out for himself and sat down across from me. "Since she had the stroke, she moves slowly on land, but she's a shark in the water. It's been good for her."

"I didn't know she had a stroke. When was that?"

"A few months ago. It was pretty serious. That's why I moved home. She's recovered the majority of her mobility, but she's a little off sometimes. Like when she asked about your apartment," Jack said in an apologetic tone.

"That's not a big deal. Your mom's just as cool as ever. She always made it a point to be nice to me."

I cringed, thinking about the time we had run into each other right after I broke up with Jack. She told me I had broken her son's heart. She immediately followed that comment up by saying I would always be welcome in her home because she and Mari still wanted to see me. Even then, she had spoken her peace bluntly but with love and forgiveness leading the way. I was too young to realize how gracious her words were at the time.

Jack looked down at his cupcake and peeled away the wrapper. There was an awkward moment of silence as his large hands tore at the paper.

"I love Red Velvet cupcakes," he said before popping the whole thing in his mouth.

"I remember." The comment slipped out of my mouth.

He simply raised an eyebrow at me and made a "humph" sound. I wondered if he was remembering the same memory that was now racing through my mind.

For his sixteenth birthday, I had made Jack a dozen cupcakes. Nikki, of course, had helped. I brought the cupcakes to his house after a football game. It was the first night we kissed. The memory of him asking me to be his girlfriend was still so vivid. By that point, I had been waiting for him to ask me for a couple of weeks. I was his before he even had to ask.

"Can I get you some milk?" I asked, standing up quickly. My hip accidentally knocked the side of the table, and the remaining half of Peggy's cupcake tumbled across the table and landed right on Jack's blue shirt, frosting side down.

"Oh no," I said, reaching over and pulling the cupcake off his shirt. "Sorry. Let me get a towel."

I scrambled over to the counter and found a towel. After running it under cold water for a couple of seconds, I rushed back over to Jack, who appeared completely unfazed by the whole thing.

I reached down and dabbed at the shirt where the frosting had done the most damage.

"Don't worry about it, Kelly," Jack laughed. He held his arms up in the air like a little kid getting cleaned up.

I frantically rubbed at the area, trying my best to gather up the frosting in one hand and clean the stain with the wet cloth.

"Hey, Kel, really it's okay," he said softly and with a little urgency. His body tensed, and his hands reached down and grabbed mine to stop me from rubbing the stain clean. The cupcake had fallen further down on his shirt than I initially realized, causing me to rub areas I should not be touching.

His hands gently took the towel from my hands. I straightened up awkwardly and met his eyes. They burned into mine with that familiar desire we shared so many years ago. It shocked and excited me at the same time.

He did feel this, too.

"I'm sorry." I could feel my face flood with a crimson blush. Thankfully, his was as well. He was smiling though and chuckling quietly to himself.

"That was embarrassing," I said.

"I had no idea Chocolate Love offered that kind of service. Is that why the word love is in the name?" he joked.

"Shut up," I said relaxing. "I'm getting you milk." I planned on getting one for myself as well to calm me down.

A cold shower would be even better.

I took my time at the counter pouring the milk. Upon returning to the table, I felt a little more in control. Jack looked completely recovered.

"What are you going to do about your shirt?" I pushed his glass of milk across the table toward him.

"It's not a big deal. After this, I'll take Mom home and then go home to change. I work from home on Wednesdays." He swallowed the milk in one large gulp.

"I was wondering how you were able to be here in the middle of the afternoon on a work day."

"I'm very lucky. My firm is pretty flexible. My boss has a similar situation with his parents, so he's very understanding. On my days at home, I take Mom out for lunch or to do her shopping. Or go out for cupcakes."

"Do you want more milk?"

"No, I want to ask you something before they come back in."

The cupcake fiasco seemed to have melted some of the anxiety I sensed when Jack first walked in.

"Sure." My pulse began to quicken.

"Would you have dinner with me tonight?"

"Um, sure. At your house? I mean in town? Or what were you thinking?" Why did I need to know this? If a man asked you to dinner, and you wanted to go, you said yes. Plain and simple. No need for the twenty questions. The blush rose again on my cheeks.

"I don't think I want to scare you away with my cooking. It's pretty intense. I was thinking of something a little different. How about I pick you up and take you into the city? With all you've been through in the past couple of days, it might be nice to get out of Geneva."

A dinner in Chicago? That would mean a fifty minute car ride. A lot of alone time for two people getting reacquainted.

"I would love to, Jack." My mind raced to my closet and what was hanging in there. I'd have to scramble to put something together.

"What time?"

"How about I pick you up at six-thirty?"

"Six-thirty would be good." I did a quick calculation of all the things that needed to be done in order to make my appearance more date worthy.

"I'm glad you said yes," he said, standing up and dusting off his pants. "Mom brought her heavy cane today. If you would have turned me down, there's no telling what she would have done to you." Jack smiled and tilted his head in the direction of Nikki and Peggy, unsuccessfully trying to hide behind the door frame.

I wondered how much they had heard.

Chapter 17

After Jack and Peggy left Chocolate Love, Nikki and I spent a couple of seconds squealing like teenage girls. The store had calmed down a bit, and her staff had things under control in front, so we had a moment to ourselves.

"I hate to sound cliché, but I have nothing to wear tonight."

"You could borrow something of mine."

"Are you kidding, Nikki? What would fit me?" I laughed.

"Let's go upstairs and dig through your closet. You must have something."

"What about the cupcakes?" The table still overflowed with Red Velvet Frans that needed frosting.

"Oh, yeah," Nikki said.

"Let's finish these, and then we'll see how things are going." We turned at the same time to pick up our pastry bags.

"You know what? This is crazy. You've been working like a mad woman for me now for almost a week straight. Please just go take the rest of the day to get ready for your date. Go get your hair done. You and Mom could go shopping."

"I can't do that." I was sure Nikki thought I meant I couldn't leave. What I really meant was that I couldn't financially afford to go shopping. My mind started to mentally flip through the dresses hanging in my closet. It pretty much came down to the two dresses I wore to the wake and the funeral. Everything else dated back to my Steve time. It made me sick to my stomach to think of putting one of those dresses on for Jack.

"Hey, where is Mom by the way?" I asked, curious.

"Adelle wrangled Mom into baby-sitting this morning, so she could meet some friends. She's supposed to be here any minute."

Not only was Adelle not here helping this morning, but she'd also pulled Mom away from Nikki when she needed her to be at Fran Fest. Mom flew in to help Nikki, not to be Adelle's nanny/personal shopper. I wanted to say something to Nikki, but held my breath instead. She didn't need me stressing her out. She seemed to have let some of her frustration about Adelle go and just surrendered to the situation.

I thought again about what Bob had said earlier to me, "Nikki is not looking for Adelle's support anymore. She knows it's not there. She's looking for yours."

"Looking for me?" Mom asked, as she stepped into the room. She was already dressed in a pink apron over her khakis and white tee-shirt. "I'm here to help. Do you want me to frost those?"

"Sure, Mom. I don't know if we're going to need all of those. All of a sudden things are not so crazy. If you want you could do half. We'll be more than okay with that. I will be right back." Nikki handed her pastry bag over to Mom and crooked her finger at me. "Come with me."

"What are you two up to?" Mom asked, swooping over the table of unfrosted cupcakes like the old pro she was. Before Nikki could respond, she finished frosting five cupcakes.

"We'll be right back," Nikki said. She pulled me toward the front of the store. We made our way through the customers, stopping to greet a few familiar faces. Finally, we got to the stairs. I followed Nikki up as she charged up to my apartment.

"Got your key on you?"

"Of course," I said, stepping past her to open the door.

The minute the lock was opened, she made a beeline for my bedroom.

"What are you doing?"

"Tell me what you are going to wear?" Nikki said, as she pointed a finger at my closet.

"Are you serious?"

"Yes, right now. I want to know what you plan on pulling out of your closet in a few hours to dazzle a man you are clearly interested in," she said, raising her eyebrow and smiling at me.

"Fine."

I walked over to the closet and looked inside. The truth was, since becoming an author, I stopped needing to dress up for work every day. Casual clothes and sweats became my uniform. As time passed, the nicer clothes began to look dated and old. Eventually, I gave them away, maintaining only a couple of nice items for book signings and meetings with my editor and publisher. Those items were much too formal, though, for tonight's dinner.

Just as I thought, my options came down to choosing between the two dresses from the wake and the funeral. One was a short sleeve, gray, knit dress and the other was a simple black wrap dress. The black was my first choice, but again, it leaned toward more of a formal look than a date night look.

I hesitated for a second then reached out to grab the gray knit.

"Nope," Nikki said.

"What? You don't like it? I just wore this to the wake."

"Listen to what you just said, Kelly. You wore this to a wake, and now you want to wear this on a date with Jack?"

She was right. It was not intriguing at all.

"Can't you jazz me up a little bit with jewelry or something?" I asked sheepishly.

"Normally, yes, but we have another problem."

"What?"

She turned the dress around so the side that was facing her was now visible to me. I gasped when I saw two huge deodorant stains running up the front of the dress. It must have happened while taking the dress off on Monday after the wake.

"You always did have a bad habit of not getting things dry cleaned after you wore them."

"There is another option, you know," Mom said, standing in the doorway of the bedroom behind me. I spun around at the sound of Mom's voice. "You could let me take you shopping. A date with Jack sounds pretty important," she said.

"How long have you been standing there, Mom?" I asked.

"Long enough to know we need to get moving, or you'll be late for your date."

* * * * *

After a few minutes of negotiating who would do what, Mom and I freshened ourselves up in my apartment, so we could go shop. Nikki swore she had more than enough employees left in the shop to help her, so I wasn't worried about leaving her with too much to do. And she was excited for me to go out with Mom. We hadn't had much alone time together, and Nikki knew that.

Mom was ecstatic when I finally agreed to go shopping with her. Mom and Dad had been trying to help me financially since the day my marriage fell apart. It was just too hard to take money from my parents at this point in my life. I was in my early thirties and needed to be independent. Not to mention, my pride got in the way.

Mom finally talked me into it by saying she had intended to buy all of her girls something while she was in town. She wasn't able to spoil us like she used to when we were all living at home. This would be her chance to pick out something nice for me.

As we were making our way through the front foyer of Chocolate Love to get to my car, a familiar voice called my name.

"Kelly?"

I stopped in my tracks and waited a second before turning around.

Beside me Mom whispered, "Who is that?"

"Uh oh."

"Hi, Kelly," Gina said, as she walked toward us.

This woman would not take a hint. I thought not returning her emails would keep her away. Apparently, I needed to be more direct about not wanting to see her.

"Gina, hi," I said in way of greeting. The first thing that struck me was her change in physical appearance from when I knew her in California. She looked so much less polished now from how I remembered her. Her hair had always been perfectly coiffed and blow-dried. Now, it was much longer and cut in messy layers. The cut was so poorly styled, it looked as though she cut it herself. The layers fell in a messy wave around her face and were frizzy and dry. She also looked puffy and much heavier than I remembered her.

"It's good to see you." She moved toward me as if she was going to hug me. I stepped back, bumping into my mom. Mom grabbed my arm to steady me.

"Is there somewhere we can go to talk?" Her voice was desperate and anxious. The sound of it gave me goose bumps.

"I can't believe Steve did this to you. You can talk to me, Kelly. I will help you get through this. We will get you through this."

At the lowest point in my life, I trusted her as a friend. I had confided so much in her. Too much. She had used it all against me and exposed my innermost feelings to whichever media person came knocking for my story.

"Gina, you should leave," I said. "I don't want to see you." My mom tensed up behind me. Her hand steadying me locked on tighter.

"Let's go," Mom said, pushing me forward and out the door.

"Kelly," Gina called behind me. Her voice was inappropriately loud for a small store like Chocolate Love. She was doing it again. She was embarrassing me and exposing me in front of anyone she wanted.

Mom and I practically ran down the stairs to my car.

Chapter 18

"What is *she* doing here?" Mom asked as soon as we got into my car. We jumped in and locked the doors as if we were being chased by a wild animal. I said a silent prayer of thanks when the car started up on the first try. My car had over one-hundred-fifty thousand miles on it. I had sold the newer car that Steve and I shared in California after the divorce, knowing I couldn't afford the payments anymore.

"I have no idea," I said, pulling the car out from my parking spot behind the shop. My plan was to take an alternative route in order to avoid driving past the store. Anything to avoid the risk of seeing Gina again.

"You should call the police, Kelly. That woman was crazy." Mom knew "the Gina story" very well.

"What am I going to tell them, Mom?"

"Tell them the whole story, about how this woman is obsessed with your life." She spun her finger around her temple in a frantic gesture. Mom let out a loud sigh and dropped back into her seat.

"We should have filed a restraining order against her when all of this first happened. There is something wrong with that girl." It was clear Mom was frustrated and angry over the situation.

I knew it wasn't directed at me, but nonetheless, I became defensive.

"Mom, I had a lot going on at the time. I didn't know how crazy she was. And how can I even get a restraining order against her? She never physically hurt me. She just betrayed me."

"I know. I know," Mom mumbled. She reached out for my hand. I pulled it away from the steering wheel to give hers a tight squeeze and then returned it to the wheel. "I'm sorry, Kelly. It's just upsetting. She made a bad situation a lot worse for you when she didn't have to. It's just weird that's she's here. Seeing her probably makes you go through all of those emotions again with Steve. I know that's how I feel. It makes me so mad."

Surprisingly, seeing Gina did not make me think about Steve. In fact, it didn't make me think about what happened in California at all. It just made me upset that she was here in my present life. I had worked so hard to escape. Why did the trouble have to follow me here? I had been doing so well.

"Let's call, Nikki," I said. "I feel bad we just stormed out of there and left her with that to deal with."

Mom dug through her small purse and whipped out her cell phone. She put the phone on speaker, so we would both be able to talk to her.

Nikki picked up on the first ring.

"Gina's gone, Mom. Bob asked her to leave and not to come back. He told her if she did, he would call the police," Nikki said. She sounded cool and collected.

"Thank God," Mom said. She ran her hand down her face and slumped even further down in her seat like a deflated balloon.

"Is Kelly okay?" Nikki asked.

"I'm okay."

"What was she doing here?" Mom asked me.

"I don't know exactly. She sent me a couple of emails earlier this week to say she was going to be in town and wanted to see me."

"What?" Mom shrieked. "Why didn't you tell me?"

"I didn't think she would actually come to the shop, Mom."

"I'm telling you, she is not right, Kelly. We need to do something about this," Mom said firmly. Mom was normally pretty amicable, but when it came to her family, she could become a bulldog.

"She acted strange when Bob spoke to her, Kelly. She just kept saying, 'I just want to talk to Kelly. Just for five minutes.' I think Mom is right. That woman is crazy," Nikki said.

"Yeah, I know." I sighed, frustrated that my life seemed to be a constant whirlwind of drama.

"Wait, wait," Nikki said. "Let's not go off the deep end. She's gone and has been told not to come back. You have an important date tonight. Let's just put this aside for now and concentrate on your afternoon. You have this time with Mom. Please just go enjoy yourself and live it up."

"She's right, Kelly," I heard Bob's voice speak into the phone.

"Okay, you're right, Nikki. But we have to talk more about this later. There must be more we can do," Mom said. "Sounds like we have the problem solved for now. We're going to hang up and do some shopping."

"Have a great time!" Nikki said. "We'll talk to you later."

We disconnected as I pulled into a parking spot. Just as my hand grabbed for the door handle, Mom reached her arm out and touched my leg.

"Honey, maybe your father and I should move back here for a time."

I turned to face her. The V-neck, purple blouse she wore gave me full view of her neck and upper chest. Sitting this close to her in the car, I could see very clearly how freckled her skin was from the constant exposure to the Florida sun. At this proximity, in the clearness of day, the wrinkles in her eyes and neck were very prominent. It reminded me that my parents were getting older much faster than I liked. It would be great to have them back in town to spend these years with them.

But her face also had the same strained look now as the one she wore in court with me three years earlier for Steve's trial. I hated having her in the room, hearing all of the things her son- in- law had done, but she and my father had refused to leave my side. That week in court probably took ten years off of their lives. She couldn't go back to that dark place ever again. I wouldn't allow it.

"Mom, what are you talking about? You love Florida."

"I know, but we love you girls even more. It just seems like you all still need us."

That was the truth. Children never really stopped needing their parents, even when they were independent adults. And I did still need my mom.

"Mom, you're just here at a tough time. This isn't how things normally are. You're seeing some really bad moments."

"I know." Her eyes shifted down to the floor. "I can see you girls depend on each other. It's just so much."

"We would love for you to be back here. But it also means back to Chicago winters. It's all you and Dad ever talked about. You've dreamed about getting away from this area for a long time."

We sat for a moment in silence.

"Sometimes I wish you would have taken us up on our offer and moved to Florida. Our door is always open, Kelly." Her eyes pleaded with me and her hands anxiously grabbed for mine. "We would give you your space, Kelly. I promise. I know you're worried about that. You would have your own life."

After the news broke about my marriage, my parents had tried to get me to move into their condo. Though it was appealing to me, something in my heart told me to head back to Geneva. It was always my true home. It felt like coming back here would give me another chance at life.

While going through my own personal hell in California, Nikki had informed me that the apartment above Chocolate Love would be open for me. Knowing I could return to Geneva kept me going. During the trial, divorce, and my move, I had just kept repeating to myself, "Just get me to Chocolate Love! Give me Chocolate!" I thought the moment I moved into the apartment above Chocolate Love, my life would get better. For the most part, I had been right.

"Mom, I'm okay," I said softly, squeezing her hands.

"Really?" she asked. A flash of hope lit her eyes.

"You know what? For the first time in a long time, yes, really," I said with confidence.

My mom nodded her head up and down. A small smile bloomed on her face.

"You know what, honey. I believe you. You seem so much different this visit. You're coming back."

"I am," I laughed.

"Okay, well then, let's keep this train moving. Let's go shop for this date of yours," she said.

By six that evening, I was in my bedroom getting dressed for dinner. A small glass of wine and good music helped me relax before my night out. My make-over had left me feeling like a new woman. I was feeling like I might actually have a really good time tonight.

The outfit Mom and I picked out was laid out on the bed waiting for me. It was a light pink wrap dress, dipping into a very flattering V. The top had a delicate sparkling of sequins discreetly sewn into the fabric with a few chiffon ruffles at the shoulders.

The dress was not something I would normally pick out. Light pink usually washed me out, but there was something about this shade of pink that worked on me. The little bit of a tan I had picked up from running looked great with the color.

As soon as I had tried this dress on in the store, Mom and I both knew it was the one.

I hadn't missed the fact that Mom cringed a bit at my weight loss, but this dress best flattered me in all the right places. Even with all the action in the past couple of days, I had kept my promise to myself to keep my calories coming in on a regular basis. I could already tell the difference in myself when I looked in the mirror.

"They'll come back," I heard Nikki's voice say in my head when I looked for my curves. I swore I already saw a little hint of their return.

We had also picked out small, silver hoop earrings for a *touch of pizzazz* as Nikki would say. The dress didn't need a lot of jewelry because of the sequins. Adding too much would overdo it.

The dress shopping had taken us just under thirty minutes. When we were finished, Mom pushed for a visit to a local salon, which I had agreed to. My hair had not been cut in about a year. Because I was always throwing it up into a ponytail, there was no reason to. I was short on cash and not spending money on any extras.

As soon as I had taken a seat in the chair, a look of shock registered on the hairdresser's face. She went to work putting in some long layers and cutting a good four inches off. Now, when I looked in the mirror at home, I could see the changes the woman had made on my hair gave it a much needed healthy glow. It hadn't looked this good since my wedding day.

I just needed to slip on my dress and touch up my make-up, which was professionally done at the salon per Mom's insistence. I was worried I would end up looking like a clown, but as promised, the woman had applied the make-up subtly. The natural tones made my skin look amazing.

Mom was right, this was much needed. I should really get back on track of taking care of myself. It was worth it. I was worth it.

Deciding to take a break, I headed over to the computer to check email one last time before my date. Surprisingly, an email from my editor sat in my inbox. It read:

Dear Kelly,

Just checking in on the status of your novel. I'm excited to work with you. Can't wait to see what you come up with for your third installation in your "Antique Murder Mystery" series. Let me know if there is anything I can do to help. I would love to start reading some pages.

Sincerely, Holly Combs

Wow. This was my lucky day. Looks like Holly had finally given up on pressing me to do a tell all of my experience. It just was not something I was interested in. The best thing, the right thing for me, was to keep going with my mystery series. So far, it wasn't a blockbuster, but my books definitely sold well enough.

I shot back an email right away.

Dear Holly,

So nice to hear from you. My third book is coming along. I expect to finish it by the end of the summer. "Antique Murder #3," as it is currently titled, will involve an exciting change of location for Mary, as well as a new love interest. Let me clean some things up before sending pages. You should expect my first three chapters by the end of the week. Hope you are well. Looking forward to working with you!

Sincerely,
Kelly Clark

I had yet to meet Holly in person. My impression of her over the phone was of a hard-nosed business woman, which I liked. She had a good reputation in the industry. I was excited to work with her as well. We just needed to get on the same page, which now we were.

Hopefully, the book really would be finished by the end of the summer. With it already being mid-June, it would mean cranking out at least twenty more chapters by early August. Plus the time needed to edit and re-vamp it.

I closed down my computer and headed back to my room to get dressed for my date. When finished, I examined my appearance in the mirror.

Not bad for a thirty-three-year-old woman who's been through hell and back.

What was looking back at me in the mirror was much better than the zombie that used to stand there. The dark purple stains under my eyes had vanished, and a new sparkle glistened in the iris of my cocoa eyes. Perhaps I truly had left my past in California.

"Not bad," I said out loud.

Chapter 19

At twenty after six, I locked my apartment in order to wait for Jack in the foyer. My legs moved slowly down the stairs, a little unstable in my new heels.

Heels and I did not really have a great relationship. Luckily, flats had become the hot new trend. It probably wouldn't last, but I didn't see myself ever going back to wearing heels again unless it was a special occasion like tonight. I found them so uncomfortable. How women could wear them on a daily basis was beyond me.

Chocolate Love was deserted, except for a couple of lamps left on in the foyer. The bright overhead light, which Nikki normally left on for me, was off, and the cozier mood lights, as she called them, gave the room a warm glow. Nikki probably left those on intentionally for my date.

Knowing she was having a tough time keeping her curiosity at bay, it surprised me she was not here. Thank goodness she granted me my privacy.

As soon as I got to the foyer, it felt like a mistake. It would be better to wait up in my apartment for the doorbell. Now I was just going to look overly anxious if he saw me waiting here.

A quick peek out the front door gave me a visual of the hustle and bustle on Third Street. No Jack yet. I turned to head back up the stairs. Just as I reached the top, the front door bell rang, causing me to jump. Even though I expected it, the noise startled me.

I headed back down the stairs and walked through the foyer to open the front door, stumbling once.

Damn these heels, I thought.

Surprisingly, it was Sharon Winters, the woman raising money for charity, on the porch rather than Jack. I was a bit thrown off by her being here at this hour, but opened the door anyway.

"Hi, Sharon. Can I help you?" My eyes darted up and down the street behind her as I searched for Jack. I didn't want her here when he arrived. I was nervous enough.

"Is this a bad time?"

"The shop is actually closed right now," I said, trying to keep any irritation from my voice. Sharon was striking in a blue cocktail dress that hugged her curves in all the right places. I couldn't help but gawk at her five inch heels. Seeing them made me feel like less of a woman.

"Oh, I was hoping to catch Nikki. I have plans for dinner with a friend a block away and thought I'd take a chance to see if she was here. She volunteered to help me out a bit with the race. Should I just call her?"

"Sounds like a good idea," I said, trying to close up the conversation.

"I'm afraid I have lost her number. Could I come in for a quick minute and get it from you? I'll put it in my phone," she said, flashing me a smile. Her beautifully coiffed blond hair and perfect make-up set me a bit on edge. I remembered the way Jack laughed with her at the yoga class. The little green monster in me reared its ugly head. I didn't want to start the night with Jack seeing this perfect specimen in front of me. As foolish as I knew it was, I wanted all of his attention tonight.

Before I could respond, she snaked past me into the foyer. She must have read my non-response as an invitation to enter.

"Thank you. It will just take a second."

Sure enough, as soon as she was in Chocolate Love, the doorbell rang again.

"Just a minute," I said, heading back to the door to let Jack in.

"Hi," Jack said. "You look great, Kel."

"Thank you," I said, opening the door wide to let him in. "Come on in."

Jack stepped in wearing a dark pinstriped suit that fit so well, it looked custom made. His hair appeared freshly cut, and I caught a subtle hint of his aftershave. He always got it right with his scents. Not too much. Not too little. His familiar smell put me at ease.

I appreciated the effort of going all out with the suit. Thank God I had put extra effort into my appearance tonight. It would have been intimidating standing in front of him right now dressed the way he was if I didn't have my new dress and heels on.

"I love your dress," he commented, running his eyes down my body. He broke out into a big smile when he saw my shoes. He cleared his throat and chuckled a bit.

"Heels, huh? I'm flattered."

Back when we were dating, there had been many events where he had to listen to me moan and groan about my discomfort in heels.

"Yeah, well," I said, unable to come up with anything more. "Are those for me? Now I'm flattered."

He held a bouquet of pink tulips in his right hand. The color was a near match to the pink of my dress.

"For you. If I remember correctly, these are your favorite. I just thought I would," he paused at the sound of Sharon's heels coming closer to us. "Oh, hello, Sharon."

"Hi, Jack. I wasn't expecting to see you here. Are you two heading out on a date?" Sharon asked. The sound of her voice changed the mood in the room so quickly, it made my head spin.

"We're heading to dinner," I said, deliberately dodging the question. "Let me give you her phone number, so you're not late for your date." I chose the word date intentionally to make it clear to Jack that Sharon had somewhere to go.

"Oh, it's not really a date. It's just dinner with a friend," she said. She took the slip of paper I'd written Nikki's number on and entered it into her phone. Rather than wait for her to complete this tedious task, I walked to the door and opened it to signal it was time for her to go.

"We're running a bit late, so we'll see you at the next class?"

Sharon took the hint and headed out.

"Of course. Thanks for the phone number, Kelly. Good to see you again, Jack," she said, flashing him a smile before leaving Chocolate Love. She moved liked she was working a runway on her sky high heels.

"Goodnight, Sharon," Jack said. I watched him closely to see if he would follow her sashay out the door. He smiled back at me with an unreadable look in his eye.

I let her out and waited momentarily before returning to Jack, curious to see which direction she went. She had said she was in the area for dinner. To my surprise, rather than walking to her destination, she approached a car parked in front of Chocolate Love. Before opening the driver's door, she stopped and looked back at Chocolate Love. A strange expression passed over her face as she stood and stared back at the store. Before she could catch me looking out at her, I turned around to head back to Jack. Why would she get back in her car if the restaurant was a block away? There were no restrictions on street parking at this time. She could easily have left it there without the threat of getting a ticket. Odd, very odd.

"Let me just put these in water and then we can be on our way," I said.

A brief panic set in at the thought of finding a vase. That meant taking Jack upstairs to my apartment. As much as I'd been looking forward to spending time with him, it seemed wrong to bring him up to my private lair just yet.

"Let's go into the kitchen to see what I can put these in," I said instead, inviting him into the kitchen of Chocolate Love.

I had to turn on the lights and walk through the store in order to get to the kitchen. Jack followed silently behind me.

My hope was that Nikki still stored a couple of vases under one of the sinks. I made my way over and opened the cabinets.

"This is a great place Nikki and Bob have. It's cool to see it with no one here. I feel like I'm behind the scenes at Chocolate Love."

My hand reached into a darkened corner under the sink and fell on something cold and circular. It felt like the top of a vase. I carefully pulled it out and snuck a peek. *Bingo*.

"Yeah, they've done such a good job," I said, putting the vase under the tap to fill it with water.

"How did the rest of Fran Fest go?" he asked, leaning back against a counter.

"It was great," I said. Not that I knew any details. I had missed the rest of Fran Fest because I ran out the door as soon as Jack left to frantically shop for this date.

The mention of Fran's name changed my mood a bit. I was standing in the exact spot I found her on Friday morning. Up until then, I had not thought about the scene, even though we had worked here all day for Fran Fest. I looked down and remembered her prone body lying on the floor.

As though Jack could read my mind, he asked me, "Is it hard to be here?"

While I pondered my response, I placed the flowers in the vase, keeping my silence.

"I'm sorry," he said. "I shouldn't have brought that up. That was dumb."

"No, it's okay. I like talking about Fran. We *should* talk about her. It keeps her presence alive here. I was just thinking about your question. It should be hard, but it's not. This was Fran's home. In a way, it's right that it happened here."

"That's an excellent point," he said. "I think about that all the time with my mom. She's going downhill so quickly. We really want her to be in the comfort of her home when she passes."

Jack's eyes fell from mine, and he chewed at the side of his lip.

"I'm sorry, Jack. I didn't realize things were that bad with Peggy."

"Some days are definitely better than other days. She gets weak at night. I worry about her falling. Mari and I will have to start spending more time with her, especially in the evenings."

"She still lives alone, you said, right?"

"Yeah, I have a condo here in Geneva, and Mari lives with her family. I'm trying to give her privacy and save some for myself as long as I can. A man has to have his privacy," he said, smiling.

I nodded my head. Jack was such a considerate son. I wondered if his mother knew how lucky she was to have him. Probably.

He clapped his hands together and pulled his body away from the counter.

"What are we doing talking about all this sad stuff when we have a night out on the town planned? Are you ready? Let's go eat."

His enthusiasm pulled me back. If there was one thing I remembered Jack being passionate about, it was food.

Although inside I was dying to know which restaurant he had picked, it would be rude to ask, so I didn't. Instead, I turned off the lights and guided him out the front door, making sure to set the alarm system.

* * * * *

Jack's car, a newer model SUV, was comfortable and spacious. The drive downtown took us just about an hour. We experienced one section of bottleneck traffic, but for the most part, there was not a lot of stop and go traffic left on the highways. The conversation flowed smoothly between us, just like it always had in the past.

"Are you wondering where we are going?" Jack asked, as we drove.

"I am."

"I'm taking you to a restaurant called Spring. Have you ever heard of it?"

The name sounded vaguely familiar, but I couldn't place where I had heard about it.

"I don't think so," I said. "I'm not exactly a restaurant connoisseur. My meals pretty much consist of a peanut butter and jelly sandwich while at my computer."

"Oh boy," Jack said. He laughed revealing his perfect white teeth. It made me think of when he used to have braces. His appearance had changed so much the day he got them removed. It had been one of my first "whoa, this guy is kind of cute" moments for Jack.

"I'm taking you here because you need some Zen in your life. Spring used to be a bathhouse at the turn of the century. It was converted into a restaurant, but the owners have tried to keep some of the structures of the bathhouse intact."

"You know a lot about this place. Do you take a lot of girls here?" I asked in a joking manner.

Jack smiled at me, but when he turned back to the road, he bit again at the side of his lip. It made me regret my comment. The reason was unclear, but in my gut I knew something was off.

He recovered quickly adding, "Just wait until you taste the spring rolls. You'll be coming back for sure. Hopefully with me."

We left the car with the valet, and made our way inside the restaurant. It was smaller than I imagined, but very elegant in a simple and calming manner. The lights were low and romantic, reminding me of a very elegant spa. They certainly had done a good job with that.

Jack gave me his arm to help me down the stairs into the restaurant and stepped forward to give his name to the maître 'd.

The restaurant was busy but not overly crowded. From the looks of it, this place was way out of my price range.

The maître 'd directed us to our table. He pulled a chair out for me and handed us menus at the same time. He moved so gracefully, he reminded me of a well-trained ballerina, dancing around me and rearranging things on the table.

The sound of water running, like a gentle stream, and soothing flute music filled the room.

"This is nice," I said. "I hope I don't get too comfortable. I might fall asleep."

"I'll try to keep the conversation entertaining enough to keep you awake," Jack said, winking at me.

After a few quiet minutes of looking at the menu, he asked, "What looks good to you?"

"The wild Alaskan halibut with sweet corn and crispy Yukon gold potato. Have you had it before?"

"I have. It's excellent. The Lobster Bisque soup is a great way to start."

We ordered our dinner and a glass of wine to start. After a few sips of my merlot, I felt a warm sense of happiness and relaxation at the same time. This was already turning out to be a great night. I was so glad I had accepted his invitation to dinner.

"Jack, can I ask you something?"

Because we'd had some time to catch up in the car, I felt ready to dive in with my question. It was something that needed to be addressed.

"Anything," he said. By the sparkle in his green eyes, I could tell he meant it. If I had to guess, Jack was happy with the way things were going as well. Both elbows up on the table, he played with the stem of his wine glass and leaned in closer to me.

"I heard you got married, but you haven't talked at all about having a wife?"

Jack's eyes fell from mine to his wine glass. He leaned back slightly but kept both of his elbows on the table. Releasing his wine glass, he pushed it slightly forward and pulled his hands into a tight clasp. I watched his lips closely, but they remained locked in a straight line.

"I didn't mean to make you uncomfortable. We don't have to talk about it. It's none of my business."

He didn't confirm there was a wife, or a marriage, or even a relationship for that matter. I was working only from rumors. He didn't owe me any explanation or details about his past, but I felt compelled to know the truth.

"No, we need to talk about it," Jack said, surprising me. "I planned on telling you about this tonight." His eyes burned into mine, mesmerizing me. His right hand grabbed at his tie and loosened it.

"There's something you need to know, Kelly," Jack said.

"Okay."

"If anyone will understand this story, you will," he said, lowering his eyes for a second to his water glass. He by-passed his wine and downed a quick gulp of water. His actions were making me nervous. If there was something sinister or mysterious, I needed him to tell me quickly. I was on the edge of my seat with worry over what he was going to tell me.

"You're correct. There was a marriage. It's over now. She's gone."

Chapter 20

"She's gone?" I gulped. *Gone* drew up images I didn't want to have. *Gone* meant something very sinister in my world.

We're going to make it look like an accident. I can't have her tell my wife. I can't have this baby. I need them gone.

The phone call I overheard before Steve was arrested came rushing back to me.

I searched Jack's face, desperate for a better read of what he was trying to tell me. He licked his lips and burrowed his brows, as though he was trying to gear himself up to talk.

I leaned back slightly to get a hold of my own emotions. What was he about to spill? From the look on his face, it was obviously something big. Could I handle this? It was probably better to hear all about his past before getting too attached to him. But could I really handle this?

His hand reached out and secured mine in his.

"Wait," Jack said simply.

At that moment, our waiter returned with our soup and set it in front of us.

"Thank you," Jack and I both mumbled. He pulled his hand from mine and let the waiter arrange our dishes.

"Has she passed away?" I asked to get the conversation going again when the waiter left.

When Jack's eyes met mine again, he was more composed. He took a minute to remove his suit coat, putting it on the chair behind him. He loosened his tie a bit more and unbuttoned his shirt sleeves to roll them up. This familiar routine relaxed me. Jack was getting ready to feast. All I could think was the news couldn't be that bad if he could eat, right?

"She's alive. At least as far as I know," he said. "She's not here in the United States. We do not stay in contact. She is not allowed to contact me, I should say. It hasn't stopped her from trying though."

"I'm confused," I said.

"I'm surprised and a bit relieved you haven't heard anything about this. You, more than anyone, know how quickly gossip can spread."

"I haven't heard anything. Just that you were married," I said.

"Let me start from the beginning, then. About eight years ago, I moved to London after being offered a position there with my law firm. I met someone after living there for three years. Her name was Callie. Is Callie, I should say. We dated for a little over eight months before I proposed. I thought she was the one. We got along so well right from the start. She was also an attorney, or so she had me believe. I thought we were a good match." I nodded my head, encouraging him to go on.

"Boy, was I wrong," he said, looking down at his soup. He picked up his soup spoon and began twirling it around in his hand. "I don't want to ruin this dinner."

He looked back up at me and gave me a sheepish smile.

"No, you're not. Please, go on."

"Less than six months into the marriage, I knew it was a huge mistake. Her personality started changing on our honeymoon. Never seen anything like it. It felt like she duped me. Like I married a con artist." He paused for a second, watching me closely.

"I'm sorry," I said, but what I was really thinking was, you, too?

"This story gets strange. Hope you're okay with this stuff. I haven't told a lot of people," he said. He set down his spoon and looked into my eyes. His forehead wrinkled while waiting to see my reaction.

"Jack," I said softly. "Have you heard my story?"

"That's why I'm telling you. Number one, I trust you Kelly. And two, you can probably relate. When you marry someone and they turn out not to be who you thought they were, it's devastating. When they threaten your life, it's frightening as hell."

"Hell, yes," I said, nodding my head.

"It started with all of these strange things. She had all of these perverse ideas in her head all of the time. The way she viewed the world was off. Like everyone was her puppet. She started stealing from people and randomly shoplifting. There was this sense of entitlement. She would go to the library and steal wallets from people, then come home and brag to me about it. I tried to force her to get help, but she wouldn't. Callie started to video tape our neighbors. I didn't know she was doing it until I accidentally found some of the tapes. She would call in sick to work to stay home and video tape the neighbor's door. There were hours and hours of video recording just the *door*," Jack said.

"I also found video of people in a park. If she found the person exciting enough, she would follow them and secretly tape them for the rest of the day. Once she taped herself meeting a man in the park and taking him home to our bed. The day I found that tape was when I packed up my things and left the apartment. I told her it was over and filed for divorce shortly after."

"Oh, Jack."

"That's when she really went crazy. She became obsessed with me. I hired a private investigator to look into her. He said he caught her recording me and following me all the time. He looked closely into her background. She didn't have a law degree. She never even finished college. I met some of her co-workers, so I believed her when she told me about working as a lawyer. The whole thing was a scam. The co-workers were old friends of hers from God knows where. She convinced them to be in on the con.

"She started harassing me and wouldn't leave me alone. This went on for years. She would call me again and again, leaving threatening messages on my voice-mail. Sometimes she would just be laughing hysterically to herself. Other times, I would come home to fifty hang-ups in a row or long recorded messages of silence. She was completely undone. Her final act was to confront me outside of my law offices with a knife and threaten to kill me because I was cheating on her. I'd never been so scared in my life.

"By this time we were divorced, but she just couldn't let go. Instead of hurting me, she cut herself. She wasn't badly hurt, but finally, the police stepped in. The last I heard, she was at a psychiatric facility. I'm happy she survived because I would have felt horrible if something happened to her, but there are days." His eyes bounced from object to object on the table, but would not meet mine.

"Jack, this is not your fault."

That was what people told me time and time again about Steve. For the longest time, I did not believe them. I was starting to now. Jack's story helped me see what Nikki and Mom had been telling me for years. Mental instability was not caused by another individual, nor could it be reversed by another person. I was not to blame for what Steve did. Still, I carried shame and guilt, just as Jack seemed to.

"When the call came that Mom needed me, I was all too happy to get away from London and start a new life. I filed a restraining order against her, but lived every day of my life there just waiting for her to pop up from around the corner. It feels good that at least we have an ocean separating us now."

"I can relate," I said, nodding my head.

A resigned smile curved up slowly on Jack's face. His eyes settled back on mine. "I know you can."

"Steve and I were trying to have a baby of our own when I found out he was having an affair with another woman, Mandy. She was pregnant and he planned to kill her and the unborn child in order to avoid having to take responsibility of them. I couldn't fathom how a man who wanted to be a father to our children could kill one of his own. Right at that moment I knew I was living with a monster."

"That's when you stepped in?"

"Yes."

"How did you know he was going to do it?"

"I overheard a phone conversation with someone that was going to help him do it. At first, I thought it was a joke. When I realized he was dead serious, I went right to the police. They didn't believe me."

"It must have been horrible," Jack said.

I thought back to the night in the police station. Four hours of begging the police to listen to my story while being interrogated and treated like a crazy person. They had told me the only way they would be able to help me would be if they caught Steve in the act. Luckily, I had heard enough of the conversation to know the time and place where it was going to all go down.

"What was horrible was the way the media swarmed in afterwards and ripped up my life. It was bad enough what I went through. I didn't need the extra exposure. It made me want to crawl in a hole."

"I can't imagine having to live through that. But you did the right thing, Kelly. Steve's a psychopath and now he's locked up. You saved two lives."

"Yes, but the fact remains, he's still a psychopath. And now he's a psychopath who hates me for what I've done to his life. Those bars won't hold him forever." I shivered slightly.

"Do you want my jacket?" he asked softly.

"Thank you. I would."

He turned behind him and pulled his jacket from his chair to drape over my shoulders.

As much as it hurt to relive these memories, it felt good to talk about this with him. I never talked about Steve to anyone anymore.

Impulsively, I grabbed my wine glass and decided to lighten the mood a bit.

"To us," I said. "The survivors."

My tone was supposed to be comforting but came off a little shaky. I wanted to hug Jack and tell him it was going to be okay. That *we* would be okay. We were good people that ended up in bad relationships. It didn't have to be the end of us though. We didn't have to lose our self-confidence, our pride, or our lives. We could survive and leave the past behind.

"The survivors," he said, picking up his glass and softly touching his to mine. The sound of the glasses coming together made me smile. A victory bell.

After a delicious meal, we decided to skip dessert and head out. The only times we had physically touched each other were the few times our hands met during dinner. As we waited for the car, I got the feeling Jack was going to put his arm around me. I still had his jacket draped over my shoulders. The moment passed though when the car pulled up in front of us.

"Did you enjoy yourself?" Jack asked once we were in the car. He looked over at me and gave me a sideways smile that warmed my heart.

"I did." My body felt comfortably numb from the combination of good wine, great food, and interesting conversation. All of my nervous energy about being around Jack was gone. It felt good to have aired some of our dirty laundry. Now that it was out there, we could deal with it. I leaned out the window and gazed up at the tall buildings as we passed them by. Jack easily maneuvered his way through the city, heading for the expressway.

"Can I ask you something?" I asked him.

"Of course."

"Do you really think she might come here to the states to look for you?"

"Yes, I think about it all the time. She's not supposed to, according to the restraining order, but it doesn't stop me from worrying about it. I have nightmares she's in Geneva, and she's trying to hurt me or my family. It's a horrible way to live," Jack admitted honestly.

"I worry about Steve all the time. The California Department of Corrections is supposed to contact me in the event he escapes, is released, or given the possibility of parole. It always feels like something will slip through the system though, and they'll forget to contact me. I live my life in fear of him showing up at my front door one day."

"How long is he in for?"

"He's supposed to serve ten years. He's already been there for three."

"Is parole a possibility?"

"Yes. In the state of California, it's definitely a possibility because he had a clean record before he was arrested. The overcrowding of the prisons in California does not help the situation."

"How horrible."

"Yep."

"Can I ask you something now?" He looked over at me briefly before swinging his eyes back to the road. We were stopped at a red light. He opened a small box of mints and offered me some before shooting a couple into his mouth.

"Sure."

"Have you tried dating again?"

"To be honest, no. I haven't had the interest. My focus has been on rebuilding my life. It took a while to move back here after the trial because I had to settle my divorce. My sisters have been a huge help. I'm just now strong enough to socialize again."

"I know what you mean. I've dated a few times. Even had a couple of short term relationships. They didn't work though because of me. If the woman was late for a date, I didn't trust her anymore. My thoughts were always distrustful and anxious. I couldn't put anyone else through that. It was better to stop dating entirely.

"It wasn't just women. I didn't trust people in general. There was a lot of anger at her parents for not telling me something was off about Callie. They could have at least warned me. They admitted to me later that Callie had a history of mental illness. They said she was a very unstable youth. She was constantly rebelling and getting into trouble. They also knew she wasn't an attorney; they went along with the scam.

"I was very disappointed with myself for making such a poor choice for a partner. I even started to doubt my ability to practice law. This past year I started seeing a therapist. He's been a huge help. Working out and making time to see old friends and family has been key."

"Yeah, there's nothing like family," I said, thinking about my sisters and my parents. Even Adelle, although she drove me crazy sometimes, had been an anchor for me back in Geneva.

The rest of the ride home went quickly. We were back in front of Chocolate Love by ten to eleven. Jack parked the car on Third Street, opened my door for me, and accompanied me up the front walk.

"Do you go in the front door?"

"The front is fine."

At this time of the night, even though we had a motion detector light by the back door, the front door was lit better.

"I'm sorry I got you home so late. You said you're up early to run. Hope this is all right."

"It's okay. It was nice to get out of Geneva."

We stood at the top of the steps. I needed to open the door with my key, but I was stalling. I wondered if I should hug him. Shake his hand? After all we shared tonight, it seemed cold to just shake hands. Would he kiss me? The thought of that made my stomach jump. It had been a long time since I kissed Jack. This moment seemed very delicate, and I didn't want to mess it up.

"Do you want to keep this?" Jack asked softly, reaching his arm up to touch the sleeve of his jacket.

"Oh, no, that's okay. Here you go," I said, shrugging it off and passing it to him. "Thank you."

"Sure," he said. Jack took the jacket and smiled down at me.

"Well, thank you so much for accompanying me downtown, my lady," he said. He moved in closer. I could smell his breath mints. My body automatically leaned closer to his.

Jack's movements came deliberately and smoothly. Instead of bringing his head down to my face to kiss my lips, he kissed the top of my head, lingering for a moment. The gesture was an undeniably romantic display of respect and desire at the same time.

"I'll call you tomorrow," he whispered into my hair before walking away.

"Thanks again," I managed. A huge, goofy smile spread on my face, which I hid by turning to unlock the door. A strange combination of awkwardness and burning desire raced through me. Thank goodness I did not invite him in. I knew I was getting in over my head with Jack. And I was loving it.

* * * * *

The next morning, I woke at five-thirty to my alarm. Nikki sent a text the night before saying she would meet me at quarter to six outside of Chocolate Love to run. She was meeting me to run, but I was sure she was probably also dying to hear about the date.

I had slept very fitfully the night before but still felt rested and in a good mood. My sunny disposition was due, in part, to the warm fuzzies from my date last night.

When I opened the front door, an envelope fell to the porch. It read: *Kelly*

I brought it back inside Chocolate Love since there was no sign of Nikki yet.

My first thought was it must be from Jack. I ripped it open, and all of my warm fuzzies disappeared.

It read:

> I have to talk to you. You are in danger. Meet me today on the three-thirty riverboat cruise at Pottawatomie Park in St. Charles.
>
> —Gina

Chapter 21

"Hello?" I heard Nikki call out. "Kelly?"

"In here." I was sitting on the landing of the stairs inside Chocolate Love with the letter in my hand. The paper shook slightly in my unsteady hands.

"Why are you in here? I thought we were going to meet outside. Wait a minute, what's wrong?" she asked.

"This." I handed her the envelope.

Nikki scanned it quickly and looked back at me, her eyebrows pulled down. "Why is she doing this?"

"You don't think she's referring to Steve, do you? What else could she be talking about? Do you think he is getting out? Coming here?"

Nikki gasped before responding. "No way, Kelly, Steve is locked away for seven more years."

"How are you so sure?" I asked, shaking my head. "Maybe there's been a change."

"Because I called your attorney after you started to worry. He directed me to the California Department of Corrections website. It confirmed Steve is still there and no changes."

I let out a long exhale. "Thank God."

A great peace came over me while the news sunk in. Kudos to Nikki for taking the bull by the horns and being proactive. And protective. She took it seriously enough that she checked into it herself.

"When did you check?" I asked, suddenly worried again.

"Last Wednesday when you told me about the light on in the kitchen without Fran here."

That meant my down to earth, straight-arrowed sister thought Steve's appearance in Geneva was not completely out of the question.

"Why didn't you tell me?"

"I didn't want to worry you, Kelly. I thought it would stress you out more. Then the whole thing with Fran happened, and life just got crazy." Her eyes darted back to the envelope for a quick second.

"What?" I asked. Her eyes were filled with worry and confusion.

"Hold on," she said, pulling out the two tickets for the riverboat cruise that were also in the envelope. "When did you say Gina told you she was coming into town?"

I thought back, trying to remember her email.

"Let's see, I read the email last Wednesday night at Adelle's house. It said she was going to be flying in on Sunday night. Then in another email, she said she would be in Geneva on Tuesday or Wednesday of this week. She showed up yesterday at Fran Fest after I didn't respond to her—after we spent time with Jack and Peggy."

"Last Wednesday she told you she was going to be flying to Chicago on Sunday night," she said.

"I'm pretty sure. I remember she was going to be flying in on Sunday because it made me think how much Steve hated to fly on Sundays. He used to fly all the time on Sunday afternoons when he worked for the pharmaceutical company because he needed to be somewhere first thing on a Monday morning to do a presentation. He said it felt like he was working six days a week."

"If she told you she was flying in on Sunday, why were these riverboat tickets purchased last Wednesday? Five days earlier than when she was supposed to be here," Nikki asked, placing the tickets into my hands.

"What?" I brought them up to my face for a closer view.

"That means she's been in town for over a week. Why would she tell you differently?"

"I have no idea. When she said I was in danger, I assumed she meant Steve. If he's still in prison, what would she be talking about? Does she know something about his sentencing that we don't?"

"Jim, your attorney, said nothing has changed. He still has seven years left on his sentence," Nikki said.

"This is weird."

"I agree."

"What could she want from me?" I said, rubbing at my eyes. Suddenly, I felt very tired and overwhelmed.

"I don't know. Here's what I do know," Nikki said. "You're sure as hell not going on that riverboat cruise."

"Agreed. I wish she would just leave. How do I move my life forward with her popping up out of nowhere and bringing up the past?"

"Let's put the letter to the side for a bit and go for a run. We'll both feel better."

"Sounds good," I said, sighing. As much as I wanted to go upstairs and crawl back in bed, a nice run would clear my mind. Placing the letter on Nikki's work desk in the kitchen, we headed out the back door.

"Hey, what did you find out about the dog?" I asked.

"I'll show you later today. Funny you should bring that up," Nikki said.

"What do you mean?"

"Give me until our coffee break this morning and then I'll explain everything," she said, and gave me a wink.

On the run, we talked about my date with Jack, the email from my editor, and Nikki's future plans for her employees now that Fran was gone. She was worried about how to replace Fran, yet felt she needed to take someone else on in order to keep things running smoothly at the shop.

"I can help you out while you're looking."

"Don't be silly. You have your book to work on. You finally got the green light from your editor for chapters. I'm hoping for a referral from one of my other employees. It's the best way to bring a new person on."

"Okay, but please don't hesitate to ask if you need extra hands in the kitchen. I owe you."

"I'll keep that in mind. Just remember to thank me in your book when it sells ten million copies," she laughed.

"Yeah, right."

After we returned from the run, I headed upstairs to shower. I passed on blow-drying my hair and wrapped it into a ponytail holder. After I dressed in casual shorts and a tee-shirt, I spent the next two hours editing and revising the first three chapters of my book. I had promised Holly the pages by the end of the week. It was Thursday, so technically, I could wait until tomorrow. It would be great to send them a day early though just to look like I was on top of things.

I was confident with the direction the book was heading. My character, Mary, would be renting a space on Third Street in Geneva to re-open her antique store. The plan was to use the corner Chocolate Love was currently located on and just change it to an antique store in the novel. That way I would be able to apply my experiences with this location in real life to the book.

"Got a second?" Nikki asked, popping her head in. My whole body jumped at the sound of Nikki's voice.

"Sorry, I didn't mean to scare you," Nikki said. "You know, you should keep this door locked. We're not open yet, so it's not a big deal, but just the other day I caught someone up here looking for a bathroom. They said the one downstairs was occupied and they couldn't wait. You never know who's going to show up here."

"You're right, of course. I can't believe I left it open," I said, turning back to the computer to save my work.

Nikki handed me my coffee in a Styrofoam cup.

"Are we going somewhere?" Normally, she handed me one of the ceramic Chocolate Love mugs that said, Love Chocolate? Let it love you back. Give in to the craving. It wasn't often I received my coffee in a Styrofoam cup.

"Yeah, come with me for a minute. I have something to show you."

"How long will we be gone?" I searched for my flip-flops and took a quick gulp of coffee. I was a little fatigued from being out late the night before, but I was still on a high from being with Jack. If it wasn't for the timely deadline of getting these chapters to Holly, I would definitely be very distracted today. The feel of his lips on my forehead and the smell of his cologne still lingered in my mind.

The other thing pressuring me was that I knew Mom was going back to Florida today. With the funeral and Fran Fest over, she needed to get back to Dad. We were having one last lunch together as a family before her flight out at three.

Since Nikki was short on staff, we were bringing lunch into Chocolate Love before I took Mom to the airport. Nikki was understandably not able to leave the shop, and Adelle was conveniently busy, so that left me. I wouldn't dream of sticking Mom in a cab. A very productive morning was needed in order to get my work done and not feel pressed for time.

"Under five minutes," Nikki said. "I just want to introduce you to someone."

This gave me pause.

"What do you mean, introduce me?" I asked hesitantly. "Am I dressed okay?"

"You're fine. Trust me, she's not going to care," Nikki said, before heading out the apartment door.

"She?"

I followed her down the stairs and through the store. She grabbed a small brown bag from the kitchen counter before opening the back door. We followed the little winding sidewalk behind the building to a small knitting shop, The Cozy Corner, located behind Chocolate Love. I wondered if Nikki had scouted out a location for the book. She loved doing that.

"Is this for the book? For Mary's store?" I asked.

"Mary's store? Oh, no. Something else. But I do have an idea for Mary's store location I'll show you later."

Nikki walked up two small steps to the double glass front door. The shop was small, probably close to 400 square feet from what I could see. The glass allowed me to see into the shop. True to its name, it really did look like a cozy corner. Through the doors I saw a few overstuffed burgundy chairs set up near a small fireplace, a counter with an old-fashioned cash register, and shelves and shelves of yarn.

It was June, but inside The Cozy Corner it looked like it was permanently December. It made me want to curl up by the fireplace, knit, and wait for Santa. Right now, it appeared as though no one was in there.

"I think it's closed."

Just as we approached the glass door, a medium-sized, black, Labrador Retriever bolted from a back room. The dog came up to the glass and barked twice at us. The dog's presence made me lean back in fear.

Moments later, an elderly woman with a slight limp came out of the back room and approached the door.

"Sit, Allie," we heard her say in a surprisingly strong command. The dog sat quickly and bowed its ears downward in a submissive gesture. The little old woman was obviously the alpha in this relationship.

She unlocked the door and instead of charging out at us, the dog stayed still as a statue at her side.

"Nikki, good morning. Come on in." She beckoned us inside. "Nice to see. You brought me a treat I see." The word treat made the ears of the dog statue twitch ever so slightly. Nikki passed the brown bag to her.

"Mrs. Parks, I'd like you to meet my sister, Kelly," Nikki said, stepping into the store. I followed behind her and extended my hand to greet the woman.

"It's nice to meet you, Mrs. Parks," I said.

"Please, you girls call me Harriet. This is Allie," she said, smiling down at her dog. "Allie, come. Say hello." The dog came quickly over to us and licked the hand I just used to greet Mrs. Parks.

"Harriet just relocated her store here from Clarendon Hills, so she could be closer to her daughter who lives in town," Nikki said.

That explained why we had not met her before.

"She is normally here by six-thirty most mornings. She brings Allie with her," she continued.

"Okay," is all I said, giving Nikki a look of confused interest.

"I like to come in early most mornings to have my tea and read before the store opens at eight for some private classes I teach. I close by three, but we re-open then on most nights to teach evening classes. I'm so old now though that my daughter comes back with Allie at night to teach them instead of me. It's good to have Allie here with my daughter at night. Gives me peace of mind. Hope Allie isn't bothering you?"

"Not at all, Harriet," Nikki said. "We prefer having a dog close by. It's a comfort for us, especially with the recent break-ins."

"I heard about those. We just opened, but have been here about three months now setting up the store. We made sure to get an alarm system installed. We only worry about the store when we're not here though. Allie does the job the rest of the time. I knew you girls were coming the moment you set foot on my front sidewalk. I was holding Allie's collar in the backroom, so you could have a peaceful approach."

That explained why I didn't hear her when I ran in the morning. The dog had not arrived yet.

Mrs. Parks dipped her nose into the brown bag. Her glasses teetered low on her nose and threatened to fall off. She pushed them back up her nose with her index finger.

"Chocolate chip muffins, my favorite. Would you like to share them with me?"

"We have to head back to work. Kelly has a deadline for her next big seller," Nikki said proudly.

"Nikki told me all about it, dear. Can't wait to read it," Harriet said. "Feel free to stop in anytime."

"What was all that about?" I asked on our walk back to Chocolate Love.

"Don't you think it's a bit odd both times we thought a possible intruder was in early, it occurred just before Allie arrived at The Cozy Corner?" Nikki asked.

"What are you getting at? You still think there was an intruder the morning of Fran's death? Even though the police don't think so? You don't think Steve is connected though?"

"No way. We know it's not Steve. We confirmed where he is. You're letting that block you right now, Kelly. Let that go, and look at what we know for sure.

"It's someone who knew when you left for your run and when the dog arrived. They timed it just perfect, so they would be able to be in and out before you came down the stairs and before the neighborhood patrol dog came. They didn't break in at night because Allie would have been there while Harriet's daughter taught the knitting classes. It's got to be someone who knows the routines of the shop and the neighboring stores. It's someone we know," Nikki said matter-of-factly.

"Do you have someone in mind?"

Instead of answering me, Nikki rubbed her hands on her apron.

"Do you?" I insisted.

"Not yet," Nikki said, pulling the back door open and stepping into Chocolate Love.

Maybe she wasn't absolutely positive, but I had a strange feeling she had someone in mind and was not telling me.

Chapter 22

"Nikki," I said impatiently. "Tell me. Enough of the cloak and dagger. If you know who it is, tell me right now." The kitchen was deserted at the moment, but I spoke very quietly just to be extra careful. I didn't want anyone else overhearing our conversation.

"I don't know who it is," she snapped back. "I'm trying to piece it all together."

"Do you have a guess? One of your employees? Miguel?"

"Of course not. Why would you say that?" Nikki yanked an apron from a hook and quickly tied it on.

"Only because it makes the most sense. He was here when I found Fran, and he has a key to the store. Also, he's probably familiar with my running schedule. Remember, technically, there was never a break-in."

"Miguel is a hard-working, honest man. I don't doubt him for a moment."

"Then where are you going with this?"

"You know what, never mind. Forget I said anything." She turned and put her finger on one of the clipboards hanging on the wall.

"Nikki, what's wrong? Why are you acting like this?" I asked.

"I think what happened in my store was linked to the other burglaries. The police have just pushed Fran's death under the rug. Just because something wasn't taken doesn't mean someone didn't break in. Maybe they just didn't know what to take. Maybe they couldn't find the cash on Wednesday morning and came back on Friday morning to finish the job. Maybe they didn't know the money from my cash drawer goes home with me every night."

"Right there—that tells us it couldn't have been an employee. Your employees would know you take the cash home. It would be pointless to break into the store in the early morning hours."

"Yeah, my employees know," Nikki said, turning back to the clipboard.

We stood in silence for a moment. I watched Nikki closely as she moved her finger over the schedule.

"Okay," she said more to herself than me.

"Have you asked the police what time the other break-ins in the neighborhood occurred?" I asked.

"I have a message into Detective Meyers. In the meantime, can you do me a favor and keep the code to yourself?"

"Of course. Why? Who else knows it right now?" I bit at my lip, anxious to know who was in the circle of trust.

"You, me, Bob, and Miguel. We will be the only ones to open or close the store right now. I want someone I trust."

"Got it." She obviously trusted Miguel. I didn't know she felt that strongly about him. With Fran gone, he was the senior employee at Chocolate Love.

"Sorry for snapping at you," she said. Her hands pulled away from the clipboard and ran up and down her apron. I pulled one of her hands into mine, trying desperately to offer my sister some comfort. Nikki had been so strong over the past couple of days, putting on a big show for Fran Fest. It was easy to forget she lost a beloved employee and a trusted friend. Things were probably very scary for her right now.

"We're going to figure this out," I said simply.

"I know," she said, meeting my eyes. "I just want to feel safe again."

"We will." I knew what she meant. For some reason the phrase "absence of malice" popped into my head. My subconscious was trying to tell me that we both wanted to live in a world again where we didn't fear our surrounding inhabitants. Where we trusted our loved ones, and didn't secretly wonder when our closest friends, employees, or family members would turn against us. An absence of malice. Let this be a stranger, please, I hoped. If there were break-ins and someone was trying to steal from Chocolate Love, it would be so much better if it were a stranger.

At that moment, Miguel came back into the room from the storage basement located off of Nikki's office.

"Hey guys," he said brightly. "Slow morning so I thought I would restock some stuff."

"Thanks, Miguel. Is Yasmine in yet?" Nikki asked, referring to the other employee working the morning shift.

"Not yet. She should be here any minute," he said.

"I'm going to get to work," I said.

"Check in with you later," Nikki said, nodding at me.

"You're okay?" I asked.

"Totally. Go work."

Miguel set down the bag of flour he brought up from the basement and stopped at the corkboard in the kitchen. He reached into his back pocket and pulled a picture from it.

"Got an updated one from my wife today."

Nikki had set up this board so that everyone could see the faces of their kids or spouses while they worked. It was loaded with family photos.

"This is Lupita," he said proudly. "She turns five next Tuesday. We're throwing a big party this weekend."

"She's beautiful," Nikki said. "I haven't seen her since the Christmas party."

"These kids are growing up so fast," he said, smiling. "Maria is talking about adding another one. Yikes!" he laughed.

I felt so bad for doubting Miguel. Watching him pin his pictures up, it was hard to think of him with any kind of sinister side. After all of the years he had worked here, Nikki probably had a good read on him by now.

"I'm going to head back upstairs until lunch. Do you need any help preparing for it?" I asked Nikki.

"No, I'm ordering from Donatello's down the block," Nikki said, referring to our favorite sandwich place. "Don said he will deliver our order himself. Mom and I called ahead last night. We got you spicy Cajun turkey on pumpernickel. Is that right?" Nikki asked.

"That's the one." Nikki and I frequented Donatello's when we wanted to get out for lunch. "What time should I come down? Do you need me to pick Mom up?"

"Noon. Mom wants to walk over here, get some exercise before the plane ride home. She said she will have her bags already packed. When we finish up lunch, can you swing back to my house and pick up her bags before you head to the airport?"

"Of course. Who else will be joining us for lunch?"

"I think it's just the three of us. Bob and Mike have to work, and Adelle had to take the kids to their classes."

"Okay, see you at noon." I rushed up the stairs, anxious to get back to my pages. It would be great to send Holly the three chapters before lunch. That way, I would not have to stress about rushing back from the airport. Mom and I could have a cup of coffee at the airport before she went through security.

Even though she had been here for almost a week, we hadn't gotten a lot of time to talk one-on-one, and I was looking forward to spending time with her.

I sat down at my desk, crossed my legs up onto the chair and did a neck stretch. It was time to get back to work. But first, a check on email. I was pleasantly surprised to see one from Jack. It read:

Dear Kelly-

I had a great time last night. Is it too forward to say I have not stopped thinking about you since I left your doorstep? If it is too forward, delete this email immediately and pretend you never saw it. Ha!

Would you like to go out for ice cream after yoga? I know it's kind of counter-productive, but let's be reckless. We'll deserve a reward for our workout.

In case you were wondering, I got your email address from Mari. Hope that's okay. She lectured me about client/yoga instructor privacy laws but was more than happy to hand it over.

-Jack

It was nice to see Jack be so open with me. He didn't appear jaded or as guarded as I expected him to be. Even though I had hurt Jack in the past, he seemed to be able to put it behind him and approach this opportunity to be together with a pureness of spirit. I expected though, at some time, we would talk about our past. We needed to.

I wrote back immediately. There was no reason to play games with Jack.

Dear Jack-

I also had a wonderful time last night. And, no, you're not too forward. It's nice to have someone to talk to.

Thanks for sharing your stories. I had no idea you were in such a bad situation. Can't get over how much we have in common.

I would love to go out for ice cream with you. Let's be reckless! ☺

Love, Kelly

I wanted to put in something along the lines of "I'm so happy to have you back in my life" but was not able to figure out a way to do it without coming right out and saying it. Now that would be too forward.

I settled with what I had written and hit send. Enough was enough. There was work to do.

The rest of the morning was spent channeling the frantic, nervous energy I had from writing Jack's email into getting my first three chapters cleaned up. Finally, at three minutes after twelve, the chapters were ready. After sending them to Holly, I checked my email one last time. No response from Jack yet. I logged off and closed my laptop.

Downstairs, I found Nikki in the kitchen with Don sorting out the sandwiches.

"You're not sure of the time?" I heard Nikki ask.

"All I know is my cash was stolen. I told Debbie not to leave anything in the store, but she forgot," Don said in his deep Italian accent. He wore his signature uniform black pants, a white tee-shirt, and a Donatello's apron.

"Hi, Don. What are you guys talking about?" I asked. The closer I got to the table where the sandwiches were laid out, the stronger the smell of my spicy Cajun turkey sandwich. It made my stomach growl.

"I was just telling your sister we were robbed last night," Don said, throwing his arms up in the air. "Can you believe that?"

"What?"

Chapter 23

Nikki's eyes met mine over Don's shoulder. She tucked her hair behind her ear and returned her gaze to Don.

"Yeah, they broke the lock and everything," Don said. "We should have gotten a better system with locking up at night. You happy with the alarm system you set up, Nikki?"

"I am," Nikki said. "What did the police say?"

"They told me whoever did it didn't leave any prints, or any evidence of who they were. Did they tell you the same thing?"

"Actually, they never investigated mine as a robbery because there was no break-in and nothing was taken."

"You leave your cash here?" Don asked.

"I used to have a safe here, but not anymore. Bob and I take the cash with us when we leave every night. Since the break-ins, we've started doing nightly deposits. I don't even trust it in my own house anymore."

"That's a good idea. I usually just take the cash home at night with me and make deposits at the end of the week. I should start nightly deposits. With this economy, people are pretty desperate out there. You just don't know what they are capable of, you know?"

"I know," Nikki said.

"Did they take anything else?" I asked quietly.

"Nah, just the cash. They were real sloppy about it. Left a couple of drawers open and spilled some napkins on the floor. Like they were in a big rush or something. You know this all comes down to budget cuts. Geneva cut the number of patrol officers because of the town's budget. If they had more patrol cars, I'm sure they could catch this guy. That makes, what, four or five of us in this area now? This has to stop. We can't afford to lose cash like this. We're struggling to get by just as much as the next guy. Like I said, they just happen to hit me on the right night when I forgot to take the cash out. Thank God they only got me for one day's work. I don't know what I would do if they cleared me for more," he said.

"I hear you, Don," Nikki said, nodding her head.

"Hello?" Mom said in a singsong voice as she entered the room.

"Well, Mrs. Barbara Clark, so nice to see you," Don said, opening his arms in way of greeting Mom.

"Don, it's been a long time," she said, walking into Don's embrace. He gave her cheek a quick kiss.

"Look at ya', will ya'? Florida is doing you some good. How is the hubby?" he asked. "Why isn't he here? Too good for us Genevans now?" he joked.

"He's home with the dogs. He wanted to be here for Fran's funeral, but we couldn't find a dog sitter.

"The poor thing. My wife and I were out of town, or we would have been here for the wake and funeral. Don Jr. told me you guys did a wonderful job honoring her memory. She'll be missed, that's for sure. She was like clockwork, tuna on rye every Tuesday and Thursday afternoon. God bless her," he said. He made the sign of the cross with his right hand and then kissed his fingers before opening them and floating them up into the air.

"We're just heartbroken. My girls will be all right though. They're fighters. And they have each other," Mom said proudly.

"Yes, indeedy, I wouldn't mess with these girls," he said, and winked at me. "You should be very proud."

I lowered my eyes.

"That's why I was surprised someone tried to break in here," he said.

"I thought the police determined it *wasn't* a break-in?" Mom said. Her eyes jumped to Nikki for confirmation.

"Well, with them robbing my shop last night, isn't that a little suspicious? Maybe they'll look again at your place as a target," Don said, turning to Nikki. "I'm going to head back now. Got a lot of orders to fill, and poor Don Jr. looked a little overwhelmed when I left. I just wanted to personally come by and see you girls to tell you I'm sorry for your loss. Call me if you need anything, Nikki. I'll keep you posted if I hear more from the police.

"I will, Don. Thanks for dropping off lunch," Nikki said.

Don nodded. "Take care, Barbara. When are you heading back?" he asked.

"I was going to fly back today, but now I'm not so sure. There's too much going on here. I can't leave my girls alone with all of this happening on Third Street. What if something else happens?" She looked straight at Nikki.

"I'll just see myself out," Don said. "Enjoy the sandwiches, ladies."

"Thanks, Don. I'll call you later," Nikki said, waving goodbye.

He seemed embarrassed to be here during what was obviously going to become a heated family discussion. My mom's question of should I stay or should I go had been a long standing debate in our family. Of course, we wanted her here.

A lot of things would work better if Mom and Dad still lived here—their children and grandchildren were here, a lot of their friends were here, and they loved Geneva. But the winters and the inability to get away from all of our problems could drag them down.

"I'm worried about your safety, Kelly," Mom said. "First this thing with Gina and now more questions about the morning Fran passed. There's no question about it. Chocolate Love must have somehow been broken into on the morning of Fran's death. This is just too much of a coincidence with all of these other break-ins." Her voice rose in pitch as she spoke, and she visibly shook with worry.

"Mom, I will be okay. The alarm system Nikki set up is state of the art. No one is going to try anything here again. Especially with what happened to Fran. That would be stupid."

"What's stupid?" Adelle asked, as she walked into the room with Cindy and Craig in tow. Her arms were filled with more shopping bags. She set them down on the floor and put her hands on her hips, waiting for one of us to fill her in on what was going on.

"I thought you said you weren't able to make it for lunch today?" Nikki asked. She opened her arms out to the kids. Both ran into them to greet her. As usual, Cindy's eyes darted around the room, while she hugged Aunt Nikki.

"Hi, guys," I said. They came over to me next, so I could squeeze them hello.

"Turns out ballet is cancelled, so we're here," Adelle said.

"I hope you have food in those shopping bags because we didn't order enough. I didn't expect you to be here," Nikki said.

"Should we call over to Don and see if he can send over a couple more?" Mom asked.

"Don't be silly. Don's sandwiches are big enough to split," Adelle said.

I was hungry enough to eat an entire one by myself. There went Adelle messing things up again.

"Let's just unwrap and see what we have. We'll make it work," Mom said.

"I want some of yours, Aunt Kelly," Cindy said, reaching up to help me unwrap my sandwich.

"I heard you had a date last night," Adelle said.

"What do you mean *a date*?" Cindy asked. "My mom and dad go on dates. I thought your husband was dead, Aunt Kelly?"

"Um," I said, trying to stall for an explanation.

"Is that what you told her?" Nikki asked, abruptly stopping from biting down into her ham and Swiss.

"No, remember we said Uncle Steve went away and is never coming back," Adelle whispered soothingly into Cindy's ear. Cindy looked like she might burst into tears.

"I thought that meant he was dead," Cindy said, her voice trembling.

"Young, beautiful ladies, such as myself, don't have to be married to go on dates." I made my voice sound funny to alleviate the tense vibe of the room. "You should have seen me, Cindy. Grandma took me to get my hair done and bought me a new dress."

"I bet you were beautiful, Aunt Kelly. Like a princess," Cindy said, pushing her glasses up high on her nose. "Can I see the dress?"

"Of course. And yes, Grandma bought me a princess dress. If you don't have to leave right away, you're welcome to come up to my apartment after lunch and take a peek at it."

Cindy's eyes lit up. She loved being in my apartment.

"I have to take Grandma to the airport, so we can't spend a lot time up there. We'll just take a quick look."

"The airport! Can I go to the airport, too?" Cindy asked. She whipped her head back to her mother.

"Not today, Cindy," Adelle said.

"Why not?" she whined.

"Because we are busy for the rest of the day," Adelle said matter-of-factly.

"I thought you said we had nothing else to do today," Cindy pressed.

When Mom asked Adelle to take her to the airport because Nikki and I would be working, Adelle told her she had things going on all day with the kids. Cindy didn't know she'd just revealed her mother to be a liar.

"That's not true, we have a play date with Molly," she said calmly to Cindy.

"We do?" asked Cindy, delighted by this news.

"Yes," Adelle said. "She's coming over in an hour."

"Oh my gosh," Cindy said, clapping her hands together.

I knew exactly what Adelle was planning. When they got home, she would tell Cindy that Molly was not able to come after all. It would break Cindy's heart.

"I can take her with me?" I offered.

Cindy looked totally confused now. Nikki gave a little snicker under her breath. Adelle shifted her head in Nikki's direction and shot her a look. Nikki coughed to try and cover up her laugh.

"Can I go, Mommy? Please? Please? Can I go with Auntie Kelly to the airport?"

"Only if you don't mind missing a play date with Molly?" Adelle countered smoothly.

Cindy hesitated for a second to contemplate her decision. I wanted to reach over the table and slap Adelle across the face. It was such a cruel thing to play games with her kids. We all knew there was no play date with Molly planned. The only one who was fooled was Cindy. From the look on little Craig's face, sitting on my mom's lap, I swore he even knew it was all a bunch of baloney.

"Can you call Molly and tell her we can do it later?" she begged Adelle.

"I guess," Adelle said.

"Thank you so much, Mommy!" Cindy's arms reached up to hug her mom. Adelle's eyes met mine for a second, completely void of guilt. She could be such a pain.

"Okay, let's see the dress," Cindy said, turning back to me with a huge smile.

Mom, Cindy, and I made it to the airport in record time. The highway traffic was still light at this time of the day.

We stopped for a quick coffee and an ice cream swirl for Cindy at the airport before Mom's flight departed. While we sat and chatted, Mom made me promise to check in with her on a daily basis until everything settled down. I also promised to call the police if Gina contacted me again. The only way we were able to convince her to head back to Florida was because she planned to be back soon with Dad.

I tried my best to tell her we would be fine and that she should focus on getting settled back at home with Dad.

Cindy and I hugged her good-bye one last time before she walked through to airport security, promising to call us when she landed.

I would miss Mom. It was nice to have her here.

Although Cindy no longer took naps, it had been a long day for her, and she fell asleep in her car seat on the ride home. Her rosy, red lips hung open as she snored. I couldn't stop myself from peeking up in the rearview mirror every couple of seconds to observe her in her slumber. She looked like a little angel asleep in my backseat. All of the excitement of getting to the airport was a bit much for her.

I was anxious to get home and back to my work but wouldn't mind extending our ride just to have more of this precious time with her. There really was something special about a sleeping child.

My cell phone rang, disrupting my quiet thoughts.

"Hello?"

I heard only shallow breathing.

"Hello?" I repeated.

"Why aren't you here?" a voice on the other end asked. Her voice was broken and anxious, but there was no mistaking who it was.

My eyes darted down to the digital clock on my dashboard. It was twenty to four.

"I..." Her voice was so disturbing; I wasn't sure what to say.

"I'm not coming, Gina. How did you get my cell number?"

"You're not coming? Are you kidding me?" Gina shot back. "You need to be here, Kelly. Your life depends on it."

I felt it now.

Fear.

Chapter 24

S ilence.

A few seconds passed. My instinct told me to hang up the phone, but for some reason, I found myself unable to. My eyes darted up again to the rearview mirror to check on Cindy in the back seat. She was at least twenty miles west of us now, but her harsh tone made it feel like Gina was sitting next to me in the passenger seat.

"Did you hear me, Kelly? Hello?" she said.

She was acting like I was late to a mutually agreed upon appointment. There was never any intention on my part to meet her. Did she really think I would show up after what she had done to me?

"Gina, I don't know who the hell you think you are. Do not talk to me that way. Stop calling me, and stop trying to meet up with me. I'm not interested in what you have to say. Do you understand that?" I tried to speak as quietly as possible so as not to wake and frighten Cindy.

At first, Gina didn't respond. For a second, I thought she hung up.

"You just don't get it, do you?" Gina said slowly.

"No, you don't get it. I'm going to call the police if you don't leave me alone!"

"I'm only trying to help you," Gina said again with that clear, slow, spooky voice. "You have no idea the danger you are in. He's not who you think he is."

When she said the word *he* it felt like two strong ice-cold hands gripped around my heart, making it stop for a split second. What the hell was she talking about?

"What?"

"Listening now?" Gina asked, sounding self-satisfied.

I hung up and tossed the phone on the passenger seat in disgust. Something must have stopped her from calling me back because the phone didn't ring again. Maybe Mom was right about looking into that restraining order.

I spent the next thirty minutes making my way back to Geneva. Part of me did not want to go back, because it would bring me closer to Gina. What if she was waiting for me at Chocolate Love? It was clear she wasn't going to give up on trying to contact me. Why did she care? Why was it so important to her? Knowing Gina, she wouldn't give up until she got what she wanted.

When we had been friends, it was a quality I admired in her. I had met her at one of my husband's Christmas parties where she also worked as a pharmaceutical sales representative. We became instant friends, bonding over our love of books and reading. She had left the company a couple of months afterward to start her own marketing and sales company. That's when she got her star tattoo as a way to mark her new venture, as she had told me.

She had been driven and hard-working, so things started off well. Even though she was busy with work, she had always made time for us to hang out. She had loved hearing about my books and even enjoyed brainstorming with me about my plots and ideas for my characters. She had a very active imagination and was never scared to reveal some of the crazy ideas she came up with for my books.

She had been very giving of her time and patient when it came to my career and helping me along.

That was why it had hurt so badly when she betrayed me. When I lost Steve, I had lost her, too. A double whammy for me. The love of my life and best friend gone at the same time.

Just as I was getting off the highway, I quickly leaned over to my passenger seat to grab my phone. I needed to wake Cindy up soon, so she wouldn't feel like she missed the whole adventure.

"Hello?" Adelle answered.

"Hi."

"What's wrong? Your voice sounds funny. Is Cindy okay?" Adelle asked.

"Everything is fine. We're just getting off of the expressway now. I just got a weird phone call from an old friend." I looked up in the rear view mirror and noticed Cindy was awake. She stared out the window with a glazed over look on her face.

"Do you want to talk about it?" Adelle asked.

Surprisingly, I did want to talk about it with her. When she wanted to be, she could be a great sounding board. She had been the one that pushed me to follow my dreams when I first got into writing my books. But at some point, she had just shut down.

Sometimes, I blamed it on the responsibility of the three kids, but this behavior was there before there were children in her life. She was like a radio that just tuned out sometimes. I would love her ear right now but held back because it would not be appropriate for Cindy to hear the whole story.

"Not right now. Maybe later."

Maybe this was what Adelle went through in her daily life. If you had three kids constantly present, and you were a full-time mom like Adelle was, maybe your radio couldn't tune in to other people. Your children took priority.

"I'm here to talk if you want," Adelle said.

"Thank you."

"Why don't I meet you at Chocolate in ten minutes? I left some of my shopping bags with Nikki. I'll just pick-up Cindy there," she said.

"Sure. Sounds good."

After we hung up, I turned to give Cindy a quick smile. Her glasses sat crooked on her face, and her pig tails had fallen out. She looked rested but slightly disturbed.

"Are you okay, sweetie?"

"Sometimes my mom and dad fight." I couldn't tell if she was referring to a dream she just had, or if she was talking to me about something bothering her in real life. Either way, I scrambled to try and think of a way to comfort her because I felt she was waiting for words of wisdom from Aunt Kelly.

"That's normal, Cindy. Moms and dads have a lot of responsibility in their lives, and it can be very stressful on them."

I paused for a minute to see where she was going to go next. If she was having the nightmares like me, it would take time for her to process my words.

"Am I an irresponsibility?" Cindy asked.

"You are a blessing." I said, sounding almost too much like my mother.

"But do they fight because of me?"

These questions did not stem from a nightmare. She was not spacey or frightened the way I was after a nightmare. This was a little girl confused with what was going on in her home and trying to get some help.

"Of course not, Cindy. You make their life wonderful." I didn't want to pry but wished she would give me more information about the specifics of her parent's arguments. How could I help unless I knew more?

"Aunt Kelly, what's the konomy?"

"The economy?"

"Yes."

Yikes. I wasn't prepared for this.

"It's about the money and the businesses that keep the world going." Hopefully, my answer sounded intelligent, yet easy enough for a five-year-old to understand. What the heck did I know about the economy? Obviously nothing. I was flat broke and living under my sister's roof because I couldn't afford to pay rent.

"Why has it been so bad? Does it have to go for a time out? There's Mommy!"

The excitement in her voice upon seeing her mom outside of Chocolate Love made me smile. Adelle was doing something right. These kids adored her.

Traffic on Third Street was busy, but I was able to slide into a parking spot right in front of the store.

"How about we continue our economics talk another time," I suggested. How nice to be five and so distractible.

I helped Cindy out of the car and locked it. Maybe Adelle and Mike really were having financial problems. It would make sense with Mike owning a construction company. Who was building new homes or businesses these

122

days anyway? I had no idea how the rental side of the business was holding up.

They must have been arguing about money in front of the kids. How else would Cindy have known the word economy? I would never know though from the amount of shopping bags Adelle walked around with. It was best just to stay out of it. I had no interest in getting knowledgeable about their personal finances, seeing as I had enough problems of my own.

Cindy ran up to Adelle, who bent down to pick her up into her arms.

"I missed you, my sweet girl," she said. Craig stood next to Adelle and pulled at her pant leg in protest, showing his distaste for all of the attention on his sister. "Let's go in and get Mommy's stuff, so we can get home and make dinner. How was the drop off?" she asked, turning her attention to me.

"Great," I said.

Once we got inside Chocolate Love, we ran into Nikki in the hallway speaking to Sharon Winters. The store was crowded with customers. It was the pre-dinner rush, when the store filled up with people picking up desserts and treats for the evening.

"Hi, guys," Nikki said. "Do you remember Sharon Winters?"

"Of course," I said. Standing next to Nikki, who was also petite, put Sharon's height in perspective. She was so tiny, she reminded me of Tinker Bell.

"It's nice to see you again, Kelly," she said.

"Yes, you, too." I never did ask Nikki if Sharon contacted her after getting her phone number from me the other night. I assumed they were able to hook up since she was here today.

"This is my other sister, Adelle, and her children Cindy and Craig," Nikki said.

Adelle reached out to shake her hand.

"It's nice to see you all," Sharon said.

"Nikki has allowed me to hang up some of my signs for the race next weekend. There's going to be a pre-race dinner at the Lutheran Church right across the street on Friday night. Hope you all can come," she said, flashing her white teeth at us.

"We'd love to come," Nikki said, sneaking a peek at me to make sure that was okay.

"Are you running as well, Adelle?" Sharon asked.

"Probably not. It's just too hard with the kids," she said.

"Of course," Sharon said. "I'll go ahead and post the signs. I was thinking of putting one on the cork board in the hallway and then one on the door, if that's okay?"

"Sounds good," Nikki said.

"Can we talk for a second?" I asked Nikki, pulling her to the side and widening my eyes.

"Sure. Let's go back to the office," she said, tilting her head toward the kitchen.

Chapter 25

Nikki and I excused ourselves from Sharon, Adelle, and the kids to go talk in the kitchen.

"What is going on?" Nikki asked once we were in her office.

"I don't know what to do, Nikki. Gina called me on the way home from the airport. She was upset because I didn't show up. She sounded crazy. She told me I don't know everything about *him,* whoever *he* is. I'm scared, Nikki. Maybe we should talk to the police. I told her I was going to get a restraining order against her," I said, trying to keep my voice down. This did not need to get around the shop.

Nikki swiveled her head around to the work table. There were three other employees putting together some type of dessert platter.

"Are you guys okay for a second?" Nikki called out to them.

"We're fine. We're ahead of schedule with this, and the front of the store is covered," Miguel said.

"Let's go upstairs and call Detective Meyers from your apartment. Maybe he can help us," she said.

Back in the foyer, we bumped into Adelle holding the shopping bags she left at Chocolate Love earlier.

"Can you watch the kids for one second? I have a PTA meeting I have to attend tonight. I just want to pick up some chocolates for it. It will take me two minutes," she said.

"No problem. Make sure they give you the family discount," Nikki said, scooping Craig into her arms. Cindy reached out and tucked her hand in mine. We sat down on the bench with the kids in the foyer near the small public bathroom.

"Thank you." She rushed off to put in her order at the counter.

"Hey, just to let you know, I switched the code on the alarm. What we had was too common. It's now 2253. Or just remember the word *cake*."

"Cake," Cindy said.

"What do you think?" Nikki asked.

"Sounds good to me," I said, bouncing Cindy up and down.

"Cake, cake, cake," she laughed.

A clanging sound in the bathroom startled both of us. The door was slightly ajar, so I had assumed it was empty. We heard someone mumble a muted swear word. A couple of seconds later, Sharon stepped out of the bathroom and into the foyer.

"Oh, hi. Dropped my pushpin and then I knocked over your paper towel stand. I think I got it fixed. Hope you don't mind. I hung one of my posters in your bathroom," Sharon said, smiling at us.

I found it comical to know she was the one swearing in the bathroom. It was hard to believe this woman ever got frustrated at anything. She always seemed so darn polished.

"That's no problem, Sharon," Nikki said.

"Good. I don't like to take advantage of anyone's support for my charity. I just figured since there was so much hanging in there already, you wouldn't have a problem with it," Sharon said. "See you both tonight, right?"

"Tonight?" we asked in unison.

"Yoga!" she laughed. "I'm addicted now. Mari is such a fabulous teacher. Got to do something to keep me in check. Especially if I keep coming to Chocolate Love for Walnut Turtle Yummies," she said, holding up a bag with the Chocolate Love emblem on it.

"Of course," Nikki said. "We'll be there."

"See you both later," Sharon said as she walked out of the shop.

"Do you think she heard the password?" I asked.

"No way, you wouldn't be able to hear us from in there. Hold on," she said. She set Craig down on the bench and stepped into the bathroom.

"Ouch," she said when she came out.

"What?"

"She put her poster right over the Fran Fest announcement I had up. I wasn't ready to take it down yet. Here comes Adelle."

"Thank you," Adelle said, scooping up Craig from Nikki's arms. She held a large white box sealed with an elaborate pink bow.

"Let me get someone to help you out to the car," Nikki said.

"That's okay, Nikki. I'll help her," I offered, carrying Cindy in my arms.

"No, no, that's okay," Adelle said. "Cindy can walk and carry the box."

"Are you sure?" Nikki asked.

"Yes, of course. Thank you, though. You both have your hands full."

I was anxious to get upstairs and see what we could do to get the police involved with Gina's episodes.

We started to head upstairs but stopped when we heard Adelle at the foot of the stairs calling out Nikki's name.

"Just one last thing. I have these keys in case of an emergency still for Chocolate Love, but what about the security system? Do I need some kind of code if I need to get in here?" Adelle asked.

I was standing right behind Nikki. From the way Nikki's shoulders tensed up, it appeared Adelle's question made her uncomfortable. She pulled her right hand up to push her hair back behind her ear, one of Nikki's tell-tale signs of nervousness.

"We're still working on the alarm system," Nikki said.

"Oh, I thought it was all set up," Adelle said.

"We did have it installed, but there have been problems with it. I'll let you know when we have it figured out," Nikki said.

"Okay, talk to you both later. Thanks again." Adelle turned and directed the kids out of the store.

"What was that about? You're not even going to give Adelle the code?" Nikki turned her dark eyes on me before she bolted past me on the stairs.

"I will," she stumbled. "Just not yet."

"You don't think...."

"I don't want to talk about it right now," Nikki said, making her way up to the top of the stairs.

"Uh, sure," I said.

* * * * *

"There's not enough at this time to be able to justify a restraining order. If there is no direct threat made to your life, there's really nothing we can do, Ms. Clark. And history shows that when you file a restraining order, it can elevate the situation."

"Are you kidding me?" Nikki barked. We had been on the phone with Detective Meyers for about ten minutes now, and Nikki was starting to sweat. I couldn't help but think she was harboring some ill will from the way he handled Fran's death.

"I'm sorry, ladies. We're here to help you, but this situation does not call for our involvement."

"Yet," Nikki snapped. "What has to happen? She needs come at her with a gun?"

I ran my index finger slowly across my neck to give Nikki the universal signal to stop. She needed to chill out.

"Why don't you give me a physical description of the woman so we have it," Detective Meyers requested calmly.

"Fine, then be on the lookout for a five-foot, five-inch crazy woman with long, brown hair, weighing approximately one-hundred-sixty pounds, Detective."

"Maybe a little bit more," I added as I made an upward motion with my thumb to indicate to Nikki her weight approximation was off. "And she has a small black tattoo of a star behind her right ear," I said.

"Here's another distinguishing feature. You'll know her because she'll be the one with a manic look in her eye. She's trouble, we're sure of it," Nikki said before disconnecting. I felt bad we were rude, but also frustrated.

Nikki left my apartment in a huff to go have dinner with Bob before she had to pick me up for yoga. Poor Bob. He had no idea what he was about to walk into when he got home tonight. Hopefully, she would calm down so they could enjoy their time together.

I went into the kitchen to make myself dinner and to check to see if I had a reply from Holly.

* * * * *

By the time Nikki was back to pick me up, she was a totally different person. Bob had calmed her down or cheered her up somehow.

"Feel better?" I asked when I sat down in the passenger seat.

"I do," Nikki said. "I spoke with Bob. He gave me some ideas on how we could document the things Gina is doing, so we can eventually get the restraining order we want. You saved the letter about the riverboat cruise, right?"

"Yes."

"Are you saving the emails?"

"Yep. Now, I'll definitely keep them in my inbox."

"Just save everything you can. We're going to nail this witch," she said, a new level of determination filling her voice. In a way, Nikki was a lot like Gina. Determined, independent. A woman that got what she wanted. Only Nikki wasn't crazy.

Yoga class passed quickly. It was exciting to have Jack next to me in class, especially knowing we had a date afterward. I had styled my hair and put on a little extra make-up before class. I looked a little overdone compared to some of the other participants, but Jack seemed to appreciate my efforts.

Sharon Winters spent a few minutes after class promoting her race for next Saturday morning and pre-race pasta party.

"You can pay for your registration to the 5K race by check up until Thursday. On Friday night at the pasta party, it will be cash only," she said. The mention of the word pasta made my stomach growl slightly. I snuck a peak in Jack's direction to see if he noticed, but his attention was on Sharon's talk.

I no longer worried about Sharon's interest in Jack. Even if there was something there on her end, I was pretty confident Jack's interest was with me.

"I want to talk to her about the dessert I am donating for the pre-race party in honor of Fran," Nikki said when Sharon had concluded her talk. "You're heading out with Jack, right?" Nikki's eyebrows bounced up and down.

"Yes," I said, breaking into a huge smile, unable to stop myself.

"See you tomorrow," she said. "If you go home, don't forget to set the alarm tonight."

"What do you mean 'if I go home'?" Of course I was going home after ice cream. I was not ready for Jack and I to be more intimate yet. Well, truthfully, my body was ready, but my heart and brain were not.

"Are you being assigned a curfew?" Jack asked from behind me. I didn't have to look at him to know he was smiling. I could hear it in his voice.

"Just the opposite," Nikki laughed. "You guys have fun. See you

127

tomorrow." Nikki left to go talk to Sharon.

"Are you ready for some sugar?" he asked. He put his hand on the small of my back to lead me out the door. "Sorry, that came out kind of lame."

I laughed and allowed him to steer me toward the exit. We walked through Shannon Hall and waved goodbye to Mari, Nikki, and Sharon, who all watched us intently.

When we got out to the parking lot, Jack opened the car door for me. Two new water bottles had been placed in the cup holders.

"For me?"

"I thought you might need it after class." He closed the door and walked around to the driver's side.

When we pulled out of the parking lot, my eye caught a woman walking out of Shannon Hall I hadn't seen before. It struck me as odd that she wasn't dressed in work-out clothes. Her jeans and long-sleeved tee shirt were totally inappropriate for the warm weather. My heart picked up a beat when I realized she was staring at Jack's car.

It was Gina.

Gina's furious eyes met mine. She was probably in there the whole time, watching me during class.

Was there anywhere I could go without her following me?

Chapter 26

I contemplated telling Jack about Gina. But something kept me from opening up to him. He was smiling and playing with the radio in search of something. I really didn't want to spoil the mood. There was also a part of me that didn't like revealing that the problems I had in California may have followed me here. Jack knew what it was like to be stalked and harassed. He was able to escape it, but it had obviously done some damage. I didn't know how he would react if he knew Gina was doing the same thing to me. It could bring up a lot of bad memories for him. He may not want to continue our relationship if it meant having to relive his nightmare with Callie. Instead, I held everything I was feeling inside.

"What's wrong," he asked, turning toward me. We had circled around Shannon Hall and were about to head west toward downtown Batavia.

"What do you mean?"

"You're quiet and pulling at your lip," he said, reaching out and gently taking my left hand down from my bottom lip.

"You used to do that when you were worried about something," he said. He placed my hand onto my lap and rested his hand for a second on top of mine before returning it back to the steering wheel.

"Nothing is wrong."

"Is it about us?" he asked, glancing my way briefly.

"Oh, no. I was thinking about something completely different."

"About Steve?" he asked.

"No." In a way it was about Steve. The only reason Gina was in town had to be related to Steve. It was the only thing we had in common anymore. "He's not who you think he is" was what she had said on the phone on the way home from the airport. I didn't want to hear what she had to say. What was the point? I didn't trust her anyway.

"I can understand if that's what it is. You can tell me, you know. I remember how hard it was to start dating again after Callie. You compare everyone you're dating to your ex."

"Jack…."

"You can tell me, Kelly. If this is too much for you, too fast, we don't have to do this. We can wait, take our time. Whatever is going to make you feel more comfortable." He turned the car north on Island Avenue and then right into the parking lot of Batavia Creamery.

It was situated just west of the Fox River with a small outdoor seating area, allowing customers a nice view of the main business district.

"No, I am not doing any kind of comparisons, trust me. Just trying to bury some skeletons in the closet."

"I get that." The corner of his mouth pulled up into a smile. He pulled the car in front of the shop, put it in park, and turned his body in my direction. A moment passed where we looked at each other, waiting for the other person to speak. There was so much to say, yet where did we begin? We had not changed after the class, so the smell of Jack's perspiration lingered a bit in the car. Mixed with the smell of his aftershave, it was a nice, familiar scent. The fact that we were still dressed in our work out clothes gave this date a very casual feel, which was just what I wanted. He squinted his green eyes, studying me, and put his left arm up on the steering wheel.

He seemed to make a decision and reached for the keys to turn off the car.

"Okay, so, the reason I brought you here is because they have an excellent mint chocolate chip ice cream. Probably not as good as Chocolate Love's, but if I remember correctly, mint chocolate chip is your favorite. It might be a good way to see how your competition is doing."

"How did you remember that?"

"I remember a lot about you, Kelly Clark," he said, pulling the keys out and shooting a hesitant glance my way.

"Kelly Clark remembers a lot about you, too, Jack O'Malley," I said boldly.

Jack's eyes widened, and he gave me a big smile.

"Really? Well, why don't we grab some ice cream and go for a walk along the river. You can fill me in on some of those memories."

I laughed and stepped out of the car.

After purchasing a scoop of mint chocolate chip and a strawberry shake for Jack, we walked west until we ended up on the Batavia Riverwalk. We passed the sand park located near the Peg Bond Center, the central activity hall for Batavia, located right where the Fox River flowed into a little pond called the Depot Pond.

"Do you know why this is called the Depot Pond?" I asked, trying to read a plaque.

"It's because of the Batavia Depot Museum up there," Jack said, pointing to the small museum on the west side of the pond. That museum used to be a train station until the line was moved. That's how those running paths along the river were formed. They're all from the old train line. In fact, I believe the paths will be where Sharon's race takes place on Saturday."

"Let's go check out the museum," I said.

"It's probably closed now, but why not."

The museum was painted a bold red and looked like a new roof had been recently added. It was closed but a nice explanation of the museum was framed in a display case outside of the building.

"According to this, it says the top floor of the museum holds all of the information on the history of the train, as well as a section dedicated to Mary Todd Lincoln. She was held in Batavia in the Bellevue Place, a private, upscale sanitarium, ten years after her husband, Abraham Lincoln, was assassinated. This museum has the bed and dresser she used during her stay at Bellevue. Want to come back here when this is open to come see it?" Jack asked.

"I would love to. What else does it say?" I asked. All of this information was making my head churn with ideas for my book. This would be great material for The Antique Murder Mystery #3.

"The bottom floor of the museum contains all of the history of the early settlers of Batavia, including the Early Woodlands Indian tribe."

"Isn't it funny that we lived here for so long and never appreciated the history of the area?" I said.

"I guess we were busy being kids."

We walked back toward the Peg Bond Center, on a newly installed brick sidewalk circling the pond. Nearly every brick was dedicated to a sponsor or community member.

Our conversation had been light since leaving Batavia Creamery. We continued our walk, ate our ice cream, and ended up near the Batavia Dam on the east side of the river.

With the rain being light this year, the river was low, but still moved rather quickly around the dam area. We sat down on a small bench and took in the beautiful scenery.

"The water flows fast right here," I said, speaking the obvious and referring to the cycling motion of the dam.

"It's a dangerous river. Seems like every summer, there are multiple drownings," Jack said.

"I just remember Mom drilling it into our heads that we should never try to swim in it. I also seem to remember the fire department talking to us at school about the dangers of the Fox."

"Remember this— 'A civilian never saves a civilian'?" he asked.

"No."

"They told us most drownings occur because someone falls in and whoever they are with tries to jump in and save them. But unless you've had some professional training, the first victim ends up fighting the second victim because they struggle too much, causing them both to drown.

"That has stuck with me since the Geneva Fire Department came to speak to our fifth grade class. I remember thinking it must feel so wrong to watch your friend or loved one drown. How do you not jump in and at least try? That's why the drownings keep happening. It's irresistible. Any normal person would dive in," he said.

"I can't imagine. It must be awful to watch."

Jack's hand reached out and took mine onto his leg. With the index finger of his other hand, he traced the lines on the inside of my hand.

"I would try and save you." He gazed out onto the water, his smile telling me he was trying to lighten the mood.

"Jack, do you want to talk about us?"

His green eyes met mine.

"What do you mean exactly?" he said. His finger lay still over my hand.

"I mean our past. We should talk about it. We have to before we can move forward, don't you think so?"

"Kelly, we're together now. It's not quite the past, but it's like the past in a way. I haven't felt this young and hopeful in a long time. I really enjoy being with you."

I grabbed hold of the hand that was tracing mine and moved it into motion again. I liked what he was doing.

"Does that make any sense?" he asked gently.

"Yeah, it does. I'm just happy you're able to be open with me after what I did."

"What did you do?"

"The way I ended things," I said. This was why I started this conversation in the first place. Now I just had to muster up enough courage to say what was on my mind.

"Jack, I still had feelings for you when we broke up. I was really young and unsure about how serious we were. That's not saying I didn't move on. When I got married, I did it with the best intentions. But I can't help but think my life would have turned out a lot differently if we, maybe, ended up together."

Jack raised one eyebrow in an amused look.

"Are you laughing at me?"

"No," Jack said, as he reached out to me and pulled me swiftly into a hug. His body wrapped around mine, crushing me against him and engulfing me in his intoxicating smell.

It was one of the clearest things I could remember about Jack from when we were dating. He never held back his affection.

"You have no idea how good it is to hear you say those words." He moved in quickly and planted a soft kiss on my lips. Before I could properly return the kiss, he pulled away.

"I was not done kissing you, damn it," I wanted to scream in protest.

"It's not too late for us, Kel," Jack said. "You know that, don't you?"

"Yes. I think you're right," I said, smiling.

Instead of leaning back in to kiss me again, Jack hesitated and looked deeply into my eyes.

In answer to his question that I saw there, I leaned in to give him a hungry kiss. We spent a few minutes making out like two naughty teenagers on a warm summer's night. It felt great.

By the time Jack dropped me off at home, I was exhausted and exhilarated at the same time. I wanted desperately to invite him in but that would be rushing things. It was important for us to be careful this time around Besides, building a relationship with Jack was going to be fun. It was just easy with him.

I opened the front door, disarmed the alarm system with my code, and let Jack walk me into Chocolate Love. We walked slowly into the foyer. I turned and caught him looking upstairs to my apartment. Considering the way we were kissing on the park bench earlier, it wasn't hard to guess what he was thinking about.

He smiled down at me and took a hold of my hand.

"I think I better say goodbye here. I don't know if I can resist you, my little temptress," he laughed, using the nickname he gave me back when we used to steam up the windows of his car.

"I can't believe you remember that name," I said, stepping in closer to him and tilting my head up, so he could kiss me goodbye. He smiled down at me but did not initiate a kiss.

"I remember a lot more," he said, as he leaned his face closer to mine, stopping just short of meeting my lips. His smile broadened, and he made a quick motion like he was going to kiss me but stopped. He was teasing me.

Two could play at that game.

"Remember the night after our homecoming game in your parent's basement?" I teased back, raising my eyebrow.

His mouth dropped open slightly.

"Okay, now I really have to leave," he said, as he dropped a quick kiss on my lips and pulled away. He laughed when his lips came back to mine a second time. Just as he was about to pull away, I pulled him closer to me and kissed him more aggressively. My body moved in close, so my legs were pressed up against his and my hands wandered down the back of his black athletic shirt. The feel of his muscles under my hands made my stomach do a somersault.

I ended the kiss, disconnected my body from his, and stepped back onto the landing of the stairs.

"Thanks for a great night," I said, smiling at him and shooting him his signature wink.

"You're killing me," he said, a little out of breath.

Mission accomplished.

Chapter 27

I watched as Jack ran out of Chocolate Love after we ended our kiss, mumbling something nonsensical about "those yoga pants are going to be the death of me."

Our kissing had obviously rocked him.

After I locked my door to my apartment, I leaned back on it to soak in all that happened in the short couple of hours we had tonight. It all had gone by so fast.

It was exciting to know I could still turn Jack on. Although we hadn't had one sip of alcohol tonight, I felt a bit drunk and dizzy as I pulled my body away from the door. I wondered what was next for us.

I started a bath to help me wind down, knowing I would not be able to fall asleep with all of the emotions pumping through me. While the bath filled with lavender bubbles, it hit me that I had not heard from Mom since dropping her off at the airport.

Most times, no news was good news. According to the little digital clock I kept in the bathroom, it was nearing ten o'clock, which meant it was eleven o'clock her time. She and Dad were normally in bed by nine-thirty. I made a mental note to call first thing in the morning to check on her. It would only worry her if I called this late.

I tied on a robe and turned on my computer, thinking Mom might have sent an email instead of a call. She often did that if she was too tired to speak live.

Sure enough, the first email was from Mom, addressed to all of us.

Hello Ladies,

Thank you for a wonderful visit. I was so lucky to be able to spend time with all of my daughters, son-in-laws, and grandchildren. Wish I could have stayed longer. Dad and I are already talking about plans to come back at the end of next month for Nikki's birthday. We'll be able to make plans for Mickey and Rooney then. Let me know if that would work for you three. Love you all and miss you already.

Love, Mom

At least I would be able to put the worry to rest. Mom was home safe and sound. It would be nice to have her and Dad back soon. If they came at the end of next month, that should be more than enough time for me to have a rough draft of my new book. Mom could take the draft for her initial read through and give me comments for the revision. It was always a great motivator to have an event like a visit from relatives to push me to finish my work.

I went back into the bathroom and shut off the water, sticking a big toe in to see how the water felt against my skin. Just right.

Slipping into the water, the lavender bubbles circled around me. The warmth of the water and the smell of soap relaxed me immediately and loosened up my muscles.

Sure enough, the instant I allowed myself to relax, my cell phone left by my computer rang.

My initial thought was that it might be Jack. I smiled and heaved myself out of the warm bath. Throwing a towel around my wet body, I padded my way over to the phone. The screen read "Withheld." Strange. It had to be him though. Who else would call me this late?

"Hello?" I said, trying to make my voice sound sexy, just in case it was him.

There was no response from the other end.

"Hello?" I said again, a little louder this time.

There was definitely someone there. I could hear breathing.

"Jack?" I said, giving it one last try.

Just as I was about to hang up, the breathing picked up in pace. It sounded very labored and deliberate now. Like the person on the other end was taunting me.

"Who is this?" I demanded.

When the breathing abruptly stopped, I ended the call and threw the phone down on the chair. I turned to make sure my apartment door was locked and bolted. Seeing that it was, I relaxed a bit. Being in such a daze after the date, it wouldn't have been a big surprise if I had forgotten.

Suddenly a sinking feeling washed over me.

Although I locked the apartment door, I never enabled the alarm system again after Jack left. I didn't even lock the door behind him because I had been so intent on getting upstairs, forgetting that I was responsible for securing the store.

Crap.

I sat down for a minute, still dressed only in my towel, and tried to figure out what to do. The thought of going down there to lock up was terrifying.

It had probably been Gina on the phone since she seemed so intent on harassing me. I wouldn't put it past her to make obnoxious phone calls, especially after our heated phone call earlier today. My mind drifted back to the image of her outside of the yoga class. She looked strange, so off. Her slovenly appearance made her look different from the Gina I used to know.

This wasn't even the same person. She was like the maniac version of Gina.

Now I regretted I didn't tell Jack what I saw. I should have told him the whole story. Maybe he would have stayed here with me tonight. Why did I have to be so damn chaste about our time together? Didn't I learned in the case of Jack, we shouldn't waste time? We should have been together tonight. He would have never forgotten to lock up, and we would be safe and happy in each other's arms.

No use wishing for what could have been. If I was going to do this, it had to be now. I couldn't just sit here and wait for someone to walk into Chocolate Love, if they weren't here already.

I stood up and walked into my bedroom to get dressed. There was no way I was going down there in only my bath towel. It was always the half-naked woman who was the first one killed in horror movies.

After pulling on sweats and a tee-shirt, I considered calling Nikki, but in the end chose not to. I was too upset and angry with myself for doing something so stupid. It was embarrassing after all of the hard work she put into the alarm system to ensure my safety.

I unlocked my door and turned on the hallway light to illuminate the winding staircase. My eyes dropped to the landing at the bottom where Jack and I were earlier in the evening. All I had to do was get down those stairs, lock up, and enable the alarm system.

But that wasn't true. The entire building needed to be searched because if someone got in already, they could be hiding anywhere in Chocolate Love.

Still clutching my cell phone in my hand, I punched in the numbers 9 1 1 and placed my thumb over the call button. If anything seemed off, I was calling the police.

"I've called the police. They'll be here any minute!" I yelled at the top of my lungs.

I was angrier now than scared. Something had come over me. Tonight was a glimpse of what my life could be like, and I wanted it. I desperately wanted to have a life with Jack. I was tired of living like this.

Creeping slowly down the stairs, I allowed my eyes to adjust to the darkness. The door leading out of the foyer was wide open, just like Jack had left it on his way out. I couldn't tell from this distance if the front door on the other side of the hall was locked. Who was I kidding? I knew it wasn't.

At this point, if it was, then that would mean someone else had been in here, because I knew I didn't lock it.

I stepped off the landing and reached to turn on Nikki's mood lamp on the small table near the stairs. That allowed me to see into part of the store, but the back kitchen was dark and out of my line of vision.

"Hello?" I said aloud, giving it one last attempt for my presence to be known. "I see the lights from the police car outside. I'm going to let them in."

Instead of walking to the front door, I took a deep breath and walked quickly into the front room of the store. I braced myself, waiting for someone to pop out from behind the display counters.

"Is anyone here?" I called.

The store was empty. I continued on into the back kitchen, inspecting every angle where someone could hide. Nothing. The back door was locked up safe and tight.

The last room to inspect was the front display kitchen where Nikki's employees prepared the chocolate for the viewing pleasure of the public. I saved this area for last because it was the least likely place someone would hide due to the fact that it was all glass. Sure enough, the room was empty.

Relieved, I went back to the front door to lock-up and enable the alarm. It appeared as though I was alone here in Chocolate Love, so I closed my phone and put it in my pocket.

Back in the foyer, I locked the second door. If someone got in the front door, not only would the alarm go off, but they would also have to figure out how to open this second door, which had a completely different set of locks.

I had done some really stupid things tonight considering what was going on with Gina and the break-ins. I had turned off the lights in Chocolate Love when Jack left, but completely tuned out my responsibilities to lock up. It was great to be falling for Jack, but I needed to keep my head on straight.

Just as I was about to head upstairs, I noticed the closed public bathroom door, and a chill ran down my spine. Freezing in place, I steadied myself by holding onto the banister.

Seeing this door reminded me of the small storage basement off the kitchen. I was not even close to being done. There were so many more places someone could hide.

I reached slowly into my pocket, trying to make as little noise as possible, and pulled out my phone to dial 9-1-1 again. Moving my thumb over the send call button, I walked over to the bathroom door. Sweat beaded down my neck as my heart picked up rhythm. I pictured Gina in there laughing at me when she heard me lock up the store.

If she was in there, what the hell was she planning? Did she want to hurt me? Was she going to sneak up to my apartment in the middle of the night?

Before getting any closer to the door, I rethought my strategy. I left the overhead light on and reached down to unplug the lamp near the stairs as quietly as I could. Its chrome base was rather heavy and could serve as a weapon if needed.

When I tried to remove the lamp shade, it slipped slightly in my hand, almost falling to the floor.

"Damn," I said quietly. My heart was pumping so fast by this point, I thought I might faint. I set it down quietly on the table and moved closer to the bathroom door.

The lamp was in my right hand and the phone in my left. One of them would have to be released from my firm grip in order to open the door.

Placing the phone in my pants pocket, I threw the door open and jumped back as if someone was going to charge out at me and attack. When no one did, I reached my left hand in and turned on the light. Empty.

Now that only left the storage basement to explore.

Making my way back through the kitchen, I opened the door and turned on the light. It seemed quiet, but if I was going to be thorough, I had to go down the steps.

I tiptoed slowly down the stairs, wincing at every creak the stairs made. Each step gave off a distinct sound. Like playing a piano with my feet. So much for the element of surprise. If someone was down here, they were definitely aware of me now.

"The police are here," I called weakly. "We're coming down." I forced myself further down the stairs. When I finally made it to the bottom, my heart relaxed. The sweat on the back of my neck cooled. It would be impossible for someone to hide down here due to its small size. Unless they were hiding under the stairs.

I moved quickly to inspect. It was dark, but I was able to tell right away no one was under them. I let out a manic laugh and sat back on the ground, not caring that my pants would be filthy from the basement floor. It was over. I could go to bed now.

Suddenly, my laughing came to an abrupt halt. The first time I looked, it wasn't visible because it was balled up so tight under the bottom stairs. I leaned in closer to get a better look.

"What is that?" I wondered out loud.

Chapter 28

Nikki kept this area pretty clean except for a couple of plastic boxes filled with Christmas and other holiday decorations. Those were tucked neatly against the wall though, so the fact that there was a random shopping bag shoved under the bottom two steps looked completely out of place.

The shopping bag was from a high end department store with a number of locations here in the Chicago area, including one in our local St. Charles Mall.

Why was it there? Such an odd place to put it.

I reached for the bag and peered inside. There was one large white box inside of it. The distinguishable red markings on it told me there might be a product from Coach inside of it. I couldn't resist opening the box. My sisters and I had been having a love affair with Coach purses since high school. Steve used to buy me a Coach purse for Christmas every year when we were married. It had been years since I received one of those, but it didn't stop me from filling my free time gawking over their products online.

Inside the box was a Kristin Leather Pleated Satchel in Emerald Green from this year's upcoming fall collection. I had been eyeing it online. It was tough not to drool on it, it was so beautiful. The price tag read four hundred dollars. Why would this beautiful piece be sitting here bunched up in a corner under the stairs of a stinky cellar? Who would do such a thing?

My first thought was it had to be a man, someone who did not have the right respect for a beautiful piece of leather like this. Maybe Bob bought it for Nikki and hid it here in the store. It was not like he could hide it at home. She would definitely find it there. Of course, it wasn't too smart to keep it here either. Nikki kept this store in tip-top shape. She would notice anything out of place. But there was no reason for her to look under the stairs until her Halloween decorations were needed, and that was months away.

Maybe Bob chose well after all, as long as he planned to give it to her before Halloween. Her birthday was soon. That had to be it. Now I felt bad for opening this up. This was none of my business.

While carefully wrapping the purse back up into the box, my cell phone rang again.

"Hello?" The phone number was not recognizable, but at least it was not blocked. It was coming from a local area code.

"Hi," Jack's voice said on the other line.

"Hi, there," I said, happy to hear his voice.

"What are you up to?"

I looked around, trying to decipher what to tell him. I felt quite foolish about this whole thing. The lamp base sat next to me on the floor, a reminder of the danger I thought I was in a few moments ago. Now I just felt like an overly emotional snoop with Nikki's purse box sitting in my lap.

"Oh, nothing," I said, setting the box back into the bag. I pushed it back under the stairs, hoping it looked like it did when I found it. Didn't want to have to explain to Bob about snooping around his basement. Both Nikki and Bob put a lot of trust in me.

"Why does our connection sound so bad?"

Probably because I was in the basement. "Hold on, let me just move to another part of my apartment. Sometimes my cell phone connection breaks up in my kitchen." I grabbed the lamp in my other hand, ran up the stairs, closed the basement door, and then ran through the store, shutting off lights as I went.

At the stairs leading up to my apartment, I carefully placed the lamp back in its position on the table and headed back upstairs.

"Hold on one second more." I bolted up the stairs, opened my apartment door and then locked up for the night. It felt good to have my little adventure behind me. Now I could rest safe and sound for the night.

I took a moment to catch my breath and then put the phone back up to my ear.

"What are you doing, Kelly?" Jack asked, laughing. "How big is your apartment anyway?"

"It's pretty big," I said, short on breath.

"As if I wasn't curious before, now I really want to see it," Jack said in a husky voice. I pictured him sitting on a couch in his condo with a smile on his face.

"That could be arranged," I said, thinking back to my earlier thoughts on us spending more time together. We were both adults. We knew we wanted each other. What was the sense in waiting?

"Oh, yeah?" Jack said.

"If you play your cards right, Mr. O'Malley," I said with a laugh.

We spent the next hour catching up on the parts of our lives we needed to fill each other in on. Most things we talked about were more casual, like the fact that he was becoming a gourmet cook. He had started taking classes to distract himself from all of the troubles he was having with Callie in London. It made sense to me with the way he loved food. He promised to make me a nice dinner very soon.

"Do you know what Mari's daughter asked me the other day?" Jack asked.

"What?"

"How come you don't have a lady that sleeps in your bed with you like mommy and daddy?" Jack chuckled.

"Oh, my," I laughed. "What did you tell her?"

"I pointed to an ice cream truck and said let's go get some. Done."

"Yeah, they are very distractible. That's the best way to handle it. My niece thought my ex-husband was dead. I think that's what my sister may have told her. She asked me about it the other day."

"What did you tell her?"

"Want to go see my new princess dress?"

We both laughed together at that.

"I do want them someday."

"What?" I asked.

"Kids. A few. I think they are hilarious. Hanging out with Mari's family has really had an impact on me. It's making me want a family of my own," Jack said. His words hit me hard.

"Yeah." I didn't think Jack realized what shaky ground he was walking on. My infertility issues had to be discussed at some point, but this was not the right time for me. It needed to be done though. I had not realized up until now how much Jack wanted kids.

"What's your schedule like for tomorrow?" I asked, trying to change the topic as quickly as possible.

We wrapped up the conversation around eleven-thirty. He apologized for keeping me up so late again, but I didn't mind. It was exciting to learn about Jack as an adult. Some things about him were still the same, but some things were also very different. He still had the same moral compass, but his interests and his passions had blossomed.

Jack promised to call me in the morning. We made tentative plans to get together again tomorrow night for dinner at his place. After we said goodnight, I fell into a deep restful sleep, excited for another evening with Jack.

When the alarm went off the next morning, all I wanted to do was roll over and go back to bed. I knew, however, Nikki would be waiting for me. We only had a week left to train for the charity race. I was not worried for myself. Completing a 5K race would be easy. But Nikki was just back into running and needed all the training she could get.

I forced myself out of bed and walked to the kitchen for some breakfast. Although I had a good night's sleep, it was laden with dreams. No nightmares this time, but my mind felt like it had been working out all night. While I brewed my first cup of coffee, various images popped into my head from my dreams, like a television show on fast forward. All very unclear.

After my coffee, I dressed in my running shorts, sports bra, and a sleeveless, pink running shirt. Down in the store, Nikki was standing in the foyer, studying the lamp I had used last night in my manhunt through Chocolate Love.

"Is he still here?"

"Who?" I asked, stopping abruptly on my way down the stairs.

"Jack," she said, laughing. "Who did you think I'm talking about?"
"Oh."
"He is!" Nikki squealed.
"No, he's not. Why do you think he's here?"
She tilted her head and looked at me.
"You did not get a lot of sleep last night, did you? And check out this lamp. The shade is all askew. You guys must have been making out on the way up the stairs, and when things got hot and heavy, you knocked into this lamp."
She was not too far off. We were making out a couple of feet away from the lamp. If we had allowed things to go further, we could have easily bumped into the lamp shade.
"No, that is not what happened." I smiled, refusing to kiss and tell. "I must have bumped into it last night on my way up the stairs. And although I will not go into detail, I will tell you we had a wonderful time last night. We are seeing each other again tonight, and don't even ask. I have no intention on filling you in on every detail."
Nikki smiled and jumped up and down like a fifteen-year-old pumping her fist in the air. "Yes! That is fantastic news!" Nikki said. "You needed this. I'm so happy for you, Kelly. Your life is officially on the fast track to happy town. Good riddance, old crazy life. Whoo-whooo!"
"You're nuts." I made the decision not to tell her anything about the situation last night. Nothing horrible happened. It was all a false alarm. Plus, if I told her, I would have to work like crazy to not tell her what I found under the stairs. Nikki would know I was hiding something. I didn't want to spoil anything for her.
On the run, we talked about Gina outside of yoga and the anonymous call last night. We agreed to be on high alert for any Gina spottings or phone calls. Nikki said she also put together a log last night for us to write down any encounters we had with Gina. She had already recorded the two emails, the call on the way home from the airport, and the time she came into the store. The plan was to build a case against her, so the police had to pay attention to the situation.
When we returned home, I headed upstairs to shower and get to work. Before showering, I checked my email. I was pleasantly surprised to find another email from Holly:

Dear Kelly,

I like what I'm reading so far. Send me more. Can you send me the next ten chapters with an outline?"

—Holly Combs

I was thrilled to see her interest but was only just finishing up on my eighth chapter. It had taken me some time to get moving on the book, as it always did in the beginning of a novel. It normally took me six months to write a book. Ninety-five percent of the work happened in the last two months. I was like an express train once I hit my stride. This one was taking me much longer. Technically, I was in my fourth month of trying to write this book, so I was hoping the express train was about to leave the station.

An outline? That was tough. I missed my old editor, Maggie. She never asked me for an outline. She knew those didn't work for me. I had a rough idea in my head as far as how the story would go. But a professional outline on paper? Ugh.

I didn't bother drying my hair because my plan was to take another shower before my date tonight and spend a lot of time primping. Right now it was time to get to work. This was what I had been waiting for.

The next couple of hours were very productive. When Nikki came in with our coffee at eight-thirty, it was a welcome break.

"Whoa," she said, after I opened the door to let her in. She held two steaming mugs of coffee and a legal pad under one of her arms.

"What?"

"You look like a mannequin. You're so stiff and tough. What did you do with my sister? It must be getting good," she said, sitting down on her chair. I pulled the legal pad out from under her arm to prevent her from dropping it when she tried to place the mugs down on my desk.

"Good? What's good?"

"The book, Kelly. You turn into a freak when you're deep into the book."

"I do?" I pulled my hands up to my face and thought about the creepy, plastic mannequins I saw in stores.

"Don't worry. It will go away by your date tonight. Maybe you should get a quick nap in. You might be up late again tonight," she said, throwing me a scandalous wink.

"Shut up," I laughed.

"Are you working tomorrow?"

"I'm working every chance I get. Check out this email," I said, pulling up my email from Holly.

"Yes!" Nikki stood up and broke into her choo-choo dance again. "Whoo-whoo!" She pumped her arm in the air. "What did I tell you? You are on your way, girl!"

My computer made a noise when a new email popped up. Both of our eyes swung back to the computer screen at the same time. The name on the email was Jack O'Malley.

"Mm-hmm. You know you want to open that," Nikki said, pulling her coffee mug back up to her lips and sitting down.

"A little privacy, please." She was right. I couldn't resist opening it immediately.

She turned her body around in her chair, so she faced my bedroom.

"Go ahead. I won't peek."
I clicked the mouse and opened my email. It read:

Dear Kelly,

We are on for dinner tonight at my place. Does six work? I can pick you up at Chocolate Love.

Love, Jack

I replied to his message:

Dear Jack,

Six o'clock would be great. See you then. Can I bring dessert?

Love, Kelly

My computer dinged again immediately with another email from Jack. It read:

No. This dinner is all me. Can't wait to see you. Jack

"Come on, you're killing me."
"Alright, you can turn around. We're just making plans for dinner tonight. He's going to pick me up at six."
"Do you want me to make you something special to bring for dessert?"
"I asked him the same thing. He said no. He wants to do the whole thing by himself."
"What a man," she said, blinking her eyelashes up and down at me.
The rest of the day went by fairly quickly. At two o'clock, I turned off my computer. I was exhausted and my brain was fried. The added pressure put on from Holly made me more focused, which was great. It had taken me a good three hours to put together a rough outline. Though it was not how I normally work, I had to be amenable to my new editor. If an outline was what Holly wanted, then an outline was what she would get. I needed to show her I was a professional and could provide the materials she requested.
But putting together an outline meant I needed to think through what would happen to Mary and the logistics as to how it would happen. It also meant the majority of my research had to be done before writing the story, rather than in the midst of writing it, which was how I normally did it. Thinking of all of these changes gave me a slight headache. I popped two Tylenol and laid down, setting my alarm to go off in forty minutes.

After thirty-five minutes, I woke on my own and stayed on the bed until the alarm went off. I felt well rested and had even thought of a few new ideas while coming back into consciousness.

Normally I kept a legal pad next to my bed in case anything came to me in the middle of the night. While writing my ideas down, my cell phone rang. I didn't have any intention of picking it up but changed my mind when I saw it was Jack's number.

"Hello?"

"Kelly?" Jack said a bit hesitantly.

I could tell immediately something was wrong.

"What's wrong?"

"Nothing is wrong. I just called to let you know I have to cancel our plans for tonight."

Something was definitely wrong. He didn't even sound like himself.

"Okay," I said quietly. "Is everything all right? Is your mom okay?"

"Yeah, everything is fine. I just found out from my boss one of our clients in Boston has a financial emergency. I need to fly out there today to spend a week with him and get things straightened out."

"You're leaving today?"

"Yes," he said, not giving me any more details.

"You'll be gone all week?" I asked.

"It looks that way. I'm going to try and be back for the race," he said.

"The race," I said. My heart did a flip-flop. Something was very off here. I wasn't an idiot. I knew a brush-off when I heard one. He wasn't volunteering a lot of information, and he had not once mentioned anything about rescheduling.

"I'm sorry, Kelly." I wanted to hear more about the client, where he was staying in Boston, how he was angry at his boss for making him miss a night with me, anything. I just wanted more, but instead got nothing.

"Okay, well, good luck."

"Goodbye, Kelly. I'll call you soon," he said, hanging up.

"Goodbye, Jack," I said to a dial tone.

Chapter 29

The rest of the weekend inched along while I waited for Jack to call me. When he didn't, I fell deeper and deeper into a depression. It puzzled me as to why he gave me the brush off. Was he really on a business trip? Did I say something wrong? Move too fast?

Nikki was not happy with the way I was acting, so I locked myself up in my apartment and buried myself in my work. I didn't feel like putting on a happy act for her because I was really down about what happened.

At first it was difficult to work, but once I was able to get into the zone with my story, I checked out.

Gina sent an email on both Saturday and Sunday, trying to get me to reschedule our meeting. I ignored both of them and simply saved them to the Gina file. The whole thing with her didn't bother me anymore. My depression had numbed me so much; I didn't care if a psychotic person was stalking me. I just wanted to know why Jack hadn't called.

"You're blowing all of this out of proportion," Nikki said to me on Sunday night after she returned from her swim with Adelle. She paced back and forth in my bedroom while twirling a finger through her hair. She was trying to talk me into going to a movie with her just to get out of the house. "He's just busy. Why wouldn't he want to see you? You're still a hot piece of...."

"Stop it," I said, pulling my hair back into a ponytail. It had not been washed in days. I smelled disgusting, but I didn't care.

"Listen, this is crazy. You have been doing so well. Are you going to let the fact that Jack had to leave for work take you down again? You just have to believe he needed to work and move on," Nikki said.

Even as she said the words, I could tell even she didn't believe them.

"Nikki, come on. We both know he blew me off. It's been two days and he hasn't called. He's not going to."

"Maybe he's busy," Nikki said, sitting down on my bed next to me.

I looked up at her and gave her a look that said, "Cut the crap."

"No one is that busy," I said. "How about a text? It takes two seconds to send a text if you're too busy to call."

"Maybe he's out of network." A look of desperation crossed her face. This was not like Nikki. She was anything but a desperate person. Nikki worked in reality, facts, and figures.

"I don't want to talk about this anymore. And I don't want to go to the movies. Let me just curl up, read my edits, and go to bed early." I pulled my hand up to my hair to itch the top of my head. Not showering in the last two days had made my hair greasy.

Nikki lowered her eyes, studying my white comforter. It took a lot for Nikki to annoy me. Tonight, she was teetering right on the edge.

"All right," she said, finally accepting my wishes. "I'll go." She stood slowly and made her way to the door.

"On one condition."

"What?"

"You run with me tomorrow morning."

"Of course. I have no intention of allowing this to stop my running or writing schedule. I haven't yet, have I?"

Nikki smiled at me. "The race is still coming in six days, right? You promised me you would help train me for this."

"I know. I still plan to run the race," I said, doing my best to flash a smile back.

"Great," Nikki said, preparing to leave. "One last thing. You said this will not affect your running or writing schedule, right?"

"Right."

"What about your shower schedule? Are you planning to stick to that because the customers will start to complain if you don't."

I chucked a pillow at her head and grinned when it nailed her square on the nose.

* * * * *

By Wednesday afternoon, cabin fever had set in. The only times I had left my apartment in the last three days was to run with Nikki in the early morning hours. Other than that, I had been glued to my computer. I was more determined than ever to complete this book and make it a success.

My sadness had turned to anger in regards to Jack. Who did he think he was anyway?

I wanted the chance to tell him off. Somehow, I planned to make my feelings known. He said he would be at the race. I didn't want to spoil a charitable event by making a scene, but that might be my only time to confront him. I'd just have to see if the opportunity presented itself.

Channeling my anger, I typed like a madwoman on my computer all day. When Nikki stepped into my room at three-thirty that afternoon, she looked taken aback by my appearance.

"Whoa," was all she said. My apartment was not the orderly place it normally was. As usual, things had been let go when I was on a hot streak with my writing. Dirty dishes filled the sink, and clothes were strewn all over the apartment. Because the blinds were still closed, the entire place was dark, illuminated only by the computer screen.

"Okay, I'm cutting in here. We have got to get you out of here. Even if it's for only a couple of hours," Nikki said. Her hands went madly up and down her apron.

"Sounds good." I had no intention of fighting her. I was secretly hoping she would come up and suggest leaving. Sometime around twelve o'clock that afternoon, I had started to crave fresh air.

"Really?" Nikki said. "It's going to be that easy?"

"Yes," I nodded. "It will be that easy." I turned in my chair to face her and flashed her a quick smile.

"And a smile," Nikki said, beaming back at me. "Thank God. You're going to be okay. I thought I lost you."

"I always get like this. You should have seen the way our home looked while writing my first two books in California. It just meant the work was getting done," I said, standing up to stretch.

"I wasn't talking about the writing."

"You mean, Jack? I don't care anymore. He's forgotten. My work is my priority now."

"Great. I'm glad. Why don't you jump in the shower, and we'll grab dinner. Maybe we can even catch a movie or something."

Nikki probably knew I was nowhere near over the Jack situation, but I was grateful she played along.

"Sounds great. I need to shower and clean this place up a bit. What about Bob?"

"He's got an evening meeting tonight, so we're on our own for dinner. He won't be home until late. It will just be a girl's night tonight."

"Can we meet downstairs at five?"

"That's perfect. I have Miguel closing up tonight, so I can leave whenever," Nikki said.

After Nikki went back downstairs, I took my time in the shower washing my hair and shaving my legs. It was important to spend a little more time than usual primping. I wanted to look good just for me.

What did I need a man to dress up for?

This life was going to be about me from now on. That was the direction life had been heading after Steve. Somehow I got foolishly side-tracked with Jack. I wouldn't make that mistake again.

By the time five o'clock rolled around, I was dressed in a casual, black, cotton sundress, pulled from the back of my closet, and my hair was blown into silk. When I got to the bottom of the stairs, Nikki was waiting for me in the foyer.

"Wow, you look great," Nikki said. "Is this all for me?"

"Of course. You're the best date a girl could ask for."

"That's the nicest thing I've heard all day," Nikki said. She linked her arm in mine.

We had a quick bite to eat at Chili's on Randall Road before heading to the theater across the street. The only movie we had an interest in when we arrived was an action thriller. That worked for me. I was not interested in seeing a romance story tonight. Too bitter.

While waiting for the previews to start, Nikki and I chatted in our seats.

"Hey, I forgot to ask, did you get another one today?"

"Yep, every day this week," I said, referring to the emails from Gina. "They're all the same. Asking me to meet up with her. She needs to talk to me. I'm in danger, blah, blah, blah."

"What a psycho," Nikki said. "Do you think she is delusional? Maybe she is schizophrenic. I saw this show once on people with delusions. It can get very dangerous. They start to believe in these visions they have. One woman thought she was a messenger from God. She went into a hospital and started pulling IVs from patients and cords out of walls. A few people died because of what she did. She said she was carrying out the work of God and sending them to heaven."

"Gina's just sending emails. I haven't seen her for almost a week. Maybe she's not even here anymore. Hopefully, she went back to California," I said.

"Yeah, but what if she is still here? Maybe she's been waiting for her opportune time to strike.

"Nikki, stop. I'm out. I'm having a good time. I don't want to think about Gina."

For a moment she was quiet.

"You're right. I'm sorry."

"It's okay. I'm sorry, too. I'm just trying to stay positive."

"You know, I'm just worried about you."

"I know."

"There is a way to make up for my nagging."

"Uh, oh." I turned toward her. "Do I want to know?"

"Don't worry, it's nothing crazy. Just a run to the concession stand for some popcorn and those chocolate raisins you love."

"Chocolate covered raisins!" I clapped my hands together enthusiastically, mimicking my niece Cindy.

"I'll be right back," Nikki laughed, bolting up from her seat.

The previews began to play as she left. I sat back and relaxed. This was my favorite part of the movie going experience. It was fun to start building the anticipation of seeing another movie.

Being a storyteller myself, it was always thrilling to watch other people's ideas come to life on the big screen.

Just as I allowed myself to get sucked into fantasizing about my books on the big screen, someone sat down next to me.

Warning bells went off loud inside my head.

Chapter 30

As soon as it sunk in what was about to happen, my first thought was to get up from my seat and bolt out the door.

"You've been avoiding me," Gina said in a hushed tone.

The theater only had about ten other people in it. I couldn't comprehend how I didn't see her behind us.

"What are you doing here?" I asked. Her eyes looked sunken in her face like she hadn't slept for a long time.

"I told you I had to talk to you. I can't waste any more time. It's dangerous for me to stay here any longer," she said in an exasperated voice that was way too loud for the theater.

"Gina, how many times do I have to tell you, I don't want to talk to you? I don't care what you have to say. I need to move on with my life." I moved myself as far from her as possible in my seat.

"God, you stink." The words slipped out of my mouth. I regretted them immediately, fearing this would only agitate her more.

Someone shushed us.

"I'm sorry," she said in a more appropriate whisper. "You should see the hotel I'm staying in. You wouldn't want to shower there either."

This made her sound somewhat normal, and for a millisecond, I actually felt sorry for her.

"Kelly, I know you don't believe me, but I've come here to help you. It's all I've ever wanted to do since I did that horrible thing to you in California. My business was not doing well, and I desperately needed the cash. I sold the information about you to the press because the money kept my business afloat. It's no excuse. I just want you to know I made a mistake and am genuinely sorry about it."

As bad as she looked, Gina's plea came out genuine and heartfelt. Although our conversation started out shaky, I was able to see the old Gina again, the Gina that was my friend.

"If it's any consolation, my life has been hell since betraying you," Gina said, looking down at her hands. "I've lost my business, had to go on a ton of antidepressants, my house was foreclosed, and all of my friends dumped me. It's really important for me to make amends to you. I need to turn my life around."

She looked up at me, and her eyes met mine with a humbled expression. Her physical appearance was different, but her eyes were the same ones that used to look back at me during our countless hours at coffee shops, trips to the mall, and brainstorming sessions over book ideas and movies.

"How did you get my phone number?" This was something that had been bothering me for days.

"From the yoga class sign-in sheet," she said sheepishly.

That explained why she was outside of Shannon Hall. She was there to steal my personal information.

"Tell me what you came here to tell me," I said, keeping my voice as low as possible. The fourth preview began to play. There was not much time before the movie would start. I knew the people around us would get angry if we were still talking at that point.

"I've been digging around some and hit pay dirt. You thought you figured it all out, but there's so much more. You're not going to believe this. You really are in danger."

Her hands trembled, and her voice became loud and shaky again.

"She's here! I've seen her outside of Chocolate Love at night," Gina said.

"Mandy?" I asked, referring to the woman Steve was having an affair with in California. It was the only person I could think of that Gina would be talking about.

"No," Gina said, very agitated. "Pay attention!"

She was making me feel very uncomfortable again.

"I've been staking out your place. They're out there at night. I'm doing my best to try and scare them away. It's like the holy trinity of terror. I have his number as well and have been calling him to try and get him to...."

"Gina." I cut her off. Just when I thought she was a little better, she sounded completely crazed again. The holy trinity of terror? What the heck did that mean?

"Sometimes they go in. I guess it's just the one that goes in. It's your...."

"What are you doing here?" Nikki's voice boomed loudly in the theater. The previews had just ended.

"You need to leave," Nikki said in an authoritative voice. It made me squirm in my seat. I wanted Gina to leave, too. I was right the first time. She was still crazy.

"Fine," Gina said, standing up. "If you don't want to listen to me, then you'll just have to figure it out on your own. I'm not putting myself in danger anymore because you're too naïve to figure out the truth. You were an idiot with Steve the first time, and you're still just too stupid and stubborn to look at the truth." She shoved Nikki abruptly out of the way and bolted down the aisle.

"Best of luck to you," Gina screamed back at me from the bottom of the stairs before she left.

The opening credits ran, but no one was looking at the screen.

"Okay, folks, show is over," Nikki said before sitting down next to me. Her arms were filled with candy, popcorn, and two drinks.

We stared at the screen in silence for a second.

"What just happened?" I asked finally.

"You were accosted by a psycho," she said in response.

We sat for a few more seconds before I spoke again. "Why does this keep happening to me?"

"Want to leave?"

"Definitely."

We stood up and headed down the stairs to exit the theater. On the way out, we tossed the popcorn in the garbage but took the drinks and candy with us.

Just when things could not get any worse, I heard Nikki make a choking noise next to me right before we got to the lobby. I turned to her in a panic. She recovered quickly and simply pointed her finger.

At the front of the lobby, I spotted Jack paying for his ticket. He was not supposed to be here in Geneva. He was supposed to be in Boston.

"We can leave through the side door if you want?" Nikki asked beside me.

Jack looked up and our eyes meet. He froze in place and looked away quickly.

"Not a chance," I said.

Gina's crazy encounter had only made me more combative. I left California to get away from crazy. Now it was coming at me from all sides. I was happy here in Geneva and wanted to stay. I was not going to let Jack or Gina ruin my new home.

I walked defiantly over to Jack with my head held high. As I got closer, his mother came into view next to him. *Damn.* It was going to be too hard to tell off Jack in front of Peggy. She didn't deserve to witness an outburst. I didn't have to be mean, but I could be clear.

"Hello, Jack," I said, my tone filled with ice.

"Kelly, I...."

"Hi, Kelly," Peggy said, smiling brightly at me. "What movie did you guys see?"

"We actually didn't get to see one. We have to leave," Nikki said.

"Oh," Peggy said. She looked back and forth at us.

I said a silent thank you they had missed the scene with Gina in the theater. What if they had come to see the same movie? That would have been humiliating on top of the blow I'd already received from Jack.

"How have you been, Kelly? Have you been okay?" Jack asked.

What a strange question for him to ask.

"Of course, I've been okay." My face scrunched up in confusion.

"She's been great!" Nikki said, cutting into the conversation. "We have to leave because she just got a call from this great guy. He's only in town for one night from Paris, so we have to race home and get her ready. He's one of the dealers I import from for Chocolate Love, and he's hot!"

Give Me Chocolate

Nikki's voice was higher and louder than Gina's was when she was having her meltdown. This night couldn't get any worse. She was trying to help, but it was obviously a lie. If the floor could have swallowed me up, I would have happily allowed it at that moment.

Jack continued to stare at me with an unreadable look. I interpreted it to be one of pity. It made me want to run out of the lobby and out to the car. So much for telling him off and defending my territory.

The only one presumably buying Nikki's story was Peggy. She openly nudged Jack and looked up at him with a burrowed brow.

"Oh, and did I say he's rich, too?" Nikki said.

"Let's go. Bye now," I said, grabbing Nikki's arm to lead her out the door.

"Have a good time," Nikki said, taking my cue. She stepped up her pace and walked with me out the door.

When we got outside, I turned on her.

"Nikki, what were you thinking?"

"I don't know. I just started talking and couldn't stop myself. At least Peggy bought it, right?" Nikki said while fumbling in her purse for her car keys.

"Let's just get out of here. I want to go home," I said.

When we got into Nikki's car, she started up the engine and opened the windows to air out the warm car. Her vehicle was spacious for a compact car, but right now it was suffocating me.

"Want to come over for ice cream?" she offered as she pulled out of her spot.

"No, I just want to go home."

"Okay," Nikki said in a defeated voice. "I'm sorry I ruined your night. I've been off since…." Her voice broke off. "Since Fran," she finally said.

I looked at Nikki and saw a single tear escape down her cheek.

"Nikki, you didn't ruin my night. Gina and Jack ruined my night. Don't worry about it."

Seeing her like this made me realize how selfish I had been. Over these last few days, I should have been paying more attention to the fact that my sister was still mourning the loss of a good friend.

She swiped desperately at her eyes.

"Nikki, it's okay."

"No, it isn't. Everything is falling apart. You're unhappy, Fran is dead, Adelle is in la-la land, and Mom and Dad are so far away. Our family is falling apart, and on top of all of that, I feel like someone is always right around the corner waiting to break into Chocolate Love."

"Nikki, pull over."

She pulled the car over in the parking lot and put it in park. When she did, the sobs she was trying to keep under control took over. I did my best to hug her, though I was at an awkward angle in the passenger seat.

It was frightening to see Nikki break down, but at the same time, inspiring to watch her allow it to happen. The healing process could now truly begin.

She had been this steely, brave figure, when really, she had probably been scared and sad.

When her sobs stopped, she gave me a quick squeeze back and searched for more tissues. I reached back into the backseat, where I spotted a Kleenex box earlier, and pulled some out for her.

"I'm a mess, but, man, that felt good," she finally said. "I needed a good cry."

"I can tell," I said warmly.

"I didn't realize how much I depended on Fran. Now that she's gone, it's like the heart of the store died with her." Her eyes were swollen and red.

"Don't say that. You're the heart of the store. Fran was very important, but everyone looks to you to keep the energy pumping through the store. You can't give up, Nikki. Your employees need you, the community needs you, and I need you.

"What would Geneva be without Chocolate Love? You would have people going crazy for their chocolate fix. Fights would break out in the streets."

Nikki started to laugh.

"Fights?" she said, looking at me.

"Full on fist fights. Riots, even. You're the heart of our family, too. And we're not breaking apart. Sure we have our quirks, but we're stronger than ever."

"Really?" she asked. "You feel better?"

"Yes."

I would say anything right now to make Nikki feel better. She had been working so hard to make sure I was feeling good and getting out. I should have been thinking about how much she needed to be out tonight.

"Let's go back to your place for ice cream." I said, pointing at the key for her to start up the car again. "Ice cream!" I said, pumping my fist in the air like she always did.

Nikki smiled. "Ice cream it is."

Chapter 31

By the time I got home on Wednesday night, I was exhausted but felt surprisingly refreshed. I was still reeling from seeing both Gina and Jack in the theater. At least now some doors were shut though, and I could move on.

Gina seemed to have hit rock bottom. The holy trinity of terror thing really freaked me out. She had said she was done and would not communicate anymore, which suited me just fine.

Jack and I were definitely over. It hurt. I didn't understand why he had lied to me and didn't want to be with me when we seemed to connect so well.

At least now my schedule was clear to focus on my writing. There would be no more romantic relationships in my life. Instead, my focus would be on becoming a world renowned author. It would be my new quest, a very honorable and extremely lonely quest.

* * * * *

The alarm went off early the next morning. Two more days until the race. I had to get up and meet Nikki downstairs for the run. She was counting on me.

Afterwards, I spent the rest of the day buried in my work. After finally completing a full outline for Holly, I forwarded it on, hoping she would be flexible if there were changes to the story.

Nikki and I headed to yoga that night. When I came bouncing down the stairs, Nikki was waiting for me with a big smile on her face. "You look hot! Trying to show Jack what he's missing?"

"I could care less about Jack," I said, checking my lip gloss in the mirror in the foyer before we left the building.

"Right," Nikki said, raising an eyebrow.

When we got to yoga, we dropped our purses on the old church pews at the back of the room where everyone set their belongings. We planned ahead on being late to cut down on any awkward pre-class time with Jack, if he even showed up.

I was disappointed when Jack did not show. As angry as I was with him, there was still a big part of me that would have liked to see him. We were apart so many years; it was nice to see his face, even if I was angry with him.

By the time the end of class rolled around, I was physically and emotionally exhausted. I just wanted get back home to dive into my work and bury my emotions.

At the end of class, Sharon got up and walked toward the altar to make one last plea for participants for her run on Saturday. She was dressed in a cream skirt, black, short sleeved shirt, and a pair of kitten heels. From the way she was dressed, it was obvious she had not participated in the class tonight.

Sharon spoke about the needs of her charity and how the money would be disbursed.

"Hopefully, I will see you all at the pre-race party on Friday. We'll be reviewing details of the race at the dinner as well as handing out race packets. On Saturday, we'll serve coffee, tea, and various breakfast items pre-race, donated by Chocolate Love, as well as a nice supply of food after the race. The post-race spread includes pizza, beer, bananas, bagels, cookies, bottled water, Gatorade, and much more."

Nikki and I smiled at each other. The food and goodies provided after the race were always my favorite part.

After Sharon finished speaking, Nikki spoke to her briefly to firm up some details about her dessert display at the pre-race party on Friday night.

Mari made her way over to me. I was glad she was making the effort to talk to me. Just because her brother was an idiot didn't mean we couldn't be friends.

"Kelly, I'm glad you're here," she said.

"Of course, I'm here. I love your class, Mari."

"It's really none of my business, but I want you to know I think Jack is being an idiot. He's not going about this the right way," Mari said. Her pale Irish skin was speckled in red blotches, making me think she was agitated or nervous to talk to me.

"Mari, you don't have to defend you brother. It's not your job to do that."

"No, you don't understand. I wish he would just tell you the whole story. He's not," she stopped.

"He did tell me the story. I know what happened to him."

"No, that's not what I'm talking about. He's got to tell you everything because he's going to mess this up. You guys should be working together on figuring this out." Mari appeared as though she was close to tears.

At that moment, Nikki came back over to us.

"Ready?" she asked me.

"I'll see you later, Kelly. I gotta go," Mari said, turning quickly and wiping at her cheek.

"What was that all about?" Nikki asked.

"I'm not sure," I said, watching Mari leave the room.

Friday morning I was working at my desk when there was a knock on my apartment door. It was nearing nine o'clock, and Nikki had just left to go back downstairs after our coffee break. I had been adamant about locking up, just in case Gina decided to come back for another round with me. Hopefully, she was really gone. It had been quiet since Wednesday night.

"Did you forget something?" When I opened the door, Nikki stood on the other side of it, but she was not alone.

"What's wrong?" A chill rushed over me.

"Kelly, can we come in? Detective Meyers needs to talk to us."

"Yes," I said, stepping back and allowing them to walk into the room. Detective Meyers carried a manila folder with him. He straightened his tie as he walked into the room and spent a couple of seconds looking around. It felt like he was looking for something. It made me nervous, like I was in trouble.

My mind raced back to the time Nikki and I had taken an orange from the local grocery store. She had been six and I was nine. We had regretted it as soon as we were out of the store and left it on the outside windowsill of the store because we were both too scared to go back in. That same guilty feeling ran through me now.

"Can we sit down somewhere?" Detective Meyers asked.

I waved my hand in the direction of the living room couch with the small glass coffee table in front of it.

"Can I get you something to drink?" I looked at Nikki. Her expression was eerily blank, but I could tell she knew something already. My mind jumped to Adelle. Was she okay? I thought back to the talk with Cindy on the way home from the airport. I should have spoken to Nikki about it and followed up with Adelle.

"Adelle?" I squeaked out.

"No. Everything is fine, Kelly. Detective Meyers is just here to talk to us about something he has found."

"Specifically, someone I have found," he said, sitting down carefully on the couch and straightening the wrinkles in his pants.

"Early this morning, I got a call from the captain of the Montgomery police force," he said, referring to a town about twelve miles south of Geneva. "The body of a woman was found floating in the Fox River. She was found by a runner, who spotted it tangled in the underbrush of some trees. When she was brought in, the initial examination revealed something I connected with you two."

"Oh my God," I said, pulling my hands up to my face. Members of my family raced through my mind. Why else would he be up here? My face flushed, and my voice immediately broke into hysterics. "Who is it?"

Nikki put her arm around my shoulders. "No, Kelly. It's not what you think. Just try and relax. Everything is okay."

Detective Meyers stared at me with a blank calm while he waited for me to get control of my emotions. He played with the folder he had in his hand

and held my gaze.

Tell me already, I wanted to scream.

After a few moments of painful, deliberate silence, Nikki turned to Detective Meyers.

"Tell her," she snarled.

"The woman found this morning has a distinct marking behind her right ear, a little star tattoo. We had a conversation earlier this week about a friend of yours with a little star tattoo. I think we might be talking about the same person."

"She is not a friend. We reached out to you for help to keep her away from us, if you recall," Nikki said, clarifying.

"The woman did not have any identification on her. Since you were familiar with this woman, do you think you would be able to identify her?" Detective Meyers asked, glazing over the point Nikki brought up.

"You want us to go down and see the body?" My eyes bulged out. I had been to a morgue before to get details for one of my books. The coroner gave me a tour and a little tutorial about the decay of a dead body. The difference was I didn't have any connection to the person and was able to view it with complete detachment. But someone I actually knew?

"No, nothing like that," he said. "I have pictures right here. You can identify her from these."

Before we had the opportunity to accept or reject his proposal, he whipped open the folder and laid the pictures out on the glass coffee table. There were various shots taken of the woman from many different angles: a neck shot, torso, feet, hands, and one of her face. She was bloated and an odd color white but unmistakably Gina. The water and the animals that inhabited the river had not been kind to Gina's body.

I fought back the urge to gag by taking in short labored breaths.

Nikki was speechless next to me.

"Judging from the coroner's initial review, it looks like she went into the water sometime Wednesday night. Can you ladies account for your whereabouts on Wednesday night? Say between the hours of eight and midnight?"

Before I could respond to his question, a strange rumbling noise began somewhere in the apartment. It took a second to realize the rumbling was coming from inside my stomach. Without being able to hold back or gain any control of the storm brewing inside, I retched violently, spilling the contents of my stomach onto my couch and the detective sitting on it.

Chapter 32

Detective Meyers sat in stunned silence. There was a slight widening of his eyes, but other than that, he remained cool and still, like a statue. I was humiliated but felt an immediate relief.

Nikki sprang into action and ran into the kitchen to get towels and various supplies to help clean up the situation.

"Sorry," I finally managed, not sure if he could understand me because my hands covered my mouth.

"I'm going to step into the bathroom for a moment," he said, slowly standing up and taking hold of the towels Nikki offered him.

"Are you okay?" Nikki asked after he left the room.

I shook my head, unable to speak.

"Go in your room and change your clothes. I'll clean up out here."

I did as she suggested, stopping in the kitchen to find a garbage bag for my clothes.

About ten minutes later, the situation was under control. Detective Meyers and I were both cleaned up, and Nikki had done a wonderful job disinfecting the living room. She'd taken the cushion cover off of one of my couch pillows and wiped up the area rug under the couch. The majority of my vomit had landed on his suit coat. It was now in a shopping bag by the front door. There were big wet circles on his pants, where he had obviously done some scrubbing. I offered to pay for any cleaning of his suit, which he graciously declined. He even went as far as to make a joke that perhaps it was too warm to wear a suit coat today anyway.

Surprisingly, the incident had lightened the mood in the room a bit. Detective Meyers appeared a bit more relaxed, even cracking a small smile. He reached out and cleared the pictures from the coffee table. Carefully, he put them back into his manila folder.

"Let's start again. I need identification. Can you assist me with that?" he asked in more of a polite tone. Perhaps my vomit had scared some manners into him.

Nikki and I both nodded in agreement.

"I may have rushed into that too fast. I apologize," he said kindly.

"Apology accepted," I said. Nikki stayed silent next to me, but nodded her head.

"We'll just work from two photos, the one that shows the tattoo and the one with a clear angle of the face." He looked quickly into the file and chose two before placing them out on the table. He watched me closely.

Seeing them a second time, I was able to handle it much better. It wasn't as shocking, and the overwhelming feeling that overcame me was sadness. Gina's face was bloated up like a puffer fish, but I could tell most definitely that this was her. How did this happen? How did this all come to such a tragic end?

Tears streamed down my face. I wanted her to leave Geneva, but not this way.

After we made the confirmation that this was indeed Gina Phillips, Detective Meyers put the photos away, excused himself, and made a few quick phone calls in my kitchen. When he was done, he snapped his phone shut and came back to the couch.

"When did you last see her?" he asked.

"Nikki and I went to the movies on Wednesday night. We were there for a seven o'clock show. Gina approached me during the previews. Like I told you last week, she keeps, I mean, kept trying to talk to me. I was doing everything I could to keep away from her. The way she was acting was very scary."

"Scary like how?" he asked.

"She kept telling me I was in danger. On Wednesday night, she told me there was a holy trinity of terror outside of Chocolate Love watching me. She was really, really out of it."

"Did she threaten you in any way?"

"As a matter of fact, I was relieved when she told me she was leaving town. She was frustrated with the fact that I would not talk to her. We thought the nightmare was over."

"You both stayed at the movies and never saw her again."

"Actually, we left after her outburst and went back to my house. We were embarrassed by the scene she made and wanted to leave the theater," Nikki said.

"What time did you get home, and did you stay there all night?"

"Are you questioning us because you think we killed her?" I asked, horrified by his implication.

"I'm just trying to get timeframes down. Right now we're not pursuing this as a murder case officially, but it's not every day we find an out of town guest of Geneva floating in our Fox River. We're trying to figure out the details surrounding her death."

"She was obviously delusional and disturbed. My guess is she may have killed herself. But if you must know, Kelly and I were at my house from approximately seven-thirty until ten o'clock. My husband was home by eight-thirty. He can verify this."

"Then where did you go?"

"I stayed home, and Kelly went home to her apartment."

I stayed quiet because I knew where this was going.

"You were alone?" Detective Meyers stated.

"Yes."

"A woman who was stalking you and making your life hell lands in the river and mysteriously dies right after a public incident in a theater. During which time, you have no one to account for your whereabouts?" Detective Meyers asked, raising an eyebrow.

"I guess not," I said, feeling my stomach start to rumble again.

* * * * *

Detective Meyers left after another fifteen minutes of grilling us about our whereabouts over the past couple of days. Because there was no immediate sign of struggle on the body, and all signs pointed to a drowning, he told us we were not considered suspects but that there might be future questions we would need to answer. He left with a cryptic comment about not leaving town.

"I can't believe she's dead," I said.

Nikki nodded in agreement.

"Gina wasn't a big fan of the water. She could barely swim. And it's hard to believe she committed suicide. When she said she was leaving, I thought she was leaving town, not this life. I feel horrible about all this."

"I know, but you saw her, Kelly. She was obviously going through some kind of break-down, right?"

"Yeah."

"I can't believe she did it, either. It's all just so sad."

"I hate that it had to end this way for her. It's too bad she couldn't turn a corner and get her life back."

"I'm really sorry, but I have to get back downstairs. My crew is probably wondering what the heck is going on. I left them in a middle of a project and bolted up here when Detective Grumpy showed up." She wiped her hands up and down on her apron and stood up to go. "Are you all right for now?"

"Yeah, I'm fine. I'll be down at lunch to frost cupcakes. I just want to sit here and take this all in."

"Okay. See you at lunch," Nikki said.

After Detective Meyers left, I couldn't get any work done. All I thought about was Gina's family being contacted and the horror they were experiencing. I finally gave up and headed downstairs to work with Nikki.

Nikki gave me the job of frosting vanilla buttercream on chocolate cupcakes. After working for an hour, I had enough. While passing through the foyer on my way back upstairs, I bumped into Jack. He was wearing a suit, and his tie was askew as though he had tried to loosen it. It struck me as odd that he was here at this hour. He had told me he normally worked downtown on Fridays. Of course, he had also told me he was supposed to be in Boston. I didn't know what to believe anymore.

"Kelly, I came here to see you." There was a note of desperation in his voice. "We need to talk."

Now he wanted to talk? He hadn't spoken to me in a full week. Just because he decided it was time to talk, I was supposed to drop everything and make him a priority?

"I don't think so," I said, brushing past him to jog up the stairs. The scent of his after-shave floated over me when I passed him. Damn that scent.

I turned to look back over my shoulder at the top of the stairs. He stood in the same spot staring up at me with his hands on his hips and his lips in a straight line. And damn those irresistible eyes. I raced into my apartment and locked the door.

A couple of minutes later, someone knocked on my door.

"Kelly, I'm not leaving," Jack called from the other side of the door.

I stood up from my desk and walked quickly over to the door to unlock it. On my way over, I peeked into a small mirror hanging near the door. My hair was up in a messy ponytail, and what little make-up I put on that morning had been washed away by my tears for Gina. I wiped swiftly at my tee-shirt, hoping to knock away any crumbs left over from my work in Nikki's kitchen.

"I suggest you do. I'm not in the mood right now, Jack. I have bigger things to deal with than your fickle heart," I said, opening the door.

Before I could stop him, Jack pushed his way into my living room and planted his six-foot five-inch frame in front of me.

"I have a fickle heart? Look who's talking." By the confrontational tone of his voice, it was obvious he had come here for a fight. "If I remember correctly, you're the one who dumped me all those years ago. I was the one left pining for you."

"Is that why you stood me up last Friday and left me hanging all week? Was it your little plan to get back at me? Well, if that is the case, you haven't matured a day since I dumped you. You're still a kid, and I'm glad you're out of my life again."

We were in each other's faces now. It wasn't the way we normally communicated, but nonetheless, it felt good to air these bad feelings.

Jack's expression softened. It was the opposite reaction I thought I would get.

"Kelly, that's what I came here to tell you. If you would just listen to me, you would know I didn't plan to hurt you. I was trying to protect you.

"I bailed on you last week because I was sure Callie was here in town. I started getting all of these crazy phone calls. I thought I was in danger, which might have put you in danger. The last thing I wanted was for her to find out about you. The police just told me that it was some woman named Gina Phillips. Callie was never here. I came here as soon as I found out."

"Gina? She was here for me. She drowned in the Fox River on Wednesday night."

"I know. Detective Meyers figured out she was staying at the local motel. The owners called in about a woman not paying her bills and acting erratic earlier this week. When they identified her body, Detective Meyers went to the motel on a hunch and checked her room.

"Her call history on her cell phone listed my number and yours multiple times. I had been calling the police daily, trying to get them to help me, so they linked it immediately to me. She was stalking both of us. They said she was connected to you somehow from California? I don't care what all that's about. God knows I understand sometimes your past won't leave you alone. It's all over now though, Kelly. We can be together," he said, and reached out to touch my arm, sending my stomach into somersaults as usual.

"If you'll have me." he said.

His eyes burned into mine as he leaned in closer to me.

Chapter 33

There must have been something in my expression that encouraged Jack because he was suddenly kissing me, and I didn't have the strength or the desire to stop him. It felt good to be back in his arms.

Together, we fell on the couch. He didn't comment on the fact that one of the couch covers was missing. I certainly didn't care.

"Kelly," he breathed my name. His hands crawled over my body. They ended up in my hair and pulled my face back to his.

"You have no idea how much I've missed you. I just couldn't bear the thought of Callie finding out we were together and coming after you."

"It's over now," I said.

For a brief second, I wished it was Callie who was dead instead of Gina. Gina was sick, but I still didn't think she was truly dangerous. And Jack's worries would be gone for good. It was a morbid thought.

My hands pulled at Jack's tie, trying to loosen it more.

"I want you so bad, Kelly. I've missed you so much. This sounds crazy, but one night after a particularly strange call, I got so worried, I came to Chocolate Love to try and see if you were okay. I thought if I could just get a glimpse of you through your window, I would know you were okay." The minute he stopped talking, he placed his mouth back onto mine.

"Wait, what did you say?" I said, pulling abruptly away. Something about what he said left me with a funny feeling.

I tried to sit up, which was nearly impossible with Jack's large frame on top of mine. I pushed lightly at his chest, and he responded by moving backward on the couch.

"What did you say?" I repeated.

"I know how it sounds, but I was worried. You don't know Callie. She's capable of so many weird things. She may have shown up at Chocolate Love. I know you had some break-ins and…."

"No, what you said about being outside my window." I was thinking about what Gina had told me about what she saw outside of Chocolate Love. She did say there was a man, a woman, and then she never got around to telling me who the third one was.

"Did you see anyone else when you were here that night?"

Jack's face darkened. "What do you mean?"

"It's just something crazy Gina said to me this week. I had a weird encounter with her at the theater. She probably got your number the same way she got mine — off the yoga sign-up sheet. I think that's why she was calling you. She became very protective of me. I think she was delusional about people being a threat to me. She said she saw people outside my window."

"You saw her at the theater? She was there? Now I want to know. Who is this Gina?"

"She's an old friend from California. When Steve was sent to prison, she sold stories and photos of me to the press. That's how so much about me ended up on the news. She came to town to make amends. When I wouldn't see her, she went crazy. At the theater, she appeared out of nowhere to ambush me. She told me people were watching me all the time." I shivered and Jack pulled me back into his arms again.

"She's gone now, Kelly. You'll be okay. I'm going to make sure of it." I was disturbed by the fact Gina may have been telling the truth in her own weird way. Then again, I didn't trust Gina. Part of me felt she could have been stirring up drama just to get more information out of me.

Jack left my apartment about an hour later to take his mom to a doctor appointment. Things cooled considerably for us after our discussion about Gina. Jack seemed to sense that I was no longer in the mood and did his best to comfort me and alleviate my anxieties about what had happened. As much as I wanted to be with Jack, I was left so unsettled by the week's events that I couldn't relax. Before he left, he asked to pick me up for the pre-race party. I declined because I had promised Nikki I would help her set up the dessert display she was donating.

At four o'clock, I headed downstairs to help Nikki pack up for the party.

"You're here," she said, looking surprised to see me.

"Of course, I'm here. I told you I would help."

"I know, but I saw Jack go upstairs. I thought maybe you two were busy or something. You could have skipped helping me."

"Jack left a couple of hours ago," I said, not giving her anymore details. I was thrilled by Jack's visit, but at the same time had a funny feeling in my stomach about the whole thing. One thing was for sure, I didn't want to talk about it.

"Well, I'm glad you're here, because I do need your help. These two boxes need to be packed in the van. Can you help me carry them outside?" She pointed to two rectangular pink bakery boxes on the counter.

"Miguel is bringing the van around and then we can start loading."

"Are you sure these are going to fit through the door?" I asked, staring at the size of the boxes.

"What do I look like? A novice?" Nikki laughed.

Once we arrived at the Lutheran Church, Nikki, Miguel, and I made quick work of setting up her display. When it was finished, we stood back and took in Nikki's creation.

"Oh…my…God," Sharon said behind us. "This is unbelievable!"

Nikki had created a life-size display of a female runner made entirely of cupcakes. The frame was some kind of mesh chicken wire that served as the skeleton, and the cupcakes attached onto the wire. She had on a shirt with the logo for Sharon's charity on it, shorts, a sweatband, and wristbands. I had pointed out earlier that no one wore wrist bands anymore, but we both agreed it added to the effect, so she kept them.

"Do you like it?" Nikki asked, her face beaming.

"Like it? I love it! I can't believe how talented you are," Sharon said, as she reached out and pulled Nikki into a quick embrace. "Thank you so much. You don't know how much this means to me."

"You are welcome," Nikki said. "Sharon, we recently lost an employee and dear friend of ours. Would you mind horribly if we posted this little sign beneath the display. Fran passed away from heart disease. She is the reason Kelly and I are running the race. It would be a nice way to honor her."

Nikki pulled a little gold plaque from one of the pink boxes that held the cupcakes. It read "In honor of Fran Harper."

"Nikki," Sharon said, picking up the plaque from Nikki's hands and looking at it. "What a nice gesture. Of course, you can put this up. I heard about Fran's passing. I'm very sorry."

Sharon leaned in and placed the plaque right at the base of the statue where it would be the most visible.

"I'm impressed with the generosity and good spirit of your town. You two are awfully lucky to have grown up here. All of the food tonight is donated from various vendors on Third Street," Sharon said. Her little pixie hands waved over the tables.

We saw Don from Donatello's walk in with a huge stack of bread for the pasta dinner, a vendor from the local pizza shop setting up the pasta and sauces on the main table, and a few other familiar faces.

"This was all donated?" I asked.

"Yep. There's no other way I could do it. We're just a small charity. I wouldn't be able to host something like this if it wasn't for the generosity of this community. Now all of the money from the race will go straight to the patients."

My heart warmed to see various neighbors working frantically to make the event go well for Sharon. She was right; we were lucky to call a place like Geneva home.

Across the room, I saw Jack arrive with Mari. They made their way over to us, and Sharon excused herself to answer Don's question about where to put the bread.

"We thought we would come early to help you set-up, but it looks like you have this under control," Jack said. He had changed into a more casual shirt and pants from his suit he wore earlier.

"That is so sweet," Mari said, pointing her finger at the plaque Nikki made for Fran.

"I think Fran would have liked it," Nikki said with a hint of sadness.

The party went well. Sharon gave a kick-off speech to get us revved up for the race and a precise review of the events for the morning. I couldn't wait to see how things would go. Maybe Nikki and I would sponsor a race one day. Being a part of Sharon's night made me feel like I could accomplish anything.

At the end of the night, Jack insisted on driving me home. I was happy to be in his company again, though a bit more guarded. Jack appeared relieved the whole nightmare with Gina was over. He had a happy glow about him and seemed confident about us again.

I wanted to share in his excitement, but there was a part of me that couldn't stop thinking about Gina. The whole thing was very confusing. Why did she kill herself? What was the point of taking it that far? When she left, she left angry, determined even. It just didn't add up.

I assumed when someone wanted to kill themselves, they were in the depths of despair. The Gina we saw at the theater last Wednesday night wasn't like that. She had problems, sure, but she didn't give me the impression she was done living her life.

When Jack pulled up to Chocolate Love, he opened my door and walked me to the front of the building. I thought he could sense something was off on my end because he made no attempt to come in. He leaned in to give me a quick peck and then turned his body to leave.

"I know this is not a good time to come up. Just know I'll be thinking of you tonight. Get some sleep. See you bright and early in the morning for the race."

"Okay," I said, letting go of his hand. I appreciated his ability to read my body language. He was always such a gentleman in that way.

"Make sure to lock up," he said over his shoulder.

I locked up tight and snuggled in early, deciding to pass on doing any work. I was exhausted from a long day. My body just wanted to go to bed and get a good night's sleep. Just as my head hit the pillow, the phone rang.

"Hello?"

Silence.

Chapter 34

"Hello?" I said again.

Someone was breathing, but no one spoke. I hung up the phone and scrolled back to check the screen. It read "Withheld." Gina was dead. Who could be calling me now?

My mind raced to Jack and his worries about Callie. Maybe he was right all along. Maybe Callie was back.

I contemplated calling Jack but decided not to. What was I going to tell him? Detective Meyers saw the calls on Gina's phone to me and to Jack. We knew she was the one calling.

I got up to check my apartment door to make sure it was locked. When I was satisfied, I ran back to my bed and jumped in. I should have stayed at Nikki's tonight. We had to get up early tomorrow morning for the race anyway. We had been so distracted with getting the cupcake display set-up and finding out about Gina's death, we forgot to address our plans for the night.

I was too exhausted to head over there now. It would mean getting up, getting dressed, and driving all the way over to her place. More importantly, it would mean I would have to go downstairs and walk through Chocolate Love past that spooky clock. My thoughts drifted immediately to the holy trinity of terror that might be waiting for me outside. I was better off just pulling the covers over my head and praying for morning.

I drifted off fairly easily considering the amount of stress I was under. My mind was too exhausted. I didn't like being on edge. I chose sleep instead.

Sometime in the middle of the night, I was awakened to the sound of someone rapping quietly at my apartment door. Rolling over, I looked at the clock on my cell phone. It read three-thirty.

I shot up in bed to decipher if the sound was part of a dream or if it was real. Rubbing at my eyes, I pulled on my robe and walked into my living room. I stood for a moment, letting my eyes adjust to the darkness. My instincts told me not to turn the lights on.

"Kelly?" I heard a voice whisper on the other side of my apartment door.

My body froze. This had to be a dream. If I just let more time pass, it would end.

"Kelly, let me in," the voice said again. It was frantic and persistent.

"Who...who's there?" I managed to get out. My mind went to skeletons and grave sites, the walking dead. The first person that came to mind was Gina. But that was impossible. Gina was dead. I saw the pictures.

I shook my head back and forth; causing the small hoop earrings I had left in my ears to hit the sides of my face. The fact that I could feel a physical touch told me one thing: this was real.

"Kelly!" Let me in now!" the voice demanded in a harsh, raspy whisper.

"No!" I said, as forcefully as I could manage.

"It's me, Adelle." As soon as she said her name, the puzzle pieces fell together. Of course, it was Adelle. Her voice was recognizable now. I was just too scared to decipher it.

Quickly, I unlocked the bolt. When I pulled the door open, I could only see darkness. A tall form took shape and rushed in, shutting and locking the door.

"It's me," Adelle said in a whisper, grabbing my arms.

Why was she so scared? Why didn't she have the lights on in the hallway? And the obvious, why was she here at three-thirty in the morning, and not home with her family?

"What's wrong?" I asked, raising my arms up and grabbing hold of her.

"How did you get in without the alarm going off?" I whispered. "Wait, let me turn some lights on."

"No! We have to be quiet and stay hidden."

"Why?"

"Because someone is downstairs." The fear in her voice sent a powerful jolt down my spine. It made me want to run back and hide under the covers. Adelle was strong, confident, even arrogant. She was wrong a lot, but even when she was, her voice was powerful. Even when she was desperate or overwhelmed, she was never scared. Not like this.

Seeing Adelle truly shaken made me crumble to pieces.

"Who?" I asked.

"I didn't get a look. I just heard them come in through the back door."

"Come in through the back door," I repeated. My fingers clawed at my lips. "That must mean they have a key, and the alarm is not going off. They know the alarm. Maybe it's Nikki."

"We have to call the police."

Our conversation was broken off by a knocking on my apartment door.

"Kelly," the voice said. "Please open up."

"Who is that?" Adelle asked.

"I don't know," I whispered in panic.

"Open the door, now," the small pixie voice boomed.

"What does she want?" I asked Adelle.

"I have no idea," Adelle said. "Who is she?"

"I think it's the charity coordinator, Sharon Winters."

"Ask her," Adelle said, nodding toward the door.

"What do you want, Sharon?" I asked, doing my best to sound authoritative. I had trouble, considering I was half dressed in my living room at three-thirty in the morning and frightened beyond belief.

"Let me in now. I have to talk to you. It's about your sister, Nikki. She sent me here to get you. She gave me the key and the code to get in. We met early this morning to set up the race. I'm afraid there's been an accident. Please ladies, we have to hurry. We don't have a lot of time."

As soon as Sharon mentioned Nikki, my heart dropped, and I rushed to open the door. Adelle grabbed for me to stop, but I managed to pull out of her grasp.

"Wait, Kelly," Adelle said.

Instead of listening to her, I reached up and unbolted the door. It flew open the minute the bolt turned just as Adelle said, "I think she's got a...."

I knew immediately she had been lying about Nikki. We stared into the eyes of a crazed Sharon Winters, pointing a gun directly at us. She had flipped the hallway light on just before I opened the door, allowing us to see her very clearly.

"Stupid, stupid girl," Sharon said. She was not the same woman I had spent time with last night at the kick off dinner. Her mouth was turned down in a sinister smirk, and her eyes squinted at me in anger.

"Steve always said you were the most gullible of the three. I can't believe this one got past me and ran upstairs. Steve said her survival skills were remarkable. Said she would kill any one of her sisters just to come out on top. I'm surprised you didn't attack me downstairs. You came up here to hide behind your little sister, huh? He was right. You're going to let her die first, aren't you?"

I turned to peek at Adelle huddled behind me.

"Who are you?" I asked, turning back to Sharon.

"That's right, you wouldn't know me," Sharon said. "You were always the naïve wife kept in the dark," she said, faking sympathy. "Now come on, are you that stupid? I know you found out about Mandy, but did you really think she was the only one?"

Sharon kept edging closer and closer to us. With each step, Adelle and I moved further back into the apartment. I knew if we kept moving, we'd be close to the table with my landline on it. My hope was that Adelle would be able to pick it up and sneak a phone call to 9-1-1.

I had my cell phone in the pocket of my robe, but I didn't know how to reach for it without Sharon noticing.

"Gina knew me though. She knew Steve and I have been off and on for a number of years. I'm surprised she never told you about us. She recognized me this spring when we ran into each other at a charity race I was hosting in Denver. All three of us worked for the same pharmaceutical company at one point. She came here to try and warn you about me, but you threw her away like a piece of garbage."

"I didn't throw her away," I said.

"She *was* garbage, you know. She was like a private investigator, following both of us around all the time. I did you a favor when I killed her," she said.

I gasped.

A look of pride crossed her face, making her look monstrous. Poor Gina. She really was trying to help me.

"I tricked her into meeting me Wednesday night in St. Charles near the Fox River and then pushed her in. I didn't mean to kill her at first. It was supposed to be a warning, but when the current took her down, I knew it was for the best. I certainly wasn't jumping in to save her," she laughed.

"How could you do that?" I asked.

"I didn't *have* to kill her," she said. "She made me. She was determined to tell you who I was. I couldn't allow her to, obviously." She rolled her eyes in exaggerated frustration.

When Sharon's eyes jumped up to the ceiling for a quick second, I reached into the pocket of my robe, pulled out my cell phone and handed it back to Adelle. I prayed she would be quick enough to know what I was doing. Adelle swiped the phone out of my hand.

"So, please, tell me again, who are you?" I asked, making my voice loud enough, so Sharon would not be able to hear Adelle dial the police on my phone.

"I'm the woman who came here to kill you."

Chapter 35

"What about me?" Adelle asked loudly behind me. "You don't have to kill me, do you? I won't tell anyone who you are. If you have to kill Kelly, go ahead and do it. It will be just our little secret. I promise to never tell a soul."

Adelle's bargaining caught me off guard until I realized she was merely putting on an act for the 9-1-1 operator.

"No, you wouldn't tell would you, Adelle? That's the kind of person you are," Sharon said. She seemed to know a lot about us Clark girls. I wondered how much she knew, and how she would use it against us.

"You still haven't told Kelly what you're doing here, have you?" Sharon laughed.

I turned slightly to look at Adelle. She must have hidden the phone somewhere in her pocket because both hands were at her sides. She had a frightened look on her face.

"Tell her!" Sharon shouted. "And tell her the truth. I love breaking up families."

"What the hell is she talking about, Adelle?" I whispered to her.

"I don't know," Adelle said, putting her hands up in the universal "I surrender" sign.

"Cut the crap, Adelle. Tell her! You're both going to die anyway. Let's just get it out quickly. It makes me happy to see the mighty fall. Do this one thing for me, Adelle. Now," she screamed, stepping closer to us and releasing the safety on the gun.

"Okay, okay," Adelle said, looking sheepish. "I've been coming to Chocolate Love in the middle of the night."

"What for?" And then it hit me.

"Adelle, are you the one who broke into all the businesses? Are you stealing from Chocolate Love?" I asked horrified.

Now it was clear what Gina meant by the holy trinity of terror. Jack was the *he*, Sharon was the *I can't believe she's here*, and Adelle was the third one she saw sneaking around outside. Gina said, "It's your...," but never finished what she was telling me. I think she was going to say, it's your sister.

"No, no, nothing like that. I just hide things here. I come to pick them up when no one will see me." Her eyes wrinkled up like she was looking for my forgiveness. "I'm not a bad person, Kelly. I just can't stop."

"Can't stop what?" I was totally confused now.

"I can't stop...." She pulled her hand up to her forehead to rub it. "I can't stop spending. I hide my shopping bags here, so Mike doesn't see them. He gets upset with me. I'm not trying to make him mad. It's just gotten a bit out of control. We've been trying to cut back on the spending. I just can't seem to give it up. It makes me feel better."

Adelle fought back tears. I thought back to the Coach purse under the stairs in the basement. It was probably one of the items she hid in the store.

"I think I found your purse in the basement."

"You found that? How?" she asked.

I didn't want to go into detail now about my trip to the basement.

Sharon laughed quietly next to us. Each step she took put me more and more on edge.

"Go on, tell her about Mike's business," she said.

"How do you know about that?" Adelle asked, gasping.

"Because I broke into your house, you idiot. I went through all of his paperwork in his office. I know how deep in the hole you are. You people are all the same. You have your nice house and your luxury car, in your beautiful neighborhood, but it's all fake. You're all a bunch of fakes. I know about everyone. I've been in every store. Everyone is suffering. Sometimes I took money, sometimes I didn't. Just depended on how reckless I was feeling.

"You're so careless with your purses and your security codes. I overheard you and Nikki say "cake" while hanging up my signs in the bathroom. I went into Kelly's purse at yoga last Thursday to get an indentation of your key to Chocolate Love, in order to make a copy. It's how I got in tonight. It's only when I got here I realized I did not have a copy to your apartment. Luckily, you were stupid enough to let me in."

"Did you kill Fran?" I asked.

"Kill her? I wouldn't say that. Scare her to death, maybe? What do you think, Adelle?"

Adelle gasped behind me. "You were there?" Adelle asked in shock.

"Wait, you were there?" I asked Adelle. "Why didn't you help her? Or me?" I demanded.

"I swear she was fine when I left. She came in earlier than I thought she would. I was hiding a bag behind the clock in the front hall, so I snuck out through the front door. She never saw me Kelly, I swear. She was whistling to herself when I left. Totally fine. It was only later that I found out what had happened. I didn't know how to tell you," Adelle said.

"When I saw Adelle leave out the front door, I went around to the back because I thought the store would be empty. I was surprised to see Fran there, too. She had the door open like she was expecting someone.

"Needless to say, she was surprised to see me. The gun gave her a big scare. I didn't even have to pull it on her. She saw it tucked into my belt.

You should have seen her grab at her chest and gasp for air. Have you ever seen anyone die of a heart attack? It happens just like you see in the movies," Sharon said.

I couldn't take it anymore.

"Stop it," I said. "I don't want to hear anymore."

"I thought I would try to get close to Jack, too. Jack would have been able to give me more information about you, but he didn't really respond to my advances. Seems your prince only has eyes for you. He'll be disappointed when you're gone," she said.

I gulped. "Stop," I said again.

"But you haven't heard it all. Don't you want to know why I came here to kill you?"

"No." I had no intention of playing her game anymore. Not after what she just told us about Fran. Where were the police already?

"We're going to get married when Steve gets out of prison. I've been raising the money for our life together through my races all over the country. I ran into Gina in Denver when she came to one of my talks at a yoga class. She looked shocked to see me. She was starting to figure things out, and I'm guessing she came here to warn you?"

"Yes," I answered. Now I really wished I would have listened to Gina.

"Steve and I have been in love since before you were even married. We met while you were engaged. The timing just never worked out for us. We fooled around a lot while you were married, but didn't get serious until now. Now it's our time. You were his mistake."

I wouldn't give her the satisfaction of responding to her insult. "So, you don't actually give the money to the local hospitals?" I asked instead.

"Oh, it goes to the hospitals. At least some of it does. I have to look somewhat legit. I just skim a lot off of the top. People pass money onto charity and think nothing of it all the time. If I can keep this up, by the time he gets out, we'll be very well off. We're hoping he can get early release for good behavior."

"I still don't understand why you have to kill me. I have no intention of standing in the way of you two being together. Trust me, he's all yours," I said, putting my palms up in the air.

"We can't take the chance of you running to the police with anymore stories about Steve. He doesn't exactly have a clean past. We need to erase you to secure our future. He's my soul mate, but I know he's no saint. The biggest thing we're worried about is you finding out more. Who do you think taught me about money laundering in the first place? Steve got away with it in California, but there's always the chance you might dig up something and turn him in. No. You and your sister are going to die tonight, so Steve and I no longer have to worry," she said proudly.

So there was more. Not only was Steve a philandering, murderous husband, he was a crook.

I couldn't help myself. Her story was so pathetic and desperate a giggle slipped out.

"*You* are his soul mate?" I asked with heavy irony.

"Yes," she said defensively. The gun shook slightly in her hand. Apparently, watching Fran die was easy, but hearing someone question the authenticity of her relationship with a scumbag like Steve rocked her boat.

"Don't laugh at me. Don't you dare laugh at me," she said, steadying the gun.

"Sharon, do you honestly believe Steve will not do the same thing to you that he did to me? Or Mandy? Or God knows however many countless people there are out there he has screwed over? Are you okay with him having multiple partners? And then dumping you in the end?

"You said this is your plan-yours and Steve's together-but you do realize he'll turn this whole thing on you in the end and probably walk away with the cash. Don't be a fool, Sharon. Steve is a dog."

"It's not like that with us." But she couldn't hide the uncertainty the crept into her voice.

"Are you sure?" I asked.

"Sharon, put the gun down," Adelle chimed in. "You haven't killed anyone yet. Let's just stop this before it goes too far."

"Technically, she did kill Gina," I said, unable to stop myself. Adelle nudged me and said, "Shut up" under her breath.

"I've had enough. Let's go you two. Enough talking. We're going downstairs. We need to make it look like you were killed by someone breaking into Chocolate Love. That's the other reason I've been working so hard to establish these break-ins. Adelle, it's a little weird you're here. It wasn't in the original plan, but, oh well. Maybe I'll just throw a bunch of your shopping bags around you. Mike will be able to figure out what you were up to sooner or later. He'll just have to put the story together that you were here to collect your bags and walked in on a burglary. I want to get downstairs before it gets any later. Pretty soon this whole town will come alive with eager beavers ready to run for my stupid charity. Now!" she yelled. She reached out and grabbed my arm to direct me to the apartment door. Her grasp was surprisingly strong.

I looked to Adelle, desperate for some sign that the phone call was due to bring the police any second. Unfortunately, all I saw was a frantic look on her face. Hopefully, those survival skills Sharon talked about would kick in soon.

Adelle and I made our way out of my apartment door with me in the lead. When we walked through the hallway, I was reminded of the third bride in my dream at the top of the stairs. Was that supposed to be Sharon? Did my subconscious somehow know she was coming for me?

I turned to look at Sharon. Her mouth was tense, and her eyes burned back at me. Another soul destroyed by Steve. How many more were there? If I survived this, were there more Sharons coming for me?

As we approached the stairs, two hands shoved my back violently. My first thought was I'd been shoved down the stairs. The closest person to me was Adelle. Why would she do that? This flight of stairs was so steep, a fall could be awful.

When my body slammed directly into the wall opposite the stairs, I realized I'd been purposefully shoved out of the way, rather than pushed down.

There was the sound of a struggle behind me and a screech. I turned to see Adelle and Sharon in a ball, rolling down the stairs. Adelle must have pushed Sharon down the stairs. Unfortunately, Sharon was strong enough to pull Adelle with her.

"Adelle!' I screamed out.

The clunking and banging of two bodies falling terrified me. Suddenly, the gun went off, and the women landed in a clump on the floor. The gun spun onto the hardwood floor of the foyer in the direction of Chocolate Love.

I stood for a second, trying to decipher who was alive, if anyone. When both bodies started to stir, I raced down the stairs.

Adelle was at the base of the stairs. Her body had separated from Sharon's, and blood was visible on the ground next to her. She was moaning and pointing to something. Sharon's right leg was twisted in an odd way, but she was still trying to pull herself into a kneeling position. She began to crawl in the direction of the gun.

I followed the sightline of Adelle's pointed finger. It only took a second for me to figure out what she was trying to tell me. I stepped over Adelle, shoved Sharon out of the way, and grabbed the gun. It felt heavy and awkward in my hand, but I managed to point it at Sharon and scream, "Don't move!"

Sharon slumped back on the ground and moaned. I took my eyes off of her briefly to check on Adelle. Tears streamed down her face. I could tell from the grimace on her face, she was in obvious pain, but she flashed me a brief thumbs up.

I steadied the gun and listened to the wail of sirens approaching.

Epilogue

Four months later

"You can sit right here." I pulled Cindy's chair close to me.

"But will I get in trouble?" Cindy asked, looking around in awe.

"Of course not. I know the owners. They're nice people." I shot her a wink.

We were in Town House Books, a local book shop/café in downtown St. Charles, just north of Geneva. When my book was completed last month, I suggested to Holly that we have the first book signing here, because the owners were known for celebrating local authors and giving them a lot of support. This evening they were hosting a "Dinner with the Authors" series. I was going to autograph books and give a short talk about fiction writing with three other authors.

Besides being very generous to authors, they served the most delicious soups and sandwiches. I couldn't wait to see what they had whipped up for tonight's dinner. The clan I brought with me tonight was equally excited to sample the menu.

"I'll be in charge of passing you the new pens when you run out of ink," my little protégé said. I smiled down at her and gave her a squeeze.

"I don't know if I'm going to be signing that many books tonight."

"Sure you will. I brought a whole other box of pens just in case," Adelle laughed from behind us. She pulled a brush out of her purse and ran it through Cindy's hair. She wore it down tonight, a change from her normal pigtails. Cindy said it was because she needed to look fancy in case anyone asked for her autograph.

"Any news yet?" I whispered to Adelle, referring to the phone call she'd been waiting for all day. A potential buyer for their home in Geneva was supposed to call.

After the incident with Sharon in Chocolate Love, Adelle and Mike chose to get real with their finances and put their gargantuan home on the market. It was best to downsize until things got better for Mike's business.

The economy had been extremely tough on new property development. Although Mike's rental business was okay, the construction part fell apart. Nikki and I agreed we were naïve about the whole thing. We should have had more of an idea Mike's business would be sinking and been more supportive.

As hard as this was for them, Adelle and Mike seemed stronger than ever. Adelle was getting help through a therapist to get control of her spending habits. Mike had really stepped up to the plate, trying to help his wife be more honest about their life and her worries. I was impressed by the compassion and dedication he showed his family in the last couple of months.

Adelle lifted her right arm up and down as she ran the brush through Cindy's hair. I watched for any sign of pain on her face, but saw none.

When Adelle was shot in the shoulder that awful night, I thought by the amount of blood that things would turn out much worse for her. Turned out, it was only a flesh wound. She had to wear a brace for a number of weeks and was now fully recovered. She swore there was no more pain, but I would never forget the look on her face when she laid on the floor. If I could erase the memory, I would. The clear agony on her face while she had laid there bleeding haunted me.

Things forever changed for me and Adelle that day. Her unselfish act of bravery saved my life.

A lot of walls came down between us girls. We were all more understanding and open to listening to each other's point of view.

Adelle told Nikki and me it was tough being the odd man out. Because Nikki and I were so close, Adelle always felt like she was cut out. It made her more defensive and pushed her to be perfect. The pressure of trying to raise three kids while being the perfect wife, daughter, and mom was killing her.

She also explained how being married to Mike, a once very wealthy man now rocked by the economy, caused her to shut down and be very self-absorbed. She put a lot of importance on being wealthy, and now would have to accept the changes.

Nikki and I both promised we would try to include her more and stop being so judgmental. Adelle was right. We were pigeonholing her into a stereotype and had been for a long time.

Adelle listened openly to our complaints about her not being there for us in our time of need and coming across as selfish.

Nikki also admitted she was suspicious of Adelle's presence in Chocolate Love, because she was finding shopping bags in the store in strange places. The bags would be there one day and then disappear the next. Nikki worried Adelle might be connected to the lights left on, and even possibly, the death of Fran, but she was too devoted to her sister to try and explore that further.

Adelle admitted she obtained the code to the security system from Cindy, who accidentally told her mother after she overheard us talking about it. As soon as Adelle got it out of Cindy, she started using the store again to hide her purchases. That was why she was there the morning Sharon came to Chocolate Love to kill me.

Although Sharon was injured from the fall, she was alive and living out her sentence in Dwight Correctional Center, about sixty miles south of Geneva.

I was not happy she was in prison here in Illinois. It left her in close proximity to me, but considering she was not scheduled to be released for another eighty years, I did my best to put it out of my mind.

She never did turn on Steve. She told the police Steve had nothing to do with any of what happened, and she came up with it all on her own. There was really no evidence to pursue, so the police had to let it go.

As far as the financial records, I wasn't able to trace anything suspicious so far. Perhaps Steve was a really good money launderer, or I was just looking in the wrong place.

I had a feeling I might figure it out someday. Sharon was correct in assuming I would go to the police with any information found, especially if it meant Steve would stay in prison longer.

I was glad the nightmare was over, at least for now. I would always be waiting for Steve, or some connection to Steve, to catch up with me. God only knew what evil lurked in the shadows of my past. For now though, I was happy my book was published, my family was healthy and stronger than ever, and my life was getting back on track.

"Where do I sit?" Jack asked. He was very handsome tonight dressed in a wool suit. His look was pulled together by a cranberry tie that matched my sweater dress. He leaned over the back of my seat and kissed my cheek.

"Did you do that on purpose?" I laughed, pointing to his tie.

"No, I swear. I assumed you were wearing the black one tonight. That was the one you left hanging out on my closet door. I like that one, but I'm glad you picked this one. You look great."

"So do you. I'm so glad you're here."

I looked out in the crowd from the head table across the café. The tables were decorated with fall colors, and small candles burned all around the room that was filling up quickly. Maybe my pen would run out of ink after all.

"I think Nikki has a bunch of seats held at the table over there," I said, pointing to where Bob and Nikki sat. Nikki's eyes met mine, and she waved Jack over.

"I'm going to go grab my seat then. I'm starving. Can't wait for the soup. Good luck," he said, bending down to kiss my cheek again. "We're still on for tonight, right?" he asked, close to my ear.

"Absolutely," I said, allowing my mouth to curl into a smile.

"Good. Knock 'em dead, honey."

After Jack walked away, Nikki bounced up from her chair and made her way over to the head table.

"Hey, we have a little surprise for you," she said, standing in front of me. She was wearing a gray dress and a pair of chocolate-brown riding boots. With her recently added highlights, she looked very stylish tonight.

"What?"

"Adelle and I wanted to do something special for tonight."

I smiled and looked over at Adelle. She refused to meet my eyes and turned away to look for someone.

"What did you guys do?" I was confident it was something good by the way these two were barely able to contain themselves.

"Is it Mom and Dad? Are they here?" I stood up and peered over in the direction of the front door.

There were two doors into Town House Books; one was located right at the front of the café. I could see it from where I was standing. People were filtering in, but no one looked familiar to me.

The other door was to the book store attached to the café. Whatever they were planning, whoever they were surprising me with, I could only assume would be coming through one of those doorways momentarily.

"Hold on, I'll go get them," Adelle said, walking away.

"Is it Grandma and Grandpa?" I asked Cindy. I was pretty confident now in my assumption.

"I don't know," Cindy said in a sing song way.

My eyes went back to Nikki, who was still standing in front of the head table. She had her head turned now and was also looking in the direction of the front door.

Standing with Adelle, I finally saw them. My parents were bundled up in winter coats and scanned the room. I chuckled to myself. The coats were a bit unnecessary, considering it had only dipped down to fifty degrees. Now that they were full time Floridians, that probably felt near arctic to them.

Adelle raised her arm and pointed in my direction. Mom and Dad looked up and waved when they finally saw me standing behind the head table. I motioned for them to come over.

"Thank you so much for setting this up, Nikki. This means so much to me." I waved them over and smiled, happy to have the whole Clark family here tonight. This night was huge for me. Finally the new start I had been looking for. A celebration of what I'd been feeling for a few months now. I was getting a second chance at life.

Watch out world, Kelly Clark was back.

Red Velvet Fran's Cupcakes
Yields: approximately 18 cupcakes

Ingredients:
½ cup shortening
1 ½ cup sugar
2 eggs
1 tsp. vanilla
2 oz. red food coloring
2 tbsp. cocoa powder
1 tsp. salt
1 cup buttermilk
2 ½ cup cake flour
1 tsp. baking soda
1 tsp. vinegar

Instructions:
Heat oven to 350 degrees. Cream together on medium high speed sugar, shortening, eggs and vanilla.
Make paste of food coloring and cocoa; reduce mixer speed to low and add paste to mix. Add milk and salt alternately with flour. Add soda to vinegar and blend with batter.
Using a standard cupcake pan lined with paper liners, fill ½ way using a large cookie scooper to fill (approximately ¼ cup).
Bake at 350 degrees for 22 minutes.

Cream Cheese Frosting
3 cup confectioners' sugar
1 package cream cheese (8 oz.) softened
½ cup softened butter
1 tbsp. milk
1 tsp. vanilla

Beat all ingredients together in a large bowl on medium high speed until smooth. Spread on cupcakes.

Recipe by Annie Hansen

Dear Reader,

I hope you've enjoyed **Give Me Chocolate**. Now please enjoy an excerpt from Kelly's second adventure, **Bean In Love**. I'd appreciate your review on it. Feel free to stop by my website to learn the latest news about Kelly's latest adventures and where to find me for book signings at http://kellyclarkmystery.com

Thanks so much!
Annie Hansen

Excerpt from

Bean In Love

Book 2 in the Kelly Clark Mystery Series

Chapter 1

"**P**lease, just take the money," I said.

My sister, Nikki, lounged on my living room couch with one of my gossip magazines like she didn't have a care in the world, though I knew different. She didn't even acknowledge my attempt to compensate her for allowing me to crash in her apartment above Chocolate Love, her specialty dessert shop in downtown Geneva, Illinois. I'd been living here rent free for almost a year now, and the guilt was killing me. I was starting to feel like a squatter.

"Do you think all of these photos are staged? I'm never this made up when I go to the grocery store. How could these people look like this? Kelly, see what I mean? Stars without make-up. Yeah, right. She's totally wearing make-up. And eyelash extensions! I have never even worn those, let alone worn them to a grocery store." Nikki's hand reached up and pinched at her eyelashes. "Maybe I should try them. Wow, do you smell that? They're making caramel brownies downstairs. Smells like it's going good, right? Or, wait, are they burning?" Nikki sat up and sniffed the air.

"Nikki," I said a little louder, interrupting her rant. "Will you at least look at me?"

Nikki let out an over the top sigh and tossed the magazine on the couch. She adjusted the sleeves on her pumpkin colored, zip-up fleece and finally swung her cocoa eyes in my direction.

"Please take this check," I said, holding the written check out to her. "It's time. It's long past time." The check shook slightly in my hand. I gripped it harder, trying to steady myself.

"We already did this two weeks ago. I'm not going to start taking money from you."

"Things have changed since then. I didn't know about your expansion project."

"The expansion has nothing to do with you, Kelly. We never planned on collecting rent for this apartment. I want you to spend that money paying down the debt you acquired from the divorce. Have you started that yet?" Nikki said, with a little more bite in her tone than I was used to.

Ouch. Automatically, my lips pulled up into a grimace. I fought to put them back in place.

"A little," I said, sinking down in my cushy office chair like a deflated balloon. There was no use lying to Nikki. It would be like lying to my own reflection. She knew me too well. It would take her less than a second to figure out I wasn't telling the truth. I pulled my long, brown hair out of its ponytail holder, allowing it to cascade around my shoulders like a shield from Nikki's words.

"But I don't understand. I had no idea the balance was that high. I don't even really remember opening that card to tell you the truth."

"It says right here that you did. We have your signature."

It would take me years to pay down what my lying, cheating ex-husband charged to credit cards in my name while he'd been wooing women behind my back. I hadn't even known some of the cards existed until he was sent to jail for attempted murder. Steve had been caught red-handed trying to kill a woman he impregnated while we were married. He got ten years, and I got all the debt. I also got stuck with the bills for our failed attempt at having a baby. Those IVF procedures were not cheap. With the recent sale of my new book, at least I finally had some money coming in. It wasn't enough though to cleanse me from my money woes. Still, I felt guilty living above Chocolate Love for free when Nikki could use my cash.

"I'm sorry to sound so harsh. I'm not trying to make you feel bad," Nikki said, shaking her head. "I'm so snappy today. Anyway, I'm just trying to help you get out of this hole. You're going to need all of the money you make on the sale of your books to pay off those cards and start fresh. If you start paying me, you'll be spinning your wheels. Just stick to the plan and start knocking off those high interest cards. Remember what the financial planner said?"

"I am doing those things. I just thought if I could give you a couple hundred dollars a month it would help. These are tough times," I said, referring to the struggling economy.

"Things are improving. Plus, coffee is booming during these tough times. It's where people are spending their money. If you're really serious about helping out, spend some time with me brainstorming on how we can do this. I want your brainpower, not your money," Nikki said, kicking her feet out onto my coffee table.

"Okay, then my brainpower you will get." I set the check on the table, somewhat relieved. As usual, Nikki was right. I still couldn't really afford to pay her rent.

Nikki smiled and lifted up her mug of hot chocolate. "Here's to making rent payments with your cranium," she said, lifting her mug in the air for a toast.

A knock on the door interrupted our toast. We studied each other as though we expected the other to know who it was.

"Who is it?" I called nervously.

I would never again open my apartment door without confirming who was on the other side. A few months ago, my older sister, Adelle, and I had been attacked by my ex-husband's psychotic girlfriend. She'd nearly killed us both.

So far, my experiences in life taught me you never knew what evil lurked inside of people. The ones you lived intimately day-to-day with, the strangers you passed on the street, and the ones that were on the other side of your apartment door. Everyone could turn on you. I'd become the most untrusting person on the planet. But who could blame me? Psychotic people seemed to run abundant in my life.

"It's me, Miguel."

Hearing his familiar voice, I reached for my hoodie on the back of my chair and put it on before opening the door. Miguel was Nikki's trusted right hand man at the store. He was welcome anytime, but nonetheless, I felt a bit naked in my yoga pants and skin tight, nearly see through tee-shirt I'd been hanging out in while working in my apartment. My newly added curves made me a little self-conscious. Not that I didn't love them. I'd just gotten used to life without them. I was happy to have them back. And excited to be in a place in my life where my body and my mind were healthy enough to allow them to come back. My weight loss post my divorce had not been an attractive thing. Skeleton was not a good look on me.

"I'm sorry to bother you ladies, but there is a problem. The cupcake order for Geneva High School is not right. The principal is on hold. She wants to talk to you, Nikki. I tried to work through it with her, but she keeps insisting on speaking directly to you," Miguel said, eyeballing Nikki for direction.

"No problem, Miguel. Melissa is an old friend of mine," Nikki said, bolting up from the couch.

"I'll come down with you and frost cupcakes for a bit. I need a break anyway."

"Okay, I'll run down and tell her you're coming," Miguel said.

"What about your book signing tonight?" Nikki asked as I locked up my apartment.

"I don't have to leave until five. It's an evening thing."

A small bookstore in Oak Park was hosting a book signing for me tonight. Since my book release last month, most of my time was spent promoting it and meeting fans. Because it was a Thursday in early October, I hoped the signing would go really well. In Chicago, fall was a great time to sell books and meet my target audience. The snow had not yet hit, and readers were still willing to venture outside of their homes. I had to do as many of these book signings as I could before the winter doldrums kept everyone locked inside next to their heaters.

Nikki and I walked together down the grand staircase leading from the second floor down to Chocolate Love. The smell of the caramel brownies got stronger and stronger as we descended the stairs, making me smile in anticipation. What a treat to live in a place like this. I grabbed onto the ornate, wooden railing with my right hand and ran my left along the wall. Nikki's in-laws had purchased this old Victorian home on Third Street in Geneva close to twenty years ago. Their hope had been to build a profitable business selling specialty chocolates to the wealthy citizens of Geneva. Today, the store was one of the main hangouts in the Historic District. It not only sold chocolates, but also ice cream, cupcakes, and toys for kids. The success of the store did not surprise me one bit. When Nikki went after something, she got it.

This afternoon, the store was filled with customers, mostly adults with small children inching up on their tip toes to get a glance at the delicious ice creams and fancy chocolates displayed in glass cases.

"What line is she on?" Nikki asked Miguel.

"Line one." We made our way through the crowd and slipped behind the glass counter to the back kitchen where Nikki kept a small office. Nikki had the store filled with pumpkins, gourds, and other fall décor to help put her customers in the mood for Halloween.

"What do you want me to start on?" I asked Nikki, before she grabbed the phone.

We had an agreement that whenever I was stalled on my writing, I helped by frosting cupcakes. Somehow it always got me past my writer's block and also made me feel like I was giving something back for living in the apartment rent free.

"Miguel will show you. I think we have a big order of vanilla cupcakes waiting in the kitchen," Nikki said before picking up the phone.

"Over here, Kelly." Miguel directed me to the counter where six trays of cupcakes sat.

"Wow, that's a big order," I said, nodding to the counter.

"It's for the Geneva History Museum. This month they're running the Haunted History Walking Tour every Thursday, Friday, and Saturday night. They want vanilla on vanilla and then the chocolate spiders placed on top."

"I can't believe it's already time for the ghost tours." My sisters, Nikki and Adelle, and I had gone on the haunted walk a couple of times. A member of the Geneva History Museum would lead a group of people around the town after dark while sharing urban legends. Some were based on true stories from the past, like the one about the two police officers killed while chasing a criminal down Third Street.

And some of the stories were just local Geneva folklore, like the one about the building that used to be a hospital and was now used as storefronts. Apparently, the lights flickered and merchandise moved around the store long after customers and shop owners had gone home for the night.

The town of Geneva was located right on the banks of the Fox River about thirty miles west of Chicago. In the early years, Native American tribes known as the Pottawatomi had ruled the land until the first settlers from Europe came over in the 1830s. When the railroad was laid through town in 1853, Geneva became connected to the city of Chicago, making it an illustrious location to visit or build summer homes. Although the town had grown significantly, things here were a lot slower and peaceful compared to city life.

My own parents moved here from Chicago over forty years ago when they were first married. They wanted to settle down in a nice suburban community before having children. My two sisters and I had been very happy growing up in Geneva and still lived here to this day.

After my divorce and harrowing escape from my life in San Francisco, Geneva was the first place I thought of to go. I needed a place to rebuild my life. Unfortunately, it quickly became apparent I couldn't hide from anything. Or anyone. Even in my beloved small town, evil lurked.

"What time do they need them?" I asked Miguel.

"The tour starts at seven. We should probably get them there by six for set-up."

I glanced up at the clock and saw it was inching near two in the afternoon. I threw on my apron and breathed out slowly. Time for some stress relief.

Just as I picked up my tools to start icing, the door leading from the store to the kitchen slammed shut with a bang. Startled, I dropped the icing onto the counter, causing it to splatter a couple of drops onto my pink apron that read, "Love Chocolate? Let it love you back. Give in to the craving."

My eyes jumped up to the door to see what could have caused it to slam. Normally, Nikki maintained an open door policy for the kitchen. She wanted curious shoppers to be able to look into the kitchen and see the work in progress.

"What was that?" I heard Nikki call out from around the corner.

Instead of answering her, my eyes locked on the man standing in front of the closed kitchen door. His complexion, though covered in scraggly facial hair, was a pale, milky shade of white, as though he had chosen to hide from the sun. His eyes swung frantically, searching for some unknown destination until finally landing on me.

A vampire, I answered Nikki silently in my head.

He looked familiar, but my fear blocked me from being able to grasp his name. On this warm autumn day, his sloppy, brown corduroys and wrinkled, tweed jacket seemed much too stuffy for the near seventy degree temperatures.

"I can't let them hear," he said in barely a whisper. He stayed glued to the door, but his anxious words filled the room with a nervous energy.

"Who?" I whispered back, wondering what Nikki's connection to this could possibly be. After all, he was here in her store. Although she always had the best intentions, she was a Clark sister. Trouble had the tendency to find us.

He jerked his head backward to the door.

It hit me then that this was Brian Sanders, the lead curator for the Geneva History Museum. He was nearly unrecognizable with his eyes blazing like he hadn't slept in days and his disheveled hair. What had happened to him? He'd been known to be eccentric, but right now he looked downright manic.

"What's going on?" Nikki asked, no longer on the phone. She came rushing into the room and stopped dead in her tracks next to me.

"She's back," he managed to get out. "And she wants revenge."

The sound of glass shattering on the other side of the closed door, combined with the intensity in the room, made me scream out in panic.

Acknowledgements

First and foremost, I would like to thank my husband, Brent Hansen, for always making my writing time a priority in our household. Without your love and support, this book would never have come to fruition. You keep everything running in the Hansen house.

Thank you to my parents for pushing me to follow my dreams and being supportive of my choices. Thank you, Mom, Gail McCarter, for always taking on first edits for all of my stories. Your excitement and constructive criticism continues to help mold this series. I'll never forget our 5:00 a.m. location scouting-adventure in Geneva.

Thank you to my dear sister, Mimi Cunningham, for your encouragement and feedback on the creative direction for *Give Me Chocolate*. You always steer me in the right direction.

Thank you to Cristen Leifheit for helping on design and publicity for the series. Also, a big thank you to Eddie Vincent of ENC Graphic Services for all your creative design work.

For all of my advance readers who helped edit early drafts: Mary Koll, Joan Considine, Christine Olsen, Barb Anderson, Lupita Signorella, Meghan Eagan, Elizabeth Meiers, Nicole Liwienski, Lanay Sorce, Noreen Bolsoni and Alice Hansen. I would also like to thank my editor, Brittiany Koren, of Written Dreams. A big thanks to you! You make me a better writer.

It's great to have experts to turn to—my sincere gratitude to two experts who have been a big help with the criminal aspect of The Kelly Clark Series: Thomas McCarter (Dad), Retired Special Agent in Charge, Department of the Treasury, Office of Inspector General and James McCarter (Uncle), Retired Cook County State's Attorney.

About the Author

A nnie Hansen is a graduate of the University of Illinois with a B.S. in Biology. She is a partner with Hansen Search Group, a staffing firm she co-founded with her husband and business partner, Brent Hansen, in 2001. She was named the winner of the Helen McCloy Mystery Writers of America Scholarship in 2011 for her submission of *Give Me Chocolate*. Annie is the author of The Kelly Clark Mystery Series and can be reached through her website: www.kellyclarkmystery.com. Her second book in the series, *Bean In Love*, is forthcoming in 2014. She lives with her family in the western suburbs of Chicago.

CPSIA information can be obtained
at www.ICGtesting.com
Printed in the USA
LVOW13s0324060317
526243LV00007B/565/P